the **crazy**
things
girls
do for
love

the crazy things girls do for love

Dyan Sheldon

CANDLEWICK PRESS

Copyright © 2010 by Dyan Sheldon

First U.S. paperback edition 2013

The Library of Congress has cataloged the hardcover edition as follows:

Sheldon, Dyan.
The crazy things girls do for love / Dyan Sheldon. — 1st U.S. ed.
p. cm.
Summary: When fashionista Sicilee, arty Maya, and antisocial
Waneeda risk their reputations by joining Clifton Springs High
School's Environmental Club to be near gorgeous new student
Cody Lightfoot, each finds a new way of looking at the world.
ISBN 978-0-7636-5018-6 (hardcover)
[1. Interpersonal relations—Fiction. 2. High schools—Fiction.
3. Schools—Fiction. 4. Green movement—Fiction.
5. Environmental protection—Fiction.] I. Title.
PZ7.S54144Cr 2011
[Fic—dc22] 2010048434

ISBN 978-0-7636-6468-8 (paperback)

13 14 15 16 17 18 BVG 10 9 8 7 6 5 4 3 2 1

Printed in Berryville, VA, U.S.A.

This book was typeset in Berkeley Oldstyle.

Candlewick Press
99 Dover Street
Somerville, Massachusetts 02144

visit us at www.candlewick.com

For all eco-warriors everywhere
¡Sigue la lucha!

Chapter One

Sicilee Kewe is not happy

It is a dark and rainy morning. An unfriendly wind pulls at clothes and umbrellas and rustles the plastic bags caught in branches and overhead wires so that they make a forlorn, unhappy sound. Bent, huddled figures hurry through the downpour, jumping over puddles and avoiding the sodden grass as they make their way to the sprawl of buildings that is Clifton Springs High School.

Two bright spots flicker against the gloom of the storm like flames in a starless night. They are Sicilee Kewe and her best friend, Kristin Shepl, two of the school's most popular students. Kristin is enveloped in an oversize, hooded white coat, trimmed in fur that may once have barked or even meowed, but for Sicilee this is an orange day—orange bag, orange boots, orange hat, orange jacket, orange dress over black-and-orange leggings.

The plastic bags trapped in the trees aren't the only ones making forlorn, unhappy sounds.

"It just isn't fair," Sicilee moans. "Why do we have to come back today?" The orange umbrella bobs indignantly as she sidesteps a small body of water that Kristin, her eyes on Sicilee, inadvertently walks through. "Sweet Mary, it's practically the middle of the week. I mean, really, what difference would a measly couple of days make? I swear, sometimes I really think there's some kind of conspiracy going on to ruin my life."

Christmas vacation is always far too short. There's never enough time to do all the things that need to be done. The shopping. The parties. The entertaining. The outings. The visits. The events. And then there are all the preparations for New Year's Eve — hair, nails, facial, sauna, more shopping. Not to mention the trips to the gym. You can't be stuffing your face with roast beef and cookies and not go to the gym a couple of times at least.

"I haven't really had time to recover," says Sicilee. "It's a miracle I don't have dark circles under my eyes or zits." Besides which, Sicilee hasn't even had a chance to take back all the presents that were the wrong color, make, or size. "Like that bag Aunt Clarice and Uncle Vaughn gave me? You saw it, Kris. It's a good label and everything, but it is, like, so totally last year that I can't possibly be seen with it over my arm. I might as well carry all my stuff in a shopping bag from the supermarket."

Kristin, who is now warily watching the ground for more surprise puddles, sighs. "I could've used more downtime, too, but, to tell you the truth, in one way I'm almost glad to be back at school." That one way is Kristin's mother. "Nag, nag, nag, nag, nag. . . . It's like she's on automatic or something. She didn't even stop for Christmas Day. I said to her, 'You know, this is supposed to be the season to be jolly—not the season to go on and on about who didn't empty the dishwasher.'"

"Oh, that's nothing," Sicilee assures her. "I didn't tell you what happened last night at Chez Kewe." She rolls her eyes. "It was like *Nightmare on Coldwater Drive*."

"Really? What happened?"

Sicilee sighs. "Nothing, really. All I did was very casually say that I figured it was time we did something about enlarging my closet—you know, since I can hardly turn around in it, it's so freaking small."

"Maternal meltdown?" guesses Kristin.

"Not this time. You know my mom; she prefers to talk you into submission than yell if she can. It was *him*." Sicilee's eyes (brown today to complement her outfit) widen dramatically. The orange umbrella sways with emotion. "I couldn't believe it! One minute he was all normal and talking about having the tires rotated, and the next he was all puffed up and practically drooling. It was like he was the Incredible Hulk or something. I felt like saying, 'Hey, who changed the script?' You should've heard him, Kris. He was yelling and screaming about how much everything costs and how spoiled I am and

3

how when he was my age he worked thirty-eight hours a day so he'd have some lunch money and kept his one shirt and pair of jeans in a paper bag under his bed." Sicilee is smiling as she tells her tale, but not because her father's tantrum was amusing. Like the picture on the label stuck on a package of cheap meat, Sicilee's smiles bear little relationship to what's going on inside. She is smiling because she is out in public, a place where she smiles all the time. "And then he said that if I want to be able to throw a party in my closet, I should stop buying so many clothes."

"How draconian," sympathizes Kristin.

"I told him. I said, 'Look, I'm sorry, but I can't cut back on something as important as my wardrobe. I do have a reputation to uphold, you know.'"

"Well, duh . . . Of course you do." Kristin shakes her head sadly. "They don't get it, do they? They think you get to be really popular just by luck."

"There was no explaining *that* to him last night — that's for sure," says Sicilee. "I swear, he was so overwrought, I thought he was going to have a stroke."

"My dad gets like that. I figure it's stress."

"You're probably right." Sicilee sighs. "They said on TV that stress is the disease of the twenty-first century."

"Too true," agrees Kristin. "Plus, it was Christmas. That's extra stressful. And you didn't get to go skiing this year. That probably tightened his screws even more."

The Kewe family's annual ski trip had been canceled this Christmas due to an unexpected lack of snow. Clifton Springs, apparently, is not the only place experiencing unseasonable weather.

"Well, it's not like he was the only one to know crushing disappointment, Kristin." Sicilee suddenly veers to the right, leaving Kristin on her own with the unfriendly elements. "I was looking forward to the ski trip, too, you know. I mean, I haven't been anywhere since we went to Cabo in the summer."

"Yeah, but you know what parents are like. It's all themthemthem." Kristin jogs a few steps to get back under the umbrella. "So what are you going to do about your closet?"

"Oh, you know . . ." Sicilee's smile takes on a philosophical tinge. "I'll wait for him to calm down and everything, and then I'll hit him with it again."

Having safely reached the portico of the main building, Sicilee makes a sudden, unscheduled stop to check out her reflection in the glass doors. "Sweet Mary!" She tilts her head first to the left and then to the right, her scrutiny both professional and thorough despite the makeshift nature of her mirror. Although Sicilee has, in fact, been exposed to the storm for only a few minutes, she is far from happy with what she sees. "Look at me!" she wails. "I look like I went down with the *Titanic*!"

The boy who was forced to stop short behind her

gives her a nudge. "Will you just go *in*?" he grumbles.

Sicilee lifts her umbrella so she can see him glowering over her shoulder. It's Clemens Reis, one of the greatest geeks who has ever lived, and the fact that he touched her does nothing to improve Sicilee's mood. She gives her umbrella a shake before shutting it, causing more grizzling at her back, and pushes open the doors.

The lobby is packed with students noisily reuniting after the holidays. All is not lost. Sicilee doesn't see anyone whose opinion she cares about among them. "I'm going to the girls' room. Right now. I have to repair the damage before anyone sees me," she shouts above the din to Kristin. "You go and find Ash and Loretta. I'll meet you by the lockers."

"OK." Kristin nods. "See you in a few minutes."

Never handicapped by the sense that she needs to be either patient or polite, Sicilee marches through the crowd, which magically parts for her as the sea did for the Children of Israel. But when she reaches the nearest bathroom, Sicilee discovers that her day hasn't started to improve just yet. Oddly enough, she isn't the only one whose hair and makeup have been adversely affected by the bad weather. The space around the sinks is packed tighter than a designer sale. Sicilee's sigh is heartfelt. *Why does everything happen to me?* she thinks. And she turns around and heads for the bathroom on the floor above.

Which is sure to be empty at this time of the morning, being so far away.

There are two girls standing together near the entrance to the second-floor restroom. Sicilee doesn't actually look at them. But, of course, she doesn't have to. She knows instinctively—by their hair (which has obviously never seen the inside of a decent salon) and their bodies (scrawny and pudgy, respectively) and their clothes (beyond hopeless)—that they are geeks from the netherworld. Which puts them way beneath her notice. Because they happen to be in her way, Sicilee pushes past them, hitting the larger of the two (the pudgy one) with her bright-orange backpack and knocking a stack of papers out of her hands.

"Hey!" snaps the girl. "Why don't you watch where you're going, Princess Pumpkin?"

Her companion quickly jumps back, banging her head against the wall.

Sicilee glances over her shoulder, like a movie star forced to acknowledge a ragged beggar because the beggar is hanging on to her ankle. "Are you talking to *me*?"

"Yeah," says Waneeda. "I am talking to *you*. Look what you did!"

"Well, maybe if you weren't such a heffalump, you wouldn't be in my way," Sicilee drawls. And, still smiling, she yanks open the door.

Chapter Two

Why Waneeda and Joy Marie were in Sicilee's way

There was no exhausting round of parties or events in the world of Waneeda Huddlesfield and Joy Marie Lutz this holiday season. They spent Christmas vacation much as they spend most of their free time: Joy Marie studied, read, practiced her violin, and completed the special project on the Magna Carta she's been doing for extra history credits; Waneeda played video games, watched television, and ate.

And now, as Sicilee searches for somewhere to repair the damage wreaked by nature and Kristin searches for Loretta and Ash, Waneeda and Joy Marie move slowly through the hallways on the second floor. Joy Marie, dressed in a gray skirt and plain white blouse, her hair in a single perfect braid, is carrying a dispenser of tape, and a box of pushpins clacks in the pocket of her gray sweater. Waneeda, her relentlessly unruly hair pulled back into a tight bun, her sweatpants and baggy pullover looking as though they are wearing her more than she is wearing them, is carrying a stack of flyers and chewing her last gumdrop. They move slowly, partly because Waneeda doesn't really "do" quickly, and partly because they have been at the school for over an hour, going up and down the corridors taping flyers to the walls and pinning them to bulletin boards, so that even Joy Marie's enthusiasm is starting to wane. The flyers say:

IMPORTANT MEETING!

THE FIRST MEETING OF THE NEW YEAR OF THE CLIFTON SPRINGS HIGH SCHOOL ENVIRONMENTAL CLUB WILL BE HELD ON MONDAY AT 3:45 P.M. IN ROOM 111.

NEW MEMBERS WELCOME!

MS. KIMODO
(HISTORY ADVISER)

COME ON, GANG! LET'S SAVE THE PLANET!

Joy Marie is here this morning because she is the cofounder, vice president, and (due to a lack of volunteers) secretary of the Clifton Springs High School Environmental Club, which has the distinction of being the most unpopular club in the history of the school. Not that this lack of popularity bothers Joy Marie. She doesn't do things because she wants to be liked; she does things because she is driven to achieve. Mr. and Mrs. Lutz expect a lot of her.

In comparison, no one expects much of Waneeda, and they are rarely disappointed. Indeed, it's fair to say that Waneeda could be the girl for whom the words "I can't," "But I'm tired," and "Do I have to?" were invented. Waneeda is here this morning only because Joy Marie slept over last night and was, therefore, in a position to make her come.

"Are we done yet?" Waneeda moans as they finally complete their circuit of the second floor. "I have to sit down. My blood sugar's really low."

Joy Marie gives her a so-what-else-is-new? look. Waneeda's blood sugar is always in imminent danger of collapse. "Almost. I just want to put a couple by the restrooms."

Waneeda sighs, but dutifully follows. Waneeda is not so much driven as pulled.

She shifts restlessly from one foot to the other as she holds yet another flyer up against yet another wall. "I don't know why you bother," complains Waneeda. "Everybody who's in the club knows about the meeting. And nobody new's ever going to join."

"You don't know that," says Joy Marie. Joy Marie's nature is basically a positive one.

Waneeda's is not. "Yes, I do know that," she insists. "Everybody thinks your club is the pits." Even the über-hip kids who wear vintage clothes and drink fair-trade coffee have stayed away from the Environmental Club the way you'd avoid a house where someone died of the plague. "They'd rather pick up litter on the highway with a toothpick than join."

"We still have to keep trying," argues Joy Marie. "They could change their minds. Rome wasn't built in a day, you know. These things take time."

"I thought time was the thing you don't have." Waneeda fumbles in her pockets, hoping to find at least an over-looked stick of gum. "I thought the end was nigh."

"Well . . ." Joy Marie's single braid bounces as she marches on. "You know what they say, Waneeda—It's always darkest before the dawn."

And it is certainly very dark at the moment. The club's official enrollment (larger than the number of people who actually show up for meetings) has always hovered at the minimum needed for school support and funding, but that, unfortunately, is not its biggest problem. Its biggest problem is a graying and portly man who, besides being famous for his amusing and colorful ties, commands a great deal of authority and respect in the community. Although he likes to be seen as politically correct, Dr. Firestone, the principal of Clifton Springs High School, has never fully appreciated the club's efforts to alert the student body to the many dangers facing the planet. The hundreds of plastic bags they dumped outside the main entrance. The posters of tortured animals they plastered through the corridors. Their picket protesting the sale of soda and bottled water on campus. All of these things annoyed Dr. Firestone, but it was last year's infamous Earth Day speech (in which Clemens Reis, cofounder and president of the club, suggested that his fellow students and their teachers were all complacent kamikaze consumers) that caused the principal to become openly critical. He said that the club, in general, and Clemens, in particular, lacked the delicacy and subtlety of the nuclear bomb.

This past November, things took a turn for the worse when Clemens began his current campaign to save the five-hundred-year-old trees at the side of the tennis courts from being cut down to make way for the new sports center. Clemens has written letters to the town council, to the school, to the administration, to the school board, to the developers, and to the local papers. More than one. Although these letters have proved no more effective than sticking a bandage over a crack in a dam, they did manage to alienate Dr. Firestone even more. "Are you aware, Mr. Reis, that you're like Don Quixote, tilting at windmills and thinking they're giants?" Dr. Firestone asked Clemens. "I suggest you stop wasting the club's resources and address some real issues, not the fate of a couple of trees." Clemens said he'd see what he could do.

And then, just before Christmas, Clemens took the mike at the end of the morning announcements, saying that he wanted to send holiday greetings from the Environmental Club to the rest of the school. What he did, in fact (as the few people who actually listened could tell you), was launch into a passionate plea on behalf of the ancient oaks and the inestimable value of the natural world. "If you eradicate a species or chop down a tree, it's gone forever," he told them. "If you destroy everything, you'll eventually end up with nothing." If there was some eloquence as well as truth in Clemens's speech, Dr. Firestone failed to see it. Dr. Firestone said it was a diatribe and summoned Clemens to his office for "a little chat." Dr. Firestone was decked out for the holidays in a Christmas-tree tie with tiny flashing lights on it. Clemens was wearing a T-shirt he'd made himself that featured a photograph of the threatened trees and the caption: *Where were you five hundred years ago? Where will they be next spring?* Dr. Firestone did most of the chatting. "You're turning what should be an ordinary high-school club into a gang of junior eco-terrorists, Mr. Reis," he accused. "You'll be setting fire to SUVs and breaking into animal labs next." Dr. Firestone made it clear that if the club didn't improve both its image and its membership, the school would have no choice but to shut it down at the end of January.

"Anyway, we do have till the end of the month." Joy Marie snaps off a piece of tape and slaps it into position. "And it doesn't say anything about trees on the announcement."

Waneeda blows fluff from the Tootsie Roll she found deep in the pocket of her sweatpants. The Tootsie Roll looks as if it may have been washed. "Does Clemens know you left out the trees?" Unlike Joy Marie, Clemens isn't intimidated by Dr. Firestone's threats. Clemens would argue with God, never mind a man whose tie lights up.

Rather than answer Waneeda's question, Joy Marie says, "What I was thinking was that we should do a serious recruitment drive. We could set up a table in the main hall . . . and do an announcement at the next assembly . . . and even go around the homerooms."

Waneeda's expression, though slightly diluted because of the candy in her mouth, delicately balances disbelief and disdain. Joy Marie is too shy to make announcements or talk to homerooms. When forced to speak in front of a class, she turns the color of tomato soup and talks so softly that even *she* can't hear what she's saying. "You're going to send Clemens out to convince people to join?"

Which would be like using wild bears and packs of hungry wolves to convince people to picnic in the woods. "Are you nuts?"

"I didn't mean Clemens." Joy Marie smooths out the paper she's half fixed to the wall. "I was kind of thinking of you." Waneeda may be self-conscious about her looks, but she is less shy than an angry bull.

"Yeah, right," snorts Waneeda. "As soon as I give up my part-time job as peace envoy for the UN."

"I'm serious." Joy Marie cuts another length of tape. "Why not?"

"Why not?" Waneeda widens her eyes. "Well, just for openers, I don't even belong to your dumb club."

"But you *could* join." Needless to say, this is something Joy Marie has suggested before.

"Yeah, right."

"No, really," argues Joy Marie. "I know you don't believe me, but it's really very inspirational."

Waneeda laughs. The only thing the Environmental Club has ever inspired is ridicule. "You mean besides causing public outrage."

"That only happened once," says Joy Marie. "And anyway, the point is that it'd be good for you to join."

Waneeda sighs.

Joy Marie is always coming up with things that would be good for Waneeda. Yoga. Swimming. Green vegetables. Jewelry making. Scrapbooking. Gardening. You'd think she was a personal lifestyle guru rather than a best friend.

"So would be being adopted by Bill Gates," says Waneeda. "But that's not going to happen, either."

Joy Marie doesn't laugh. "That's not funny; it's defensive," she says, leading the way down the hall. "It wouldn't hurt you to get involved in some kind of extracurricular activity, you know. You need to get some outside interests."

As if Waneeda has any interests at all. She sighs again.

Joy Marie stops outside the girls' bathroom. "And a little work wouldn't kill you, either." As a general rule, the only part of Waneeda that's ever been seen to work is her mouth.

"What do you call this?" Waneeda waves the flyers over her head. "Chopped liver?"

"You know what I mean." Joy Marie readies the tape dispenser for another assault. "Maybe if you really involved yourself you'd have some fun."

Waneeda is about to amend the truth slightly by saying that she already has plenty of fun, when something bright orange whacks into her arm and her stack of papers falls to the ground.

"Hey! Why don't you watch where you're going, Princess Pumpkin?" snaps Waneeda.

The other girl barely turns around. "Are you talking to *me*?"

"Yeah," says Waneeda. "I am talking to *you*. Look what you did!"

"Waneeda, shhh," warns Joy Marie. "Don't start any trouble."

"What do I care?" asks Waneeda. "I hope her eyelashes fall off in her lunch. She is such a stuck-up witch."

Chapter Three

And now it's Maya Baraberra's turn to be in Sicilee's way

Meanwhile, in the virtually empty second-floor girls' room, Maya Baraberra and Alice Shimon hug each other with the enthusiasm of people who have been tragically separated by a long war. (It has, in fact, been less than two weeks since they last saw each other, and it was distance that separated them, not heavy bombing.) Alice's Thai scarf gets caught on one of Maya's crystal earrings, and Maya's handmade backpack, heavily decorated with an intriguing assortment of iconic pins from EZLN and Che Guevara to Homer Simpson and the Sex Pistols, bangs against the sink.

"Oh, God, I am so glad to see you!" shrieks Alice, disentangling. "It was like I'd been abducted by aliens and was living with creatures with two heads who beeped. I missed you so much."

"Me too. I can't tell you how much I missed you. I mean, truly, Al, there's nothing like a week with your relatives to make you appreciate your friends." Maya swings her backpack off her shoulder with a sigh. "You wouldn't believe how soul-suckingly horrendous it was. There were times when I felt like I'd been sent to a penal colony and would never see home again."

"Oh, I believe you." Alice slides her own backpack down her arm and sets it on the edge of the sink. "Trust me, the Shimons are a world unto themselves." She makes the face of someone who understands what suffering is. "And it's definitely not a better world."

"They can't be any worse than the Baraberras. Seriously, you would not believe the junk I had heaped on me in the name of peace on earth this year. Really and truly." Words fail her for nearly an entire second. "Everything they give you is made by workers who are virtual slaves. And even if it wasn't, you wouldn't want it because it's, like, so uncool."

Their eyes now on the mirrors, Maya and Alice remove their makeup bags from their packs and set them in the sinks.

"How did they like the stuff you gave them?" asks Alice. "Mine hated my gifts. You should've seen them. You'd think I'd wrapped up roadkill or something." She reaches for her lip gloss. "Like my grandma? I gave her a box of those eco balls? So not only would she be environmentally friendly for a change, but she wouldn't have to spend a fortune using detergent anymore? She thought

19

they were shuttlecocks! You know, for badminton? 'Alice,' she says, 'I'm too old for games like that.' I didn't know whether to laugh or cry."

"I know, I know. They just do *not* have a clue. If it doesn't exist in their world, then it doesn't exist. Which pretty much limits reality to going to work, shopping, and watching TV." Maya leans into the mirror, eyeing her reflection in a critical, semiprofessional way. "I swear, if I'd had to listen to my cousin Petra drone on about her adventures as a cheerleader in the wilds of Vermont for one more minute, I think I would have run outside screaming and buried myself in a snowdrift."

"Ditto." Alice pouts at her reflection. "I'm not saying that it's not nice to see them—we do share at least part of a gene pool, and they can be really sweet and everything— but they are *so* limited." She puts on a thin, whining voice. *"Why are you wearing that? Why did you get your nose pierced? Why are you reading about that? What do you have against this? How can you drink that tea? It smells like boiled flowers!"*

"Same thing here." Maya applies more kohl. "They act like *I'm* some kind of freak because I care about stuff. Uncle Morty said that I sounded like one of those fanatical *environmentalists!* You know, like Clemens the Lemon? I said, 'Excuse me, but do I look like a nerd?'"

"Exactly," agrees Alice. "You just have to show a little concern or think a little differently and they get all warped."

"Two hundred and thirty-six plastic bags," says Maya.

"My grandmother has two hundred and thirty-six plastic bags under the kitchen sink. I counted them."

Alice whistles. "Jumping Jehoshaphat. That's got to be some kind of record."

Maya pulls roughly at clumps of her hair. The effect of her haircut is supposed to be funky and windblown, not flat and blown over. "That's what I mean, you know? They all act like there's nothing wrong with the world. It's like Grandma doesn't even know that we have an environment, never mind that it's going to be buried in plastic thanks to people like her."

"What about the food?" Alice stretches her eyes and rolls mascara on the lashes. "Did they get on your case about the food?"

"Are you kidding?" Maya shakes her head in a speculative kind of way. "It was like the sound track for the whole visit." She almost has to heave herself onto the sink to make certain her eyes aren't smudged. *What do you eat if you don't eat meat? How do you get any protein? Oh, you have to try the ham, Grandma's been baking it for the last two hundred years."*

"Praise the Lord for inventing fish and chicken." Alice, like Maya, is a practicing vegetarian — though some, of course, might say that they could practice a little harder. "I would've starved to death or been mercilessly nagged into eating some poor cow if it wasn't for them. Because, trust me, the Pittsburgh Shimons do not do tofu."

"The Vermont Baraberras do not—"

Maya breaks off as the door to the bathroom is suddenly flung open. She and Alice both turn to see who it is.

"Talk about what's wrong with the world," mutters Alice.

"The Barbie doll made flesh," mumbles Maya.

Strictly speaking, the new arrival is neither of those things. It is Sicilee Kewe.

Although Maya and Alice are staring right at her, they don't acknowledge her presence by so much as the flicker of an eye. There is nothing unusual in this. They may live in the same country, in the same state, in the same town, and go to the same school as Sicilee Kewe, but they might as well live on different planets. And rather wish that they did.

Sicilee is smiling, of course, but it is a smile that goes a long way toward redefining both loathing and insincerity.

"Sweet Mary," Sicilee says, not quite under her breath. "The dipster hipsters." And for the second time that morning, she turns and flees.

Chapter Four

What a difference a minute can make

It is almost time for the school day to officially begin. People are shuffling down the corridors toward their classrooms, but the main hall still reverberates with talk and laughter, punctuated by the slamming of lockers and the hurrying of feet on the stairs. Just like on any other morning of the school year.

Indeed, up until now there has been nothing to suggest that this day is anything but a normal day. No cauldron of witches muttering prophecies behind the library. No shower of tree frogs over the football field. No abnormal celestial activity of the sort that suggests some earthshaking event is about to take place. Even Maya, who is sometimes known for them, hasn't had one of her hunches.

But then, only minutes before the homeroom bell, the door to the office suddenly opens and a boy steps through — rather like the last person arriving at a party being held in his honor.

For the sake of our story, it is important to say here that — based on first impressions — this boy is no ordinary boy. Not an ordinary Clifton Springs boy, at any rate. It could be argued, of course, that any newcomer is going to stand out next to boys you've known since kindergarten, but it isn't simply a question of novelty. To begin with, he is closer to beautiful than handsome: full, sensuous mouth and nose; large eyes so heavily lashed that he might be wearing mascara; strong chin and brow; straight black hair. His are the kind of impossible good looks that make even the least impressionable of people think, *My God! Is that what humans are supposed to look like?* To match that, he has an air of effortless, almost alien, cool, standing there among the jeans in his vintage pin-striped suit (no tie) and plain black T-shirt, like a visiting prince — a canvas book bag casually flung over his shoulder and a class schedule, personally filled out for him by Mrs. Skwill, the overworked administrative assistant, in his hand. He shows none of the awkwardness or nervousness most of us exhibit when we walk into a crowd of strangers, but pauses for a few seconds, his eyes calmly scanning his new schoolmates, smiling amiably if vaguely, apparently completely at ease. As he starts to stride nonchalantly across the hall, one eye on the schedule he's holding and the other on the sign that says ROOMS 1–20, his new classmates turn — very much as though he is a magnet and their heads are made of iron filings—as their attention is caught. It would be an obvious exaggeration to say that jaws drop and breath is held, but it wouldn't be much of one.

It is, of course, a gloomy day, at a gloomy time of year. Which may explain why news of the arrival of a mysterious stranger in their midst will spread through the school like a wildfire raging across drought-dry plains. Speculation about the new boy starts spontaneously and immediately. He's stinking rich. He's a world-class athlete. His GPA is 4.0. He only dates models and movie stars. His mother's really famous. His father's in the CIA. He's from Europe. He speaks ten languages fluently. The only word he knows in English is "hello." Within an hour, boys who haven't seen him yet are making jokes about him; boys who haven't met him have decided whether they like him or not. Within an hour, girls who haven't seen him yet could pick him out of a police lineup. Girls who *have* seen him walk through the hallways tense as dogs that have just caught a whiff of rabbit.

In time, of course, the speculation will be replaced by facts. They will know his name, where he comes from, where he lives, and his ethnic background—plus enough trivial information to fill a quiz—but for now all anyone knows for sure is that he wasn't here before, and now he is.

Maya, descending the stairs with Alice beside her,

comes to an abrupt stop. The moment she first sees the new kid is like no other moment in her life. She feels the way someone who has never seen a body of water bigger than a wading pool might feel when she first sees the ocean. And to think how close she came this morning to putting on her silver feather earrings instead of the empowering crystals. She actually had them in her hand. It's as if some part of her knew that today would be special and she should be prepared.

"*Gott im Himmel,*" murmurs Maya. "Where did *he* come from?"

"Not around here," Alice murmurs back.

Waneeda, going with Joy Marie to deposit the leftover flyers in her locker, also stops fairly abruptly.

In much the way that someone living on the Arctic tundra never thinks about climbing palm trees or skinny-dipping, Waneeda has never shown any interest in boys. As many girls do, she has had the occasional crush on a musician or movie star—boys so far removed from her that they don't really exist—but she's never had a crush on someone who walks the same streets and breathes the same air that she does. Until, that is, the moment when the newest member of the student body, glancing at the paper in his hand, drifts past her like a satellite.

"Who is *that*?" whispers Waneeda. Joy Marie, who hasn't stopped abruptly, doesn't answer her, of course.

And, echoing the words of Alice Shimon for the first and last time in her life, Waneeda adds, "He can't be from around here."

Even she and Joy Marie would have noticed if he were.

Sicilee, in a clutch in one corner with Kristin, Ash, and Loretta, is recounting her adventures trying to find a friendly restroom when Ash suddenly interrupts her with a slightly high-pitched, "Oh, my God! Will you look at that?"

"Whoowhee . . ." says Loretta. "Do you think he's just visiting from the Planet Drop-Dead-Gorgeous or do you think he's ours?"

Sicilee and Kristin both turn to see what the fuss is about.

It's just as well that Sicilee is standing still, because the second her eyes fall on the boy in the pin-striped suit, her heart (metaphorically, if not literally) falls at his feet as if it's been shot.

"Sweet Mary," sighs Sicilee, and she squeezes Kristin's arm.

Chapter Five

Sicilee Kewe, Girl Detective

Sicilee is the kind of girl who likes to get what she wants when she wants it. Not hours later. Not tomorrow. Now. Right now, what Sicilee wants is to find out everything about the new kid that she can and then, armed with this information, introduce herself and stake her claim.

So instead of going to her first class, Sicilee spends more than fifteen minutes in the girls' room, texting her network of friends. HV U SN TH NW KD? WHR? KP ME PSTD. Needless to say, since the others are all in class and not hiding out in bathrooms around the school, she receives no immediate reply.

Sicilee's next stop is the office for a late pass.

"It was a female thing, if you know what I mean," she confides in a conspiratorial whisper to Mrs. Skwill. "If I could've gone to my class first, I would totally have done that. But I just couldn't. It was a super emergency. It was like the time my mom took me to New York to see *The Phantom of the Opera*? And this pigeon dropped one right on her head as we came out of the hotel? So even though we knew we were going to be late and everybody was going to be really annoyed, we had to go back inside so she could wash her hair."

Mrs. Skwill is one of the many people on whom Sicilee's smile always works.

"Don't you worry, honey," she assures her. "I'll write you a note."

"That is so super nice of you," Sicilee gushes. "I know how busy you are. The first day back and everything . . . and everybody depending on *you*. . . . It must be just, like, crazy."

Mrs. Skwill agrees that it has been a busy morning. There was a leak in the science block. There was a burst pipe in the gym. The main photocopier wouldn't start. Several files were missing. Two teachers are out with the flu. And, on top of everything else, there was the new student to look after.

Sicilee's smile switches from sisterly sympathy to girlish bewilderment. She tilts her head and leans into the counter. "New student? Really? Who's that?"

Kristin is waiting for her at the top of the northeast staircase for the walk to their language arts class.

"Well?" demands Sicilee. "What did you find out?"

"Not much." Kristin hooks an arm through Sicilee's as they start their descent. "Ariadne saw him in that new deli—the Portuguese one?—on Sunday, so she figures he probably lives out by her, but otherwise that's all the news that's fit to print so far. He's like the Lone Ranger, but without the mask and the faithful companion. What about you?"

Sicilee's smile is undimmed by any attempt at humility. "His name's Cody Lightfoot. He's in our grade. He's an honor student. He comes from northern California. He was living with his mother—she's some kind of journalist—but she got a job in England, so he's moved here to live with his dad. Mrs. Skwill says that his dad's a professor at the university, but she wasn't sure what the dad teaches, maybe anthropology. And besides being extremely good-looking and smart, Cody's a mechanical expert, too, because he got that photocopier that's always breaking down going in less than a minute."

Kristin whistles. "I swear, girl, you really should be a spy."

Sicilee's eyes (which, unlike her mouth, are not smiling) are on her phone. "This is unbelievable. Nobody knows where he is." If she were a spy, she would probably find herself behind enemy lines with no backup. "Nobody's in his homeroom. Nobody's in his first class." How is this possible? "Sweet Mary, nobody's even passed him in the hall." Forget the Lone Ranger; this is obviously the Invisible Man.

"It's only been, like, an hour," says Kristin. "He'll turn up."

Sicilee sighs. "Yeah, right." On the arm of some other girl. She yanks open the door to their room. And stops dead.

Cody Lightfoot, lately of northern California, has not only turned up at last, but has turned up in Sicilee's Language Arts class. His canvas book bag is on the desk directly in front of the teacher's desk, and Cody himself is to one side of it, talking to Mrs. Sotomayor in a relaxed, almost intimate manner.

He's in her class! It was starting to look as though the gods who normally smile down on Sicilee and shower her with gifts had turned the other way, but clearly they were only momentarily distracted. Here he is, where she will see him for nearly an hour every day, where she will sit next to him and talk to him and whisper witticisms and lend him a pen or borrow his. Sicilee couldn't cross the room any faster if she were on skates.

Oblivious to the fact that she has let the door slam shut on Kristin, Sicilee drops her own bag on the desk next to Cody's.

"I'm sure you'll catch up in no time," Mrs. Sotomayor is saying as Sicilee arrives on her other side, wearing a polite and patient smile on her face. And, in an atypically generous gesture, adds, "We do have an unassigned book report due on Monday, but naturally I won't expect you to do that."

Cody looks straight at Mrs. Sotomayor, which means that, since Sicilee has moved closer to the teacher, he is almost looking straight at her as well. With only a few feet and a desk between them, Sicilee now sees that she was wrong about him. He isn't merely extremely good-looking; he is awesomely, spectacularly, and uniquely gorgeous. If he were a geological feature, he'd be the Grand Canyon.

"Oh, that's not a problem." Cody's voice is warm and mellow and sounds like a hug. His eyes, it turns out, aren't blue like the eyes of regular boys, but the aquamarine of an unspoiled tropical sea. "I had some free time on my hands over Christmas, so I read *War and Peace*. Man, there is a novel that really deserves to be called great — it just has everything going for it, doesn't it? You know, once I got started, I couldn't put it down — maybe I can do a report on that? I get that we're supposed to be zoning in on American fiction this year, but maybe just this once . . ."

Mrs. Sotomayor, who in her fifteen years of teaching has no memory of a student ever volunteering for work he or she could avoid, recovers enough from this shock to say, "Well, if you're certain you have the time . . ." And, possibly because Cody is still looking into her eyes, she drops her pen on the floor. Which is when she notices Sicilee, hovering beside her like an exceptionally brightly dressed ghost.

"Sicilee?" Sicilee is not a girl Mrs. Sotomayor has ever been tempted to describe as ethereal, but she does look as though she may be having an out-of-body experience. "Sicilee? Is there something you wanted?"

Sicilee returns to reality with a start. "What?" She drags her smile from the scenic experience that is Cody Lightfoot to the dingy alley that is the head of the Language Arts department. "Oh, yeah, right, yeah. I just wanted to check with you about the book report? I know we've got a minimum length, but is there a maximum? You know, because the book I'm doing, it works on so many levels?" Sicilee steams on like a runaway train, hoping to impress Cody Lightfoot with her sophistication and intelligence. She doesn't distract herself by glancing over to see his reaction. She'll wait until she's done, and then she'll turn and give him one of her biggest smiles. And as they sit down, she'll introduce herself and welcome him to Clifton Springs. "I picked it because it really is a modern classic, and I think you could say not just an American modern classic but a world—"

"You write as much as you want, Sicilee," cuts in Mrs. Sotomayor, who knows very well that Sicilee picked this particular book because she can watch the movie and not have to read it. "Now, if you'll take your seat, I think it's about time we started this class."

"Oh, sure, right." Sicilee turns, her smile bright as sunshine. It is, perhaps, a testament to the indefatigable human spirit that Sicilee's smile doesn't dim when she realizes that Cody Lightfoot is not at the desk next to the one that holds her orange backpack. He is sitting at the back of the room. Between Kristin and Farley Hubble. Which is where Sicilee usually sits.

"Sicilee?" prompts Mrs. Sotomayor.

Sicilee takes her new seat. She is still smiling.

This, of course, is not further evidence of the indefatigable human spirit. It is simply to stop her from groaning out loud.

Chapter Six

This is how stalkers are made

Within minutes of her first sight of him, Maya Baraberra decided that it wasn't a 747 that brought Cody Lightfoot to Clifton Springs, but Fate. They were destined to meet. Didn't she have a feeling that this year was going to be seriously significant? Didn't she say? It made total sense.

But when Cody didn't materialize in her homeroom or her first class of the day, Maya realized that if she wanted to get him into her group before someone else claimed him, she was going to have to give Fate a hand.

Which is why, at this very moment, she and Alice are slouching away from school in the rain, following the figure in the old army parka (winter issue), hood up, several yards ahead of them.

"I can't believe that I let you talk me into this," grumbles Alice. "I feel like a stalker."

"Don't be so melodramatic. We're more like spies. We're having an adventure."

Alice isn't really the adventurous type. "What if he turns around and sees us?"

"I wouldn't worry about it." Unlike Sicilee, Maya doesn't feel she *always* has to smile. "I don't think he'd notice me if I was wrapped in Christmas lights." Wrapped in Christmas lights and holding a flaming torch between her teeth. "Besides, what if he does? We just happen to be going in the same direction. It is a free country, you know."

Alice's sigh is drowned out by someone shouting behind them. "Cody! Cody, man! Wait up!"

Cody stops and half turns around, and Maya stops breathing. If proof was needed that either she is invisible or he is blind, he waves amiably at someone behind her. Maya's heart resumes beating as Clifton Springs' two token goths splash past them.

"He may be seriously gorgeous and charming and charismatic and everything," says Alice, summarizing the general opinion of a large percentage of the student body as they resume walking, "but he sure isn't picky about who he hangs out with."

"Maybe he's a true free spirit, you know?" says Maya. "I mean, it's kind of Christlike, isn't it? He hung out with whoever he wanted to, too."

"I guess." Alice's shrug suggests that she isn't convinced. "But, he's new here. Aren't you supposed to try to fit in when you're new?"

And, as Maya knows only too well, the people Cody Lightfoot should be trying to fit in with, of course, are Maya and her friends.

But Cody has changed schools before, and fitting in — even with the hippest and coolest group in the school — is not his way. He prefers that things fit in with him. Although Clifton Springs is a school with a social hierarchy slightly more rigid than that of feudal Europe, he has already made it clear that he has no intention of aligning himself with any one group. He is friendly to everyone in a laid-back, effortless way — as likely to eat lunch with the emos as the jocks, as likely to walk down the hallway with the class president as the class clown. This is a method that has always worked for Cody in the past, and, on the whole, it is working now. The girls like him because, despite his break-your-heart good looks, he is neither arrogant nor aloof. The boys like him because, despite the several ways in which he stands out (he's into qigong, tai chi, all-weather climbing, yoga, swimming, and white-water rafting — not football, basketball, baseball, or wrestling), he is neither competitive nor threatening.

Indeed, the only person who has had a negative word for Cody is Jason Coombs, until a few days ago probably the hippest boy in their class. Jason thinks Cody's a little weird because of the yoga. All that standing like a tree and *om*ing, said Jason, is pretty much a girl's thing. Maya, who has been on the brink of dating Jason for the last few months, said nothing but eyed him critically, noticing new flaws.

At the end of the road the goths turn left and Cody turns right, away from town.

"What did I say?" Maya's nails dig into Alice's arm. "Didn't I say I had a hunch he was going home?" Maya has it all planned. As Cody reaches his front door, she'll suddenly call out, *Hello? Excuse me, but my friend and I are lost.* And then he'll turn around, eager to help, and she'll act all surprised and say, *Hey, don't you go to Clifton Springs? Haven't I seen you at school?* He'll hurry back to the sidewalk to talk to her, amazed that he doesn't remember seeing her before. *Yes,* he'll say, *I just moved to town.* She'll hold out her hand. *Well, welcome to Clifton Springs.* She'll smile. *My name's Maya.* He'll say that his name's Cody and invite her in.

"I just hope it isn't too far," mutters Alice. "My feet are already soaked."

But, as so often happens in life, Alice's hope is not to be fulfilled. Block after block goes by, but Cody never turns up a path or breaks his stride. Instead, he marches straight through puddles in his vintage galoshes like a man on a mission, but the girls, whose footwear is less rugged, have to scurry around the larger pools and leap across the smaller—all while trying to keep him in their sight and them out of his. Maya, warmed and protected by her fantasies, is oblivious to the distance and the weather, but as the blocks become a mile and then another, their adventure loses the little interest it had for her friend.

"This is ridiculous. Where the hell does he live?" Alice gasps. Her feet are so wet now that she feels like she's wading. "In the next town?"

Maya, deep into imagining Cody asking her if she'd like a cup of coffee, smiles into the distance.

"Maya!" Alice's voice is far too loud for surveillance work. "Did you hear me? Where is he going? To visit his mother in England?"

Maya comes back to the moment with a scowl. "Shhh!" she hisses. "He'll hear you."

"I don't care anymore." Alice comes to a stubborn stop under the relative shelter of a large tree at the curb. "I'm tired of this. I want to go home."

"But we're almost there," pleads Maya. "I'm sure we are." She tugs on Alice's arm. "Come on, he's crossing—" What she was going to say was that Cody is crossing the road—something Alice could actually see for herself if she weren't staring forlornly at her feet—but the realization of what road it is that he's crossing cuts the flow of words. "*Gott im Himmel . . .*"

"What?" Alice has added shrillness to the volume. "*Now* what's wrong?"

"Look. Can you believe it?" Maya points beyond the traffic to where a sprawl of venerable gray buildings rises from a tree-lined lawn. Students fill the paths that wind between the buildings and the quad. Cody Lightfoot has already disappeared among them, just another hooded figure with a book bag hurrying through the rain.

Alice's frown deepens. "Is that the university?" This is an accusation, not a question.

Maya nods. "I guess he wasn't going home after all." Fate is toying with her. If she hadn't been so busy jumping over puddles and trying to keep out of sight . . . "He must be meeting his father." But maybe all isn't lost. She's sure the senior Lightfoot teaches history or sociology—or, possibly, anthropology—something like that. If they can find the right building, there's still a chance they could run into Cody. She could stumble and twist her ankle in front of him. Probably his father would offer them a ride home.

"Forget it, Maya." Alice straightens up, adjusting herself in the manner of someone about to jump ship. "There's no way I'm wandering around that campus for the next hour looking for him. I'm out of here."

"But we've come so far. If we just hang around a little longer—"

Somewhere not far enough away to be reassuring, a dog starts to bark in a way that even someone less close to tears and exhaustion than Alice would describe as ferocious bordering on hysterical.

Chapter Seven

There's a chance that reality begins in dreams

Sicilee and Maya are both convinced that once they catch Cody Lightfoot's attention they are as good as on their first date with him, if not actually engaged. These assumptions, of course, are based on who they are (the most popular girl in the most popular group, and the coolest girl in the coolest group) and what they look like (model pretty, and attractive in an alternative, arty way). In contrast, Waneeda—who doesn't even register on the radar screen of popularity or cool—is a large, ungainly girl with runaway, tumbleweed hair and the instantly forgettable kind of face that would only be an advantage if she decided to commit a crime. She's not a fool. Waneeda knows that the only way she could attract Cody Lightfoot's attention would be to dump her lunch on his lap. But she still can dream.

Waneeda's dreams used to center around her favorite TV shows and arguments with her mother, but now she dreams about Cody every night. In dreams, she walks with him and talks with him and sometimes even holds his hand. In these dreams, Cody is the funny, kind, sensitive, and intelligent boy she imagines him to be—and Waneeda is someone else. Instead of shambling the way she does in real life, she sashays; instead of dragging her heels and always complaining, she is energetic and always laughing. She looks different, too. Prettier and brighter—her hair like a cloud around her head, her smile like the sun.

In last night's dream, Cody saved Waneeda's life. She was drowning in an angry sea under a hard, ash-colored sky. "Help! Help!" she was shouting. "Help! Help!" But, of course, there was no one to hear her desperate screams. There was no land in sight, no boat in the distance, not so much as a gull wheeling overhead. And then, as the icy fingers of the sea were pulling her under for the last time, Cody Lightfoot (in his pin-striped suit and black T-shirt) suddenly dove in beside her. His arms were strong and warm around her. "It's all right," he murmured. "Don't worry, dear Waneeda. Everything's going to be all right." She woke up tangled in the blankets, a pillow clutched against her.

Even now, so many hours later, as she and Joy Marie walk home together on Friday afternoon, last night's dream keeps replaying itself in her mind, making Joy

Marie's chatter no more than background noise. Until Joy Marie says something that makes Waneeda almost choke on the candy she just put in her mouth.

"What?" asks Waneeda. "What did you say?"

"God, Waneeda." Joy Marie makes her why-don't-you-ever-listen-to-me? face. "I said that Clemens says that Cody Lightfoot seems pretty solid. You know, interesting and intelligent and kind of a mensch."

"Clemens," repeats Waneeda. "Are you saying Cody Lightfoot talks to Clemens?"

Clemens Reis is the geek's geek. Waneeda, who lives behind Clemens, has known him since they were in diapers, and so can attest that he was always a peculiar child (in the video of her earliest birthday parties, Clemens is the scowling one who refused to wear a party hat or sing), but puberty has made him even more peculiar. He has an eccentric nature and an independent, argumentative mind. Physically, he is thin and gawky, with hair that is long not as a statement of cool or rebellion but because he never remembers to get it cut. His glasses are held together by a paper clip. Clemens is the kind of boy who can tell you how many helium balloons you'd need to make a cat fly (depending on its weight, of course) and who will tell you (whether you ask or not) what percentage of global greenhouse-gas emissions is caused by cows. He wears a hat knitted by his grandmother and saddle shoes. It is miracle enough that two such different examples of a carbon-based life-form as Cody and Clemens should inhabit the same planet, let alone speak to each other.

"He talks to Clemens all the time," says Joy Marie. "At least he isn't a snob like everybody else in this school."

"I guess that's true." Waneeda has, in fact, seen him talk to people even she wouldn't talk to.

Waneeda chews on a cherry-flavored ball of corn syrup and sugar in the way of someone considering the possible origins of life. No one expects less of Waneeda than Waneeda herself. Indeed, you could say that one of her strengths is that her lack of ambition is comfortably matched by her lack of expectation. But now something shifts ever so slightly, and she starts to consider the possibility that, maybe, there might be a chance that—someday, somehow—Cody Lightfoot will talk to her somewhere other than in her dreams.

Chapter Eight

Sicilee doesn't understand it when things don't go the way she wants

Since the social hierarchy of Clifton Springs High is slightly more rigid than that of feudal Europe, every group has its own table in the cafeteria.

Sicilee's group sits in the center of the room, which is both symbolic (she and her friends, after all, are at the center of the school's social life) and practical (from there they can both see and be seen).

Today, Ash, Loretta, and Kristin are discussing the weekend's trip to the mall.

"I have to take back that dress I got," Loretta is saying. "I mean, it looked great in the store, but ohmygod when I tried it on at home? I looked *enormous*. You should've seen my butt!"

Ash nods knowingly. "It's the mirrors. They have special mirrors that make you look skinnier than you are."

Kristin doesn't think it's the mirrors. She thinks the fault lies with mass production. The clothes are made to fit everybody, so they fit no one.

Loretta looks impressed. She never thought of it like that before.

Ash says that doesn't mean she's wrong about the mirrors. Everybody knows about it. She saw it on TV.

Sicilee isn't really listening. She seems to be smiling at Loretta and Ash, but really she is gazing beyond them, to a table at the side of the room where today Cody Lightfoot sits with Clemens Reis and his loser friends, looking like a movie star visiting a homeless shelter at Thanksgiving. Why is he sitting with *them*? They're nobodies. They're less than nobodies. They're crustaceous growths on the skin of society. If anybody else — *anybody,* even Kristin, even her own mother — was to eat lunch with Clemens, Sicilee would be so grossed out that she would never be able to speak to them again. But that, of course, is not the way she feels about Cody. All that really bothers her is the fact that he isn't sitting with *her.*

Last week ended much as it began. Even though Sicilee shares a classroom with Cody Lightfoot every day, she knew him no better on Friday afternoon than she had on Tuesday morning.

She watches Cody put the thermos back into his old-fashioned workman's lunch box and take out a small container as though he is doing something truly remarkable that no human teenager has ever done before. Sicilee stifles a sigh. None of the boys she considers her friend ever brings his lunch from home. None of them wears his hair the length Cody does or dresses the way Cody dresses—or causes Sicilee's heart to miss a beat when he smiles either.

Cody removes half a sandwich from the container. Her eyes follow the sandwich as it moves toward his squashy, kissable lips. Sicilee's own sandwich sits untouched on her tray. She has less interest in food right now than in learning to weave straw baskets.

"Don't you think so, Siss?" asks Loretta.

Sicilee nods automatically. "Uh-huh."

Last Friday, Sicilee finally managed to be right behind Cody as they left Language Arts and asked him, conversationally, about changing schools in the middle of the year. "It must be such a drag," said Sicilee. "Starting all over again, I mean."

Cody said that it wasn't a problem. He embraces change.

To stop herself from saying that she wished he'd embrace *her*, Sicilee offered to show him the town.

But this wasn't a problem either.

"I've been here before. You know, visiting my dad. So I know my way around."

But Sicilee still wasn't daunted. She invited him to a party on Saturday night. "You know," said Sicilee, "so you can meet everybody."

"Everybody?" Cody grinned. "That's going to be a pretty big party."

Unsure as to whether or not he was making fun of her, Sicilee laughed. "You know what I mean."

"To tell you the truth, I'm not really a party person," said Cody. And then (just when she was starting to think that, for some unfathomable reason, he was being deliberately dense) he gave her a smile that could have heated every house in Clifton Springs for the rest of the winter, lowered his voice intimately, and added, "I'm much more into one-on-one."

Now, as she watches him lick something from his fingers, Sicilee wonders again what he meant by that. Was it a come-on? Did he mean one-on-one with her? Or did he mean one-on-one with someone else?

Cody brushes crumbs from his mouth. His hand is wide and solid, the fingers delicate and long. Sicilee gulps her flavored water, stifling a sigh.

If he meant he'd rather see her alone than with dozens of strangers, then why on earth doesn't he ask her out? It's not as if she hasn't given him plenty of encouragement. The only way she could do more to bring attention to herself would be to wear bells. Risking sweat and dishevelment, Sicilee rushes to Language Arts every day in the hope of sitting beside him. She used to lurk at the back of the class with Kristin, passing notes or checking her texts, but now she puts herself right near the front, raising her hand whenever Mrs. Sotomayor asks a question, whether she knows the answer or not, and loudly agreeing with everything Cody says. *Oh, I think so, too,* she says. At the end of Language Arts, she risks broken bones again, frantic to be the person behind Cody as he leaves the room. She is always strolling through the corridor when he goes to his locker in the morning. She is always in the main hall when he leaves in the afternoon. If it weren't for the fact that she gets a ride every day from Mrs. Shepl after school, she'd be tempted to follow him home.

And does Cody notice all her efforts? He does not. Any other boy would be flattered. Pleased with himself. Any other boy would go straight to the seat she'd saved for him every day, not just when there's nowhere else to sit. Any other boy would lean close to compare notes. Borrow a pen. Compliment her. Tease her to find out if she has a steady boyfriend. Beg her for a date.

But Cody, of course, is not just *any boy.* Which is both a point in his favor and an obvious drawback, because he could only notice Sicilee less if she were invisible. Or someone else. Some dull, dumpy girl with limp hair and no dress sense. Sure, he smiles back when Sicilee smiles at him; he nods when they pass in the hallway; he talks to her when she strikes up a conversation. But he smiles at, nods at, and talks to a lot of people (including people Sicilee didn't know were in the school before she saw him smiling at them and nodding at them and talking to them). Sicilee stifles another sigh. That first glimpse of Cody, crossing the main hall with his schedule in his hand, was the last time she's ever seen him alone.

Sicilee can't figure out what's going wrong. What can the problem be? Sure, her mouth is a little small and her laugh has been unfavorably compared to the distress call of a young seagull, but, those small imperfections aside, she is hands down the prettiest, most popular, and most desirable girl in the entire school. Everyone knows that.

"He's probably just so used to looking at himself in the mirror that he doesn't notice when somebody else is gorgeous," suggested Kristin when Sicilee was trying to solve the mystery.

"But I'm used to looking at *me*," argued Sicilee, "and I notice him."

Now the other girls move on to where they'll have lunch at the mall next Saturday. The hamburger bar's getting kind of passé. Ditto the taqueria. The pizzeria is out for the moment because Loretta is back on her diet. Kristin doesn't like Chinese food. Ash won't go to the deli since the time they gave her tuna instead of chicken salad. Loretta says they could always go to that new vegetarian place, and they all laugh.

Sicilee laughs, too, but inside she is closer to tears. *So this is what it's like to be in love,* she thinks as she watches Cody clap Clemens on the shoulder like they're old, old friends. Obsessed. Fixated. Riddled with doubt and despair. It drives her totally crazy that he shows no interest in her. It drives her even crazier that she cares.

On the other side of the room, the oblivious object of Sicilee's affections suddenly pushes back his chair and gets to his feet. He starts strolling toward the back of the room. He must need something from the kitchen.

A piece of silverware clatters to the floor.

"Don't you think so, Sicilee?" asks Loretta.

"Yeah," says Ash. "What do you think?"

"I'll be right back," says Sicilee. "I need a clean fork."

Chapter Nine

Sicilee isn't the only one who is unhappy about being ignored

Maya is late for lunch. She texts Alice as she scurries to the cafeteria. IS HE THR? ON MY WY. Maya has been late a lot in the past week. She has been late for each of her classes at least once. Late for homeroom every day. Late for school this morning. Late picking up her little sister from her cello lesson on Wednesday. So late for her appointment with the dentist last Thursday that she missed it.

"But you don't understand—it wasn't my fault," she told her mother during their discussion of where she'd been when she was supposed to be in Dr. Barley's waiting room.

"Oh, really? And whose fault was it?" Mrs. Baraberra sounded genuinely curious.

"Ms. Kimodo's," said Maya. "If she hadn't given us that assignment, I wouldn't have had to race over to the library like that, would I?"

This excuse came under the heading of Necessary Lies. Obviously, there was no way Maya could explain to her mother that she is under the control of forces far greater than herself—so great that they could stop the moon in its orbit and drop every star from the sky, never mind make her miss her six-month checkup. Her mother is a practical woman who alphabetizes her canned goods and checks the spare tire in her car at least once a month. Passion is as foreign a language to her as Norwegian. If Maya told her mother that she's the Plaything of Destiny, a Victim of Love, her mother would think she's taking drugs. Even though it would have been the truth, of course: love has Maya by the heart. The realization hit her as she and Alice trudged home on Thursday afternoon. Naturally, Maya has had crushes before, but she's never felt like this. She thinks about Cody Lightfoot all the time. She turns into a bowl of hot-fudge sauce whenever she gets near him. If she even *thinks* she sees him, she feels as though she's just been pushed out of a plane. This isn't just a passing infatuation. This is l-o-v-e, love.

Which, in something of a history-making event, gives Maya and Sicilee two things in common. Being in love and being ignored.

The debacle on Thursday was, of course, not Maya's first attempt to snare Cody Lightfoot's attention. It took her two days to piece together his schedule. His locker is near Mallory's. Shelby has Language Arts across the hall from Cody's class. Jason is in his gym class and Shayla in history. Maya's lab partner, Daisy, sits behind him in

Cantonese. Daisy's boyfriend, Theo, is in his homeroom. Brion has media studies with him, and Finn has math. This information has allowed Maya to plot where Cody Lightfoot will be at the beginning or end of almost every period, and to be there, too. If Maya could be in two places at once, Cody wouldn't be able to go anywhere but the bathroom without tripping over her.

Which, of course, explains why she's always late. Late for classes and homeroom because she's upstairs when she should be downstairs, in the east wing when she should be in the west.

Not that any of this running around has done Maya any good so far. She lingers with Theo at his homeroom door every morning—and Cody nods at Theo and slips inside. She stands with Daisy outside the Cantonese classroom—and Cody gives Daisy one of his blind-that-girl smiles and sails right in. She hovers in the Language Arts corridor, but she always winds up talking to Shelby, watching Cody drift past with a girl on each side like a ship being escorted into harbor by tugboats. She has sidled up to both Brion and Jason when they were talking to Cody, grinning like a saleswoman, and Cody has finished what he was saying and walked away. On Friday, Cody suddenly appeared in the doorway of the art room, but it was to the boy next to Maya that he said, "I'm sorry to bother you, but I'm looking for Mr. Zin." And twice a day she goes with Mallory to her locker, but the only time

Cody's so much as glanced at her was when she accidentally hit him with her book bag.

"What's wrong with me?" she asked Alice.

Alice says she shouldn't take it personally. "There's nothing wrong with you," said Alice. "For the love of God, he hasn't been here a week yet. You have to cut him a little slack."

"He talked to *you*," snapped Maya.

"He asked me what time the library closes," sighed Alice. "If you'd been there, he would've asked you."

"Maybe," grumped Maya.

But if something isn't wrong with her, then something isn't right.

"Like what?" asked Alice.

Like maybe he likes girlier girls. Or shorter girls. Or taller girls. Or girls who are really thin. Or girls who look cuddly. Or girls who have curly hair. Or blond hair. Or hair so black it's almost blue. Girls who listen to commercial radio. Girls who look as though they've never seen a foreign film in their lives.

"Maybe he isn't into girls at all," said Alice.

"Oh, right." Maya laughed. "You haven't noticed that he's almost always got at least two girls trailing after him?"

"Well, then, maybe he's just shy," said Alice.

"I repeat my original question," said Maya.

It is because she spent forty-five minutes getting

dressed this morning that Maya is now hurrying down the hall. In her rush to leave the house on time, she forgot her homework for history. Ms. Kimodo made her stay after class to explain why.

Her phone starts to shiver as she nears the cafeteria. It's Alice. HURRY. C AT BCK. Maya runs the last few yards and yanks open the door with so much force that she fairly shoots into the room.

Chapter Ten

Waneeda, at least, is used to being ignored

Unlike Sicilee and Maya, Waneeda hasn't spent so much as a second brooding, plotting, scheming, or wondering why Cody Lightfoot ignores her. There would be no point. And as much as she would like Cody to talk to her and smile at her in the real world, that isn't really necessary either. Just his presence is enough. Waneeda keeps the knowledge of her crush on Cody locked in her heart, happy enough to have the secret of it, like something rare and special just for her. For Waneeda, being sweet on Cody makes her feel warm and content the way watching a movie in which everyone is beautiful and funny and endearing and guaranteed a happy ending does. It comforts her. It's light entertainment.

Excited that she is about to have the chance to see Cody Lightfoot for a matter of minutes rather than seconds, Waneeda emerges from the lunch line with her loaded tray, her eyes automatically scanning the room. She and Joy Marie, belonging to no group, sit right outside the kitchen with the other landless peasants, flanked by vending machines, garbage cans, and the recycling bins that everyone ignores, but instead of crossing those few feet to their table, Waneeda stops suddenly in the exit, transfixed by something on the left side of the room. There, sitting with Clemens and his oddball friends, is Cody Lightfoot, laughing and talking and, of course, eating.

Joy Marie, though not really interested in boys or campus gossip, has nonetheless mentioned Cody Lightfoot several times in the course of the past week, in an I-hear-he-did-this, I-hear-he-did-that type of way, but Waneeda never brings up his name in case she gives herself away and ends up with scorn and ridicule heaped on her head. Now, however, as she finally takes her seat across from Joy Marie, Waneeda says, "Do you see what I see? Cody Lightfoot's eating lunch with the Brotherhood of the Nerd!"

Joy Marie finds this piece of news so totally unnoteworthy that she doesn't so much as glance behind her.

"Didn't I tell you that he talks to Clem?" Joy Marie removes her cheese-on-whole-wheat sandwich from the reused plastic bag she's wrapped it in. "What did you think I meant?"

"I thought you meant that he asks him things like what he got for question three in the math homework. Not that he hangs out with him."

"Well, that's not what I meant. I meant that they're friends." Joy Marie takes a bite of her sandwich. "Clemens says he and Cody have a lot in common."

This seems so unlikely that Waneeda laughs. "That must be a nice change for Clemens."

"I'm serious." Joy Marie helps herself to the bowl of salad on Waneeda's tray. Waneeda doesn't really "do" vegetables. "Clem said that he and Cody are more or less on the same page. You know, about the environment and stuff like that."

"Oh, come on!" Waneeda picks up her burger. "I know you don't notice that kind of thing, but Cody is seriously attractive and—"

"And what?" Joy Marie stabs a piece of tomato with her fork. "He's good-looking so he must be shallow?"

"And pretty much the anti-nerd," finishes Waneeda. "Boys who look like Cody don't hang out with boys who look like Clemens."

Joy Marie groans. "Oh, not you, too."

It's not easy to look indignant with a cheeseburger dripping ketchup in your hand, but Waneeda pulls it off with considerable panache. "Not me, too, what?"

"Not *you* have a crush on Cody Lightfoot, too." Joy Marie points the speared tomato at her. "You do realize that practically every girl in this school has a thing about him, don't you?"

"No, I didn't realize," says Waneeda. "I didn't want

to tell you in case you got upset, but I'm actually totally blind."

"I was only saying—"

"And I was only stating a simple fact—not swooning with lust," snaps Waneeda. "Forget I said anything." Now would be a good time to change the subject, before she reveals anything else. She bites into a French fry. "So what's happening with the club? Isn't your big meeting today? You think old Firestone will really shut you down if you don't get any new members?"

Joy Marie shrugs. "I don't see how he can," she says. "I mean, you have to look at all the ramifications and issues." And she starts explaining what she sees the ramifications and issues to be.

Waneeda feels herself start to drift off—the way she does during classes that are especially boring, lectures from her mother, and conversations with Joy Marie when she's in serious, earnest mode. She's thinking about what it would be like to sit at the same table as Cody—to ask him, for instance, if he'd like a couple of fries. She is imagining him coaxing her to eat her salad—*Come on, Waneeda, vegetables are really good for you*—when she notices something out of the corner of her eye. It is Cody Lightfoot, the real Cody Lightfoot, gliding up the far aisle so smoothly that his feet don't seem to touch the ground.

Almost level with their row, Cody turns and heads toward their side of the cafeteria, edging his way between tables. Where is he going?

Waneeda glances behind her, but no one is there except Sicilee Kewe, rummaging through the silverware, and Miss Artsy-Fartsy, Maya Baraberra, looking as if she doesn't know why she's there. Waneeda turns to her right, but no one is there at all now, just a tabletop covered with crumbs and spills to show where the other girls had been.

"You know what I mean," Joy Marie is saying. "Lots of schools are starting to get on the bandwagon now— it would look pretty dumb if Clifton Springs suddenly got off."

Waneeda kicks her under the table.

"Ow!" Joy Marie scowls. "What did you do that for?"

But Waneeda, of course, can't answer. Cody Lightfoot is only thirty inches away. Twenty. Ten.

"Hi," he says, those tropical-sea eyes aimed at Joy Marie. "You're Mary Jo, right? Clem's friend?"

She blinks. "I'm Joy Marie."

"Right. And I'm Cody. Cody Lightfoot." He holds out his hand, and Joy Marie, still looking as nervous as a cat on a raft, takes it. "I just wanted to introduce myself. You know, before the meeting."

Joy Marie smiles uncertainly. "The meeting?"

"Yeah. The Environmental Club meeting? Clemens said you're the vice president and the secretary? He said you're looking for new members."

"Yeah." Joy Marie nods. "Yeah, we are."

"Right," says Cody. "Well, I wanted you to know that you can count me in. I was totally committed to the movement in my old school—we did some real cool stuff—and I want to keep it up. You know, different space but same place, right?"

Joy Marie nods.

"So I'll see you this afternoon," says Cody. And suddenly his smile is on Waneeda. "See you later."

Looking at Cody, it's actually possible to believe that you've never seen anyone smile before. "Yeah," says Waneeda. "See you later."

Chapter Eleven

"Come on, gang! Let's save the planet!"

What do you mean, you're not coming?" Kristin laughs, on the off chance that Sicilee is making a joke. "It's Monday."

Every Monday after school, Sicilee, Kristin, Loretta, and Ash go to the Nature's Way Fitness Center, where they alternate their time between aerobics, dance, and hanging out at the juice bar, looking like an advertisement for low-fat cereal in their designer spandex and sports bras.

Though not this Monday, it would seem.

"I know what day it is, Kris." Sicilee slams her locker shut. "But I can't make it. I have something else to do this afternoon."

Loretta's eyebrows go up. "Like what?"

"It's no big deal." Sicilee's smile shrugs. "There's just this meeting I want to check out."

Ash tilts her head to one side. "What meeting? I didn't hear about any meeting."

"Sweet Mary . . . It's for this club, that's all." Sicilee's hair swings like golden blades. "I didn't think I had to get your permission."

Loretta points out that she's already in a club — Diamonds, the club they all belong to.

"This is Mrs. Skelly's idea." Sicilee makes a bored, put-upon face. "She says that if I belonged to something more, you know, *serious* than Diamonds, it would look good on my record."

"Nobody ever listens to anything Mrs. Skelly says," scoffs Kristin. "Why don't you just—?" She breaks off as her eyes fall on the flyer on the wall behind Sicilee's head. Appearing to sprout out of Sicilee's shining hair are the words MONDAY AT 3:45 P.M. COME ON, GANG! LET'S SAVE THE PLANET! Most clubs meet on Friday afternoon. "Oh, God! Sicilee! You're not going to that Environmental Club meeting, are you?" Kristin is clearly a lot better at deductive reasoning than is generally supposed.

Sicilee ignores the shocked expression on Kristin's face and focuses on the small gold hoop in Kristin's right ear. "Why not?"

"*Why not?*" Ash's shriek ends in laughter. "Because it's, like, the most pathetic club in the whole universe, that's why not! Everybody in it's an industrial-strength freak."

"They're super freaks," adds Kristin. "You know that munchkin Joy Marie What's-Her-Name is in it, right?"

"And that total dork Clem the Clunk," adds Loretta. "I mean, like, *really*, Sicilee. He wears *saddle shoes*! Saddle shoes! Like some reject from *Grease*! For God's sake. I mean, where does he even *buy* them?"

"They probably still make them on his planet," offers Ash.

"And the *glasses*!" Loretta rolls on. "I mean, like, why doesn't he wear contacts like everybody else?"

"And what about all the dumb things they do?" Kristin wants to know. "Remember when they wanted us to drink water instead of Coke? Water! And it wasn't even bottled!" Her smile becomes just a little serpentine. "And in case it's slipped your mind," she adds, "you did once threaten him."

Bizarre though this may sound (rather like a lioness threatening a flea), this statement is true. Sicilee did, in fact, once threaten Clemens Reis. "You'd better hear what I'm saying, Geek Boy," Sicilee warned him. "Because if you don't stop this fascist campaign against *my* constitutional right to drink whatever I want, I'm going to put a curse on you. I'm going to make you wish that you'd never been born as much as the rest of us do."

"And those disgusting pictures they put up in the hall of tortured animals?" Ash wrinkles her nose in disgust. "They were, like, so totally gross they made me want to barf. I mean, who wants to know about stuff like that?"

"You have got to be kidding, Sicilee," cuts in Kristin. "You can't possibly join anything *they're* in. What's everybody going to think?"

"I don't care what *everybody* thinks," lies Sicilee. She raises her chin just enough to show that she is above the petty, transient concerns of lesser mortals. "What I care about is the planet, you know? Because it's, like, the only one we have?"

Ash, Loretta, and Kristin all raise their eyes to the heavens (metaphorically, of course, since there is a ceiling above them) and groan. *Sure you do.*

It is one of Sicilee's great talents to be able to flounce without actually moving. "Well, maybe you haven't heard, but everybody says the planet's going to totally *die* if we don't do something."

"That means turn off the lights when you leave a room, not become a social outcast," says Loretta.

"Oh, please . . . I'm not *joining*. I'm just checking it out. There is no way I'm going to become a social outcast just because I go to one measly meeting." It is Sicilee who decides what is in and what is cool at Clifton Springs, not other people. They wouldn't dare. "And even if I did, Loretta, then maybe there are more important things in life than just being popular? Did you ever think of that?"

They all know, of course, that there is nothing more important than popularity (unless it's money or fame).

The other girls explode in shrill howls of laughter. They've never given even the most passing thought to the possibility that there might be something more important.

Only Kristin doesn't laugh. Kristin has a serious, uncomfortable look on her face—as though her underwear is cutting into her. Kristin is thinking. What could possibly be more important to Sicilee than being popular? There's only one thing. One thing that has dominated every late-night phone conversation with Sicilee for nearly a week. "Ohmygod!" wails Kristin, too surprised to remember she's been sworn to secrecy. "It's *him,* isn't it? Cody Lightfoot! *He's* going to be there!" Yet more proof, if proof were needed, of Kristin's considerable deductive skills.

Sicilee wanted to keep her obsession with Cody Lightfoot a secret from Ash and Loretta for as long as possible because Ash and Loretta have bigger mouths than a humpback whale and she doesn't want the whole world to know about it before Cody actually asks her out. But she sees now that there is no point in trying to pretend that she doesn't know what Kristin's talking about. Better her friends know the truth than that they think she's lost her mind.

"Well." She shrugs. "I did overhear him say something about it."

Ash giggles with relief. "Well, why didn't you say so? I mean, *that* I get. He is, like, totally awesome."

"Now that makes sense," agrees Loretta. "He's the hottest thing in this school next to the boiler."

"God, Sicilee . . ." Kristin laughs. "You really had me worried for a minute."

Chapter Twelve

Desperate times call for desperate measures

Come again?" Alice cups a hand to her ear and leans toward Maya. "I know it couldn't possibly be true, but I thought I heard you say you're going to hang out with the Geek Squad this afternoon instead of coming home with me."

"Hello? Hello?" Maya calls into Alice's ear. "Is anybody there?"

Alice jumps back, laughing. "You don't have to shout, Maya. I'm not deaf."

"Are you sure?" asks Maya. "I mean, I did tell you Cody's going to the Environmental Club meeting."

"Uh-huh." Alice nods. "But you didn't say anything about *you* going."

"Well . . . *duh* . . ." says Maya. "I didn't think I had to." It's not as if Maya's been keeping how she feels about Cody a secret from Alice. "I thought that it was kind of glaringly self-evident, you know?"

"You did?" Alice looks puzzled for a second, then slaps her forehead as though several very large (and possibly environmentally unfriendly) lights have just switched on inside it. "Oh, I know what must've confused me. It must've been the part where you said that you'd rather be buried in eels than go to one of those meetings again."

Maya gives her an uncertain smile. "What do you mean, *again*?"

"I mean, *again*—you know, like, after last time? When the dreaded Clemens talked for about ten hours, and you said that you figured the only thing the planet needed to be saved from was *him*? Because of all the hot air?"

"Are you sure?" Maya squidges up her face and squints, trying to remember. "We went to a meeting?"

"Uh-huh. You made me go with you."

"I did?"

"Uh-huh. You fell asleep."

"Well, I'm not going to fall asleep this time," says Maya. "You'll see. It'll be totally different."

"*I'll see?*" Alice automatically takes a step backward. "You're right—it *will* be totally different. Because I'm not going with you."

"What do you mean, you're not going with me?" Maya certainly wasn't planning on going alone. Alone among the geeks. "Why not?"

"*Why not?*" Alice's is an expressive face, and right now what it's expressing is indignant disbelief. "I'll tell you why not. You may not remember all the way back to last Thursday, Maya, but I was the one who nearly got pneumonia because you thought it was a great idea to play Follow That Boy in a monsoon."

"I said that I was sorry. *Gott im Himmel,* how was I supposed to know he wasn't going home?"

"I was almost bitten by an insane dog."

"You *weren't* almost bitten. He was just barking to protect his house."

"He came after us."

"Alice, it was a dachshund, not the Hound of the Baskervilles."

"And my shoes were totaled by the time I got home."

"But nothing like that's going to happen today. I'll call my mom. She'll come and get us."

"No. If you ask me, hugging trees is even more humiliating than climbing them."

"Please, Alice? It's just one meeting. And then me and Cody will be friends, and I'll never ask another favor from you as long as I live."

"No. I'd rather go over Niagara Falls on a surfboard."

"Pleasepleaseplease!" Maya clasps her hands in supplication. "I don't want to be all by myself with Clemens and the geeks."

"You don't have to be." Alice nods behind her. "I bet that's where they're going. You can sit with them."

Maya follows Alice's gaze. She sees Joy Marie and

Waneeda all the time, but she hardly ever looks at them. They don't seem real to Maya—Joy Marie with her intense expression and nervous movements and Waneeda, slow and ungainly, shuffling beside her. They look like cartoon characters. A mouse and a bear. Joy Marie and Waneeda come to a stop at the stairs. A mouse and a bear who are bickering. Maya has gone to school with Joy Marie Lutz and Waneeda Huddlesfield her whole life, and yet she has probably never said a word to either of them. She probably wouldn't even recognize their voices in the dark. Maya sighs. "Oh, goody."

Chapter Thirteen

Waneeda and Joy Marie
discuss motivation

I'm not saying that it's not great you decided to come to the meeting, Waneeda," Joy Marie is saying as they make their way to Room 111. "I just don't understand why all of a sudden you changed your mind—that's all. I've been trying to get you to join since we started the club and you've always been dead set against it."

Waneeda sighs. As soon as Cody said he was joining the Environmental Club, Waneeda knew that she was going to join, too. How could she *not*? She may be lazy, but she's not stupid. But, not wanting Joy Marie to jump to the obvious conclusion, she waited till five minutes ago to tell her. She should have known that Joy Marie would jump to the obvious conclusion anyway. As soon as Waneeda said that she thought she'd come along to the meeting after all, Joy Marie got that I-think-someone's-been-smoking-in-the-bathroom look on her face.

"I don't know why you're making such a big deal about it." Waneeda slows her already slow pace, hoping that Joy Marie will keep steaming ahead and finish the argument without her. "A person is allowed to change her mind, you know, Joy Marie."

Joy Marie, of course, stays in stride. "You said you'd rather be run over than join. You said your image was bad enough without being in the club. You said—"

Sometimes being friends with someone like Joy Marie is something of a trial for someone like Waneeda. "What've you got? A photographic memory?" Waneeda's book bag bangs against her thigh. "I was just joking when I said that stuff. Can't you tell when someone's joking?"

"Yes, I can." When irked, Joy Marie has a habit of sucking in her cheeks as if she wants to make them disappear. "That's why I'm asking *why?* Did you have a vision? An epiphany? Did you suddenly realize how lonely it's going to be when there aren't any other species left on the planet?"

Waneeda's whole body harrumphs. "Does it matter?"

It does to Joy Marie. "You know how I feel. The club and what it's trying to do are really important."

"I know they're important." Waneeda has a vague idea. "Obviously, I think so, too." She couldn't care less.

"I'd just hate to think that you aren't taking it seriously."

God help me, thinks Waneeda. *She's like a pit bull terrier. Once she gets her teeth into something, you have to call the fire department to get her off.*

"Of course I'm taking it seriously. That's why I'm coming with you!"

Joy Marie's jaw sets in a way that means she knows she is about to say something Waneeda probably doesn't want to hear. "I'd just like to know that you're not just coming because of Cody Lightfoot—that's all." They cross the main hall to the west-wing staircase. "It'd be nice if you actually cared a little about the environment, too."

All Waneeda cares about, of course, is being in the same room as Cody. Breathing the same air. Hearing him speak. Being close enough to touch him, should she ever dare. Seeing that smile again and again.

"I'm not saying that Cody didn't influence me," says Waneeda. After all, if someone like him wants to join, then the club must be better than Joy Marie has always made it sound. "But mainly I thought that I was doing you a favor." Waneeda comes to a mulish stop at the bottom of the stairs. "You're the one who needs new members, remember? You're the one who was begging me to join." She scrunches up her face and puts on a thin, baby voice. "*Oh, Waneeda, it's so important. . . . Oh, Waneeda, it'll be fun. . . .*"

"Well, yeah . . ."

"Because if you've changed your mind, just say so, Joy Marie," snaps Waneeda. "Personally, I'd just as soon go home. I do have other things to do."

Joy Marie, of course, is unaware that the membership of the Clifton Springs Environmental Club is about to rise, if not quite as sharply in the next twenty minutes as sea levels are predicted to rise in the next ten years, then significantly nonetheless. As far as she knows, they can't afford to lose a potential member—even if it is Waneeda and she's joining for the wrong reason.

"Forget it," says Joy Marie. "I'm sorry I said anything. I'm happy you're coming." And she charges up the stairs to stop any further argument.

Waneeda smiles to herself as she lumbers after her.

Chapter Fourteen

Ms. Kimodo can be forgiven for thinking she's gone to the wrong room

Ms. Kimodo looks at her watch as she leaves the office and heads to Room 111.

Ms. Kimodo is running late.

Unlike being the faculty adviser for the school newspaper or the Drama Club (both of which have won state and national recognition and are enthusiastically supported by local businesses), being the faculty adviser for the Environmental Club has no kudos attached to it. The only time the club got any outside attention was last spring, when it tried to have the soft-drink machine in the cafeteria replaced with a water fountain — and even then it was the mass protest by the student body, not Clemens Reis's scrupulously well-reasoned arguments, that received the coverage. None of its small but significant successes — the school's recycling program (modest and largely ignored), the free showing of a landmark documentary on climate change (unfortunately scheduled for the same night as a basketball game—a detail Clemens could never be expected to know), and its campaign to persuade the administration to use energy-saving lightbulbs wherever possible (victorious but largely unnoticed)—has done anything to improve the club's image. Everyone, except the four or five stalwart members who actually show up for meetings, regards it as the club of either whining nerds or fanatical activists.

Clemens doesn't help. Indeed, Clemens can probably be held responsible for this negative image. He is a very passionate and committed young man, with no interest in spin or in sparing people's feelings. Last year's major campaign to get people to eat less meat—You Are What You Eat—can be cited as an especially painful example. (Just the memory makes poor Ms. Kimodo flinch.) Featuring photos of horribly distressed and mutilated animals plastered all over the school—even on the insides of the stalls in the bathrooms—as well as the screening of a documentary on industrialized farming that emptied the viewing room in a matter of minutes, the You Are What You Eat campaign alienated far more people than the one person it converted (Ms. Kimodo wouldn't eat meat now if she was starving). Ms. Kimodo doesn't allow herself to remember Clemens's infamous Earth Day address.

Ms. Kimodo stops in front of one of the dozens of flyers with which Joy Marie with her daunting efficiency has more or less papered the walls of the school. (Joy Marie doesn't help much either.) Next to the exhortation COME ON, GANG! LET'S SAVE THE PLANET! are several penned comments (*I'd rather have a date. Try and make me. Your planet or OURS?*). Ms. Kimodo rips it off the wall, sticks it in her bag with the others she has found throughout the day, and hurries on.

It has to be said that, though not a glamorous job, being the faculty adviser of the Environmental Club is not a demanding one, either. Clemens and Joy Marie are both far more knowledgeable about ecological issues and have much better organizational skills than Ms. Kimodo (not, given the low membership and even lower attendance, that there is much to organize). All Ms. Kimodo has to do, really, is show up for meetings and try to talk Clemens out of his more alienating ideas. The least she can do, she feels, is be on time.

Ms. Kimodo is running late today because Dr. Firestone wanted to have a word with her. In fact, Dr. Firestone wanted to have several words with her, none of them particularly good. "I thought, perhaps, as we start this new year, that I should remind you of the conversation I had with young Mr. Reis before the holidays." It may be Clemens whom he holds responsible for the club's "extremism," but it is Ms. Kimodo whom he holds responsible for Clemens. After all, it was she who suggested that he and Joy Marie start the club in the first place. Dr. Firestone would have preferred it if she'd chosen students who were less serious and intense (students, for example, like Maya and Jason, who could be counted on not to give him a hard time).

Ms. Kimodo assured him that she hadn't forgotten.

"Well, someone has." Ms. Kimodo isn't the only person to rip Joy Marie's posters from the walls. Dr. Firestone had half a dozen in front of him. He picked one up. "Have you seen these?"

"Of course I have. They're —" began Ms. Kimodo, but broke off with an, "Ah . . ." Quickly she added, "No, I haven't noticed any like that."

Someone had also written on the flyer in Dr. Firestone's hand. But it wasn't a rude or sarcastic remark. What it said, in red, was: *We will be discussing phase two of our ongoing campaign to protect our primordial oak trees from senseless slaughter.* The flyer dropped back to the desk. "I told him to forget about the trees." Dr. Firestone has a deep, resonant voice that (especially at times like this) always makes Ms. Kimodo think of God talking to Abraham. "I told him that it's time to get his priorities straight. If he wants to do something really useful — such as plant some flowers or hang up bird feeders or raise some money to adopt a rain forest or an orangutan, anything of that ilk — well, then, the whole school would be right behind him."

"The whole school's right behind him now," murmured Ms. Kimodo. "By at least ten years."

Dr. Firestone's fingers tapped a tune on the edge of his desk, which might have been why he didn't seem to hear her. "But you know what he's like. He doesn't listen. All he does is argue. He doesn't understand how to win friends and influence people. He upsets them with his extremism and left-wing ideas."

Ms. Kimodo leaned forward, trying to make out the tune.

"Are we talking about the drinking-tap-water idea or the not-sticking-electrodes-in-the-heads-of-monkeys idea?" she asked.

But Dr. Firestone has not gotten where he is today by being hampered by a sense of humor.

"You know what we're talking about, Jocelyn. The sports center has the approval of the town council and the school board. It's about progress, not global warming. It has nothing to do with the environment."

"Well . . . The trees . . . I believe Clemens feels . . ." began Ms. Kimodo.

"He's being unreasonable. I've told him that we'll plant three trees for every one we take down. What more does he want?" Dr. Firestone got to his feet. "The bottom line is that your club has six members, Jocelyn—and that's on a good day. If it doesn't have at least a dozen by the end of January, I'm afraid that's it. The school can't be squandering its resources on lost causes. Am I making myself clear?"

"You couldn't be clearer if you were made of glass," said Ms. Kimodo. She said this with a smile.

Now, Ms. Kimodo finally reaches the door of Room 111 and pulls it open. The first thing she notices is that there are more people inside than usual. Many more. Even Waneeda Huddlesfield, who has never been known to join anything except the lunch line, is sitting next to Joy Marie.

And then Ms. Kimodo sees Sicilee Kewe, smiling as though delighted to be there, but standing off to one side as though also afraid that she might catch something. Today is a pink day for Sicilee. Ms. Kimodo would be far less surprised to be told that every soldier in the world has put down his or her weapons and taken up needle-point than to see Sicilee Kewe at an Environmental Club meeting. Not only is she the unofficial poster girl for overconsumption, but she did once come fairly close to threatening Clemens Reis's life as well. This can't be the right room. Her talk with Dr. Firestone has discombobulated her. Ms. Kimodo takes a step back to check the number over the door, and bumps into someone behind her.

Ms. Kimodo looks around.

"Cool, man," says Cody Lightfoot. "I was afraid I was late, but it hasn't started yet."

Ms. Kimodo smiles the way she does when she is given an unexpected present. But by the time she takes her seat, Ms. Kimodo's smile has vanished. There is obviously going to be a blue moon tonight, thinks Ms. Kimodo. Either that or the world is going to end. Ms. Kimodo's pessimism is based on her discovery that not only has Sicilee Kewe shown up today, but Maya Baraberra is there as well. Maya is also standing off to one side (the opposite one from Sicilee), looking bored and not smiling. It is fairly common knowledge that neither Maya Baraberra nor Sicilee Kewe would join anything—not even the last lifeboat off a sinking ship—if the other was in it. And then she sees Sicilee and Maya—cleverly able to glare at each other while looking elsewhere—insert themselves into chairs on either side of Cody Lightfoot as though they're bodyguards protecting an important politician.

Ms. Kimodo's smile returns.

Chapter Fifteen

More than one person thinks of leaving, but doesn't

You might think that, confronted with this sudden surge of interest in saving the planet, Clemens would be a little nonplussed—or at least surprised. *Where did all these girls come from?* he might wonder. *Why are they here? Are they lost? Drunk? Hypnotized? Is someone playing a joke?*

But Clemens (unlike some people) has fewer sides than a circle. It is part of his charm that he is so sincere in his own beliefs and motives that he assumes the same of others. Which means that, in this instance, after months of mockery and hostility, he takes it for granted that the Clifton Springs Environmental Club is experiencing the first packed meeting in its history simply because his fellow students are listening to him at last. They've woken up and smelled the toxic waste. They've seen the light pouring through the gaping hole in the ozone layer. They finally realize that it's better to have a few very old trees at the edge of the campus than a state-of-the-art sports center with an Olympic-size pool. Clemens looks around the crowded room and smiles. Gloating isn't really in his nature, but oh how he wishes that he could see Dr. Firestone's face when he hears about this.

At exactly 3:45 p.m., Clemens gets to his feet (knocking Joy Marie's pen and notepad to the floor and stepping on the pen) and calls the meeting to order.

"Hi," says Clemens. The paper clip holding his glasses together seems to wave in greeting as he adjusts them. "Firstly, I'd like to thank you all for coming." Today, in honor of the occasion, he is wearing another of his homemade T-shirts: *Trees Don't Grow on Money*. "It's a gratifying turnout." He removes a red bandana from his pocket and blows his nose. "I see a lot of unfamiliar faces, so for the benefit of all our new members, I'd like to start the meeting by saying a little about the club and why we set it up and what it hopes to achieve and so forth."

Chairs scrape and feet shuffle. The old members glance at the clock and sit back, resigned. The smiles disappear from the faces of the new members, to be replaced with looks of concern. Only Cody, who, of course, was not here for the Christmas diatribe or the infamous Earth Day speech, smiles back as though he thinks this is a pretty awesome idea and can't wait to hear what Clemens has to say.

Reassured by Cody's smile, the others all relax again,

prepared to believe that this won't be as bad as they fear. But sadly, like so many beliefs, this one is ill founded. Clemens "saying a little about the club . . . and so forth" includes a list of the crises facing the world. It's a very long list.

Within only minutes, Sicilee is so done that if she were a cake in the oven she'd be burning. She cups her hands over her mouth as if she's giving every word that Clemens utters serious thought, but really it's so Cody doesn't see her yawn.

Up until now, the most soul-destroyingly boring experience Sicilee ever had was the summer her father decided they should do a family road trip instead of flying to a foreign beach with cabanas and waiter service for their summer vacation. The car broke down approximately two million miles from nowhere in some Podunk mountains. And because they were in some Podunk mountains, the cell phones didn't work. Nor did the entertainment system, the AC, or the radio (though that was not the fault of rural America, but of whatever was wrong with the car). It was over two hours before help arrived, and during that time there was nothing to do but sit by the side of the road, looking at trees and, for a change of pace, the sky. Sicilee thought she would die. Listening to Clemens yammer on about how we're killing the planet and consuming our way to oblivion, however, is much, much worse. What can all of this depressing stuff about dwindling forests and melting glaciers and polluted rivers possibly have to do with her? Merciful Mother, *she's* not in the Amazon. And she's definitely not about to be stranded on a chunk of ice with the last polar bear or go fishing in some toxic river, either. There is only one thing that prevents Sicilee from galloping from the room—and you would be wrong to think that that one thing is Cody Lightfoot.

It is the presence of Maya Baraberra, perched like a vulture on the other side of Cody, that keeps Sicilee sitting there as if she's been cemented into her chair. There's no way she's leaving now. She wouldn't give Maya the satisfaction. She wouldn't give her the opportunity. Sicilee swings one foot back and forth, almost brushing Cody's leg. She might have known Maya the Barbarian would be after the best-looking boy ever to walk the streets of Clifton Springs. Indeed, she should have known. Really. She really should have known. As soon as Maya strolled through the door with that you-can-start-now-that-*I'm*-here look on her face, a series of images from the past week flashed through Sicilee's mind like a slide show. Maya lurking in the corridors. Maya hanging around outside classrooms. Maya skulking along the hallway where Cody's locker is. Maya, just this afternoon, hurling herself into the cafeteria, clutching her phone, as if she knew Cody was near the door. How could Sicilee have been so blind? Her teeth grind away behind her inattentive smile.

Meanwhile, on the other side of Cody, Maya keeps

herself awake by remembering how much she loathes and detests Sicilee Kewe. Indeed, her first thought when she walked into Room 111 and saw Sicilee, aloof from everyone else like a visiting princess, was: *Gott im Himmel! Barbie and the troglodytes!* She was tempted to take a picture to post on the Internet. Her second thought was: *No boy is worth this. I'm out of here.* But then Sicilee's perpetual smile, cold as the back of the freezer, fell on her like a dead hand.

And all at once, as though someone had turned on a projector in her head, Maya saw a moving montage of scenes from the past few days. And in every scene was the blindingly monochromatic Sicilee Kewe (in orange, in yellow, in mauve, and in turquoise), teeth gleaming like miniature glaciers as she sashayed past Mallory's locker as if she were on patrol . . . strolling along with her hair swinging and her eyes moving down the corridors like heat-seeking missiles . . . loitering in the lobby at the end of the day as though she were waiting for a bus. She was everywhere Maya was — everywhere Cody was likely to be — hunting him down as if she were the sheriff and he a wanted man.

Which was when Maya had her third thought: *She's here for the same reason I am.*

After that, of course, Maya wouldn't have gone home for the chance to show her paintings in a New York gallery. The last time she and Sicilee wanted the same thing was in the sixth grade. Then it was Sicilee who won the lead in the class production of *The Sound of Music*. This time, however, Sicilee is *so* going to lose. There is no way Maya plans to stand by and watch Sicilee Kewe con Cody Lightfoot into believing that they have anything more in common than species and language. It's totally ludicrous. She is so awesomely not his type. As if! As if someone so devastatingly cool might possibly be that dumb. Does she think he's not going to notice her fur coat and her mother's Cadillac Escalade? Does she think he's not going to notice that Sicilee doesn't care about anything besides her self-centered self? That she has a carbon footprint the size of the footprint of a yeti? Or that the girl never wears anything *twice*, never mind secondhand?

Because of Clemens's egalitarian principles, the chairs are always arranged in a circle at these meetings. Waneeda sits across from Sicilee and Maya, her face turned toward Clemens as though she's the king listening to Scheherazade tell her astonishing stories, but her eyes constantly move to Cody. Except for this afternoon when he came over to talk to Joy Marie, this is the closest she's ever been to him, and the longest she's ever had just to look at him. She could sit like this forever—watching him scratch his head, watching him cross and uncross his legs, watching him twine his fingers together and then untwine them again, watching expressions of agreement and outrage cross his face like sunlight and shadows. And, as an added bonus, any twinge of guilt Waneeda may have felt about Joy Marie's questioning of her reasons for coming this afternoon disappeared the second Sicilee and then Maya stepped through the door. She kicked Joy Marie, glancing at her with a smirk on her lips and one eyebrow raised. *So what do you think their motives are? Are you going to ask them why they came?*

"But there's a serious crisis happening right here, in our own backyard," continues Clemens.

And then he starts talking about trees.

Chapter Sixteen

Climate change

A certain restless tension shimmers in the growing gloom of the afternoon. More yawns than Sicilee's are being stifled. Butts are shifting in seats. Feet are scraping on the floor. Songs are being hummed under breaths. Several heads are discreetly bending to check for phone messages or to see if time has actually been stopped in its tracks. Waneeda is surreptitiously searching in her pockets for something made of chocolate. Ms. Kimodo is in danger of nodding off.

Clemens, of course, is oblivious to the fact that he is now in the midst of people who would rather be stranded in a desert in a sandstorm with a pregnant camel than stuck in this room listening to him.

Cody, on the other hand, is well aware that in a mere matter of minutes (though, clearly, it seems a lot longer) Clemens has begun to undermine all his hard work. Over the last week, while seeming to ease effortlessly into his new life like a foot into a slipper, Cody has actually been tireless in his efforts to persuade all these girls to come to the meeting. Sicilee and Maya may have heard about Cody joining the club by sheer chance, but the others were all charmed into coming, lured by that break-your-heart smile. Why? Cody would say that he did it because he was raised to be Green, and because he likes Clemens and wants to help out a brother and kindred soul. All of which is true. But what is also true is that, like an immigrant opening the first Chinese restaurant in town, Cody saw a gap that he could fill. In thousands of schools across the nation, environmental clubs are the cool "in" thing—as popular as pizza. They're guaranteed to make everybody feel good and look even better. But not in Clifton Springs. Cody plans to change all that. He's going to make the club hip. He's going to give it a higher profile than the football team. And in the process transform himself from being an outsider to being at the heart of campus life—and all without stepping on anybody's toes.

"Those trees remember what we've forgotten," Clemens is saying. "Do you know what they'd say if they could talk?"

Someone near Cody groans.

Someone else mutters, "Yeah. Shut the hell up."

It is then that Cody suddenly gets to his feet, surprising Clemens so much that the club's president stops speaking.

As Cody rises, the movement of everyone else coming to attention and straightening up in their chairs sounds almost like a sigh of relief.

"Clem, man—" Cody shakes his head as though he's been dazzled rather than dazed by Clemens's speech. "That is sharp. That is really sharp. You're like Radio Free Nature. The Voice of Freedom. A beacon of hope."

Clemens, his mouth still open for the words that Cody cut off, blinks.

"I'm telling you," says Cody. "I'm, like, blown away by the multitude of things you know." Although his arms hang by his side, he somehow gives the impression that he is shaking Clemens by the hand. "Man, you've got it all down: chapter, verse, and date of publication. It's awesome. Totally awesome. Myself? I'm so inarticulate, I'm lucky I remember my name when I'm trying to explain what I believe. But you? I can only salute a class-A pro."

Clemens pushes his glasses back up his nose. "Well, the—"

"But, you know, before we get too deep into all the heavy global-destruction and who-does-what-to-whom stuff, there's a couple of things I'd like to say. Or try to say." Cody laughs good-naturedly. Everyone except Clemens smiles back. "You know, just about why I'm here and where I'm coming from—that kind of autobiographical-detail thing. Fill in my little piece of the big picture."

Clemens says, "Well, I—"

"I think some of you already know who I am." When Clemens speaks, he focuses on a point over the heads of his listeners, but Cody spreads his smile around the room like butter over hot toast. No one is looking at their cell phone now. "But for those who don't, I've been involved in the Green scene since junior high. Last year, at my old school, I was really active in our environmental club—we called it Mayday?—and I had a truly awesome time." Cody was, in fact, the president of the club and receiver of a special personal achievement award from the EPA, but this is an autobiographical detail he chooses not to mention just yet. "Well, not just me—we all did. It was as incredible as walking on the moon. It was like opening the back door but instead of there being the deck and the grill and a couple of chairs, you walk out into the stars. And it wasn't just life-changing—it was really fun, too."

There is something about the way Cody speaks that makes his audience smile and nod in agreement, even when they have only a vague idea of what he's talking about. "I'm not saying this isn't a really important thing we're doing here," he continues. "It's terminally important. And to tell you the truth, yours truly has a Green rap sheet, like, a mile long." Cody's laugh is infectious. "No, really," he says with a grin. "I'm, like, Mr. Crunchy Granola." Cody, though looking more like Mr. Heart-stoppingly Gorgeous, turns out to be so seriously concerned about the environment that he buys a lot of his clothes second hand and usually walks to school or rides his bike. He doesn't patronize chain stores if he can help it. He's a vegan. His parents buy organic and local as much as they can. Since it's only birds who *have* to fly, he made the trip from California on a train. His mother drives a hybrid car. They reuse everything possible at his house, from jars and bottles to paper and envelopes, and what they can't reuse, they recycle. One night a week, they even do without electricity. Cody grins self-mockingly. "And so forth."

Even Ms. Kimodo laughs.

"I'm not telling you all this to brag or anything. I just want you to know where I'm coming from." Cody has somehow drifted into the middle of the circle. "I don't want you to think I'm just one of these weekend eco-warriors." Several heads shake. They would never think that. "I'm, like, totally serious and committed. But lots of people think being Green is some kind of torture and punishment. They don't get how much fun they can have." In some miraculous, or possibly magical, way Cody manages to smile at every person in the room individually but at exactly the same time—as if each of them is sharing an intimate joke with him. "I'm telling you, man, a night without the lights on can be a very cool thing."

An almost electric current of giggles and smiles runs through the room.

"Anyway, I don't want to take up all our precious time talking about myself. I've got a lot of ideas I want to share with you guys—things we can do to get the school right behind us and have some real impact. But first I think we should hear about *you*. You know, just a few words about yourself so we know where you're coming from." Cody smiles back at all the faces smiling at him. "How about it?" He opens his arms, embracing the room. "Who wants to start?"

While the others are all glancing at each other to see who'll be brave enough to go first, both Maya Baraberra and Sicilee Kewe leap to their feet as though tied together by invisible strings.

"I'd love to start," says Maya before Sicilee can. Her smile bobs back and forth between Sicilee and Cody. "I know it's going to sound kind of weird, but I'm a lot like Cody, really." Maya, it seems, has been into the environment for as long as she can remember, possibly because of her artistic nature and her love of animals. "And I've been a vegetarian for practically eons, and I decided over the holidays that it's time to go vegan. You know, because of all that Christmas carnage?"

"Me, too," interrupts Sicilee. She can't seem to decide who she's looking at, either. "You know, into the environment? I believe we can change our ways. Like my parents? My parents wanted to go skiing over Christmas, but I insisted we stay in town — so we didn't have to take a plane?"

"Oh, and of course I ride my bike everywhere. I only go in the car when there is no other choice." Maya edges forward, slightly blocking Sicilee from Cody Lightfoot's view. "And obviously I wear vintage clothes. And I recycle everything."

"Well, I've been doing the Green thing for, like, *ever* now," says Sicilee, sliding to the left. "The bottles . . . the lightbulbs . . . the whole vegan scene . . . I believe that we all have a responsibility. You know, to the polar bears and the trees and everything?"

"*Gott im Himmel,* you know what?" Laughing as though she can't imagine how she forgot about this, Maya moves in front of Sicilee again. "I actually once had a sit-in, you know, all by myself, in this tree they were going to cut down?" She doesn't mention that the tree was in her backyard or that the "they" who were cutting it down were her parents.

"But the whole point of a club like this is that no one's an island." Sicilee shifts to the right this time. "I believe that it's not about one person doing one thing every now and then. We all have to pull together. Then we'll be able to save the planet!"

"Well, of course. That's why we're all here today."
Everybody knows that, Sicilee. The unspoken words shimmer
on Maya's smile. "Isn't that right?"

This last question is meant for Cody, and both Maya
and Sicilee, who have slightly forgotten about him in their
attempts to outmaneuver each other, turn to him now.

Only to discover that he's no longer standing there
but has sat back down.

Chapter Seventeen

Warrior Greens

As a further example of things they have in common, both Maya Baraberra and Sicilee Kewe imagined that they would be leaving the meeting with Cody Lightfoot. Each of them was prepared not just to walk all the way home, but to walk all the way to someone else's home if it meant she walked with him.

But neither of these scenarios happened. Somehow, when Cody stood up at the end of the meeting, Maya and Sicilee were left looking at each other across the space where he'd been. Sicilee tossed her hair and shrank her smile so small that she seemed about to spit. Maya stared back unblinkingly. If looks were curses, Maya would have been turned into a toad and Sicilee would have vanished completely, and probably forever.

By the time they picked up their things and stood up, Cody was walking out of the room with Ms. Kimodo.

And so, against all the odds, Maya Baraberra and Sicilee Kewe ended up leaving the school side by side.

"You know, you really are incredible," Maya says as they cross the lobby. She puts on an exaggerated shrill and girly voice. *"Ooh, I've been doing the Green thing for, like, ever now . . . the bottles . . . the lightbulbs . . . the whole vegan scene!"*

"Oh, look who's talking!" Sicilee fumes. "You made it sound like you and Cody were virtual twins."

Maya's laugh will later be described by Sicilee as sounding like the squeal of a panicked pig. "At least everything I said was true!"

Naturally, Sicilee had been prepared to embroider the truth a little—to claim she turned off lights and things like that—but how could she with Maya standing there looking like the cat that had swallowed every pigeon in the park? She had no choice. What was she supposed to say? That her mother gives her old clothes to the church thrift store and that every time he gets the electric bill, her father stomps around the house turning off lights? She had to lie. Boldly. Baldly. The worst thing was that once she got started, she couldn't seem to stop. By the time she was done, she'd altered the truth so much that it wouldn't have been able to recognize itself.

Sicilee yanks open one side of the glass doors. "Are you saying you don't believe me?" she asks as she sails through.

"Oh, heavens to Betsy! I wouldn't dream of such a

thing." Right behind her, Maya catches the closing door with her hip, her expression sour as she pushes through. "I am *so* sure you're Greener than grass." She leans her mouth close to Sicilee's ear. "Like *not!*" If the planet thought it had to count on Sicilee to save it, it would shoot itself now. "If there was one word of truth in anything you said, it was the word *I.*"

"That just shows how much you know." Sicilee strides on, hair swinging, heels clicking against the pavement. "It just so happens that *I* am not a liar, Baraberra. I leave that kind of thing to people like you."

Maya's laugh pops like a blister. "Oh, please. Spare me the self-righteous crap. I bet you don't even know what a vegan is."

"Of course I do." Sicilee doesn't. She thinks that *vegan* is short for *vegetarian.* She slows down so that Maya can catch up with her and see the scornful edge to her smile. "Just because I don't go around drooling cool the way you do, Baraberra—shaking your stupid pins in everybody's face and thinking you're so great because you wear somebody else's old clothes—doesn't mean that I don't know what's going on in the big picture. I know what's going on."

Maya sneers. *Yeah, sure you do.* "Sicilee," says Maya with exaggerated sweetness, "we're alone now—you don't have to pretend. You don't have a clue what's going on in 'the big picture.' *Gott im Himmel,* you think *you're* the big picture. If you can't wear it, drive it, watch it, listen to it, or eat it, it doesn't exist."

"What? Unlike you, Miss Sacrifice-and-Self-Denial? Like you've dedicated your life to protecting chipmunks and drawing on the walls of the cave you live in?" Sicilee's laughter splutters like machine-gun fire. "You are such a total phony. You know, you don't look like you're doing without much to me. Your parents have two cars, just like everybody else. And you have all the stuff everybody else has." Sicilee's smile shrinks contemptuously. "Your cell phone does everything but fly."

They aren't walking anymore. They've stopped a little way down the drive, where they are squaring off like boxers.

"Sicilee," says Maya, "the point isn't whether or not I and ten billion other people have a cell phone. The point is that besides everything else you aren't—you know, like human—*you* are so definitely not the animal-rights type."

"And when did I say I was?" Sicilee has seen animal-rights types on the news. They're usually screaming, wearing balaclavas, and throwing paint on people wearing totally gorgeous mink coats. "Those people are nothing but terrorists."

"Oh, spare me." Maya purses her lips in that smug and irksome way she has. "To an animal, *you're* the one who's the terrorist, with your fur coat and those boots you wear that make you look like you've got dogs wrapped around your feet. Which is why you can't be a vegan. Vegans *are* animal-rights types, Barbie-brain."

"I know about fur and everything." Sicilee's smile shines like highly polished steel. "But, for your information, I only just started being a vegan. I can't completely change my whole wardrobe overnight."

"I know you just started being a vegan." Maya grins. "About forty-five minutes ago."

"Oh, right. At about the same time that you started riding a bike everywhere." Sicilee's arm sweeps across the empty bike rack outside the library. "Just where *is* your bike, Your Greenness? Or is its invisibility part of it being environmentally friendly?"

"It has a flat. You probably don't know this, but you can't ride a bike with a flat tire." Maya starts walking again. "And anyway, I'm a hell of a lot Greener than you'll ever be. *Gott im Himmel,* you are like a walking advertisement for the consumer society. You won't last an hour being Green." Maya looks over with a serene smile. "You won't even last ten minutes."

"Oh, really?" sneers Sicilee.

"Yeah, really," says Maya. "You're about as Green as strip mining. You probably leave the lights on when you're sleeping so you'll be able to see yourself in the mirror if you wake up during the night."

"And I suppose you're Greener than a tree, Madame I-Ride-My-Bike-in-Blizzards!" The many people who know only Sicilee's dazzling smile would be surprised at how good she is at contorting her mouth into an expression of revulsion and disgust. "You are so false, Baraberra. I bet you've never even been on a bike."

"Well, you lose, Kewe. Because not only have I been on a bike about a trillion times, but as soon as I get the flat fixed, you'll be seeing me on it every day."

Neither of these statements is much truer than Sicilee's claim to be a concerned environmentalist and vegan. The truth is that Maya has been on a bicycle only a dozen times, the last being over four years ago when she skidded on something in the road, ran into a hedge, and decided it was easier to get rides from her mother than risk her life.

"And you'll be seeing me eating nothing but vegetables," counters Sicilee (who has never thought of vegetables as more than a garnish).

"Sure I will." Maya takes a step toward Sicilee. An innocent bystander might wonder if she's planning to hug Sicilee or give her a shove, but all she does is smile — albeit in a slightly spine-chilling way. "You may think everybody's got the wool pulled over their eyes, you know? So let me be the one to tell you that they don't. It is pathetically obvious that you only came today because you have the hots for Cody Lightfoot."

"And that isn't why you came?" Sicilee smiles back. "You are such a scammer, Baraberra. You are so transparent I could watch TV through you."

"At least I have real Green credentials," snaps Maya. "Unlike some people I could mention."

"Oh, please." Sicilee's hair swings, scythe-like, with scorn. "You may be able to convince some people that you showed up because you can't sleep for worrying about the whales, but not everyone's that gullible, Baraberra. Sweet Mary! If you'd sat any closer to Cody at the meeting, you would've been on *my* lap."

"You don't stand a chance with him." Maya's voice is so reasonable and calm, you'd think she'd started talking about something else entirely (socks, perhaps, or how to bake a potato). "Cody's not one of your preppy puppets who's only interested in what a girl looks like."

"Oh, really?" Sicilee makes a face. "Then you'd better hope he's not interested in brains or character, either, because those are two more qualities *you* don't have."

Maya pretends to laugh. "But the joke's going to be on you, you know. Because I'm going to win."

"We'll see about that." Sicilee's smile stretches so that it almost seems to wrap itself around her head. "I wouldn't get his name tattooed on my butt just yet, if I were you."

Chapter Eighteen

The times are a-changin'— whether Clemens likes it or not

Waneeda may have scoffed at Joy Marie's belief that the Clifton Springs High School Environmental Club could still be saved, but Waneeda, it seems, was wrong. Something was ventured and something was gained. It was very, very dark, but now here's the dawn—all bright and golden and full of promise. In the space of just one afternoon, Cody Lightfoot has turned everything around. Room 111 buzzed with energy the way wild meadows once buzzed with bees. The geeky, whining image of the club vanished in knowing laughter. From now on, they're going to have fun. From now on, instead of laying guilt trips on their fellow students, they're going to show them the way. As Cody put it with that smile that causes everyone to smile back, "Make them aware and they will care."

Cody believes that they can inform people of the problems facing the planet and let them know what can be done about them in a laid-back, entertaining way. No pain, but plenty of gain. Cody Lightfoot is the sunny, hope-filled day to Clemens Reis's moonless, gloomy night. Where Clemens has been known to bray about "Kamikaze Consumers" and the "Shopocalypse" to come, Cody talks mildly about "The Not Yet Awares" and what a big difference it would make if everyone bought a little less now and then. If Cody and Clemens were policemen and not teenage boys, Cody would be the nice, easygoing cop who asks you if you want a coffee, and Clemens would be the one who slams his fist down on the desk and tells you that you'll never see daylight again.

"We have to get the communal chi flowing here," said Cody. "Involve people. Make them feel like they're really doing something. Let them know that we're all in this together."

To do this, this year they're going to have a major celebration for Earth Day that will involve not just Clifton Springs High but the entire town. This is what they did at Cody's school last year, and it was an incredible success that got them widespread media coverage and national attention. If it can work in California, the birthplace of photochemical smog, says Cody, there's no reason it won't work here. There will be stalls and competitions, exhibits and information, swap shops and a recycling center, music and food. Everyone will be encouraged to join in. There will be something for everyone, and something everyone can do. They'll need plenty of volunteers to run the stalls. They'll need people with special interests to run workshops. They'll need tons of donations of clothes, books, and household items. Everyone is excited. Even Ms. Kimodo. Ms. Kimodo thinks they'll have less trouble getting Dr. Firestone on board than they would have trying to fall off an ice-covered mountain. "The Earth Day celebration's just the kind of upbeat thing he loves," said Ms. Kimodo. Which is true. Nothing pleases Dr. Firestone more than a smiling photo of himself on the front page of the *Clifton Springs Observer.*

The meeting ended in high spirits. The gleeful gaggles of girls departed, bubbling with energy and eagerness, and Ms. Kimodo and Cody left together talking about how best to approach Dr. Firestone, leaving Clemens, Waneeda, and Joy Marie to put the room back in order.

Joy Marie grins when the door shuts for the last time. "What have I been saying?"

Clemens and Waneeda, who are setting down a desk, both look over at her.

"Never say die?" guesses Clemens.

"Miracles do happen?" ventures Waneeda.

"Well, kind of." Joy Marie snaps a chair into place. "What I meant was that the club was going to be saved, and it is! We're out of the woods."

Clemens brushes something invisible to the human eye from the top of the desk. "Maybe."

Joy Marie puts her hands on her hips. "Maybe?" she repeats. "What do you mean, *maybe*? We have all these new members. We have this great plan. We're actually going to have Dr. Firestone *with* us instead of against us, which should make a nice change."

Clemens's mouth shrugs. "I just mean . . . maybe. As in, maybe we're not out of the woods. Maybe we're just in a clearing." Clemens is afraid that given the speed with which things have already changed, they might lose their focus. Making the club viable is one thing; making it unrecognizable is something else. "It's only day one, you know."

Waneeda pops another chocolate caramel into her mouth and stuffs the wrapper in her pocket. "Things can still go wrong," she says.

"Oh, thanks, Waneeda. That's really helpful. I bet Columbus wished he'd had you with him when he set sail for the West Indies." Joy Marie's face flushes with annoyance. "You don't say anything throughout the whole meeting, and now you've decided to be all negative as usual."

"I'm not being negative." She is. As it happens, this is partly because she agrees with Clemens. Although her own motives are not beyond reproach, Waneeda can see that there's a difference between one person joining the club because of Cody Lightfoot and twelve joining for the same reason. It's a little like building your house on sand. Or a lake. The foundations are bound to shift in time, to crumble and collapse. But Waneeda's negativity also owes something to Sicilee and Maya. The state of bliss with which the meeting began for Waneeda ended as soon as she realized that there was going to be no way of ignoring the two of them. It was hard trying not to notice them sitting on either side of Cody like particularly self-satisfied bookends. When they popped up together like slices from a toaster, carrying on so much that Cody wound up going back to his seat, Waneeda knew that there was no way of pretending they weren't there. She could see that every meeting was going to be dominated by them out-Greening each other. *I'm Greener than you are. . . . No,* I'm *Greener than you are. . . . No,* I *am. . . . No,* I *am. . . . Well,* I'm *so Green that* I'm *going to change my name to Chlorophyll. . . . Oh, yeah? Well,* I'm *going to change my name to Spinach!* Which means that every second of happiness given by her proximity to Cody and his smile is going to be soured by their presence. "I'm only saying . . ."

"Well, don't." Joy Marie grabs another chair. "If you don't have anything good to say, don't say anything at all."

"But Waneeda's right." Clemens looks up from the task of straightening the desk so it is perfectly aligned with the one in front of it and pushes his glasses back up his nose. "OK, so there were a lot of new people—"

"Which is what we wanted," Joy Marie reminds him. "Remember what Dr. Firestone said? Expand or die?"

"How could I forget?" Although it is a talent that Clemens keeps fairly quiet, he can do an impersonation of Dr. Firestone that is so accurate you'd swear he was wearing one of the principal's lurid ties. "But what I started to say was that I don't think that most of them are very serious. They didn't seem to know very much. I'm not sure how committed they really are. Like those two girls . . ." There is no need to specify which two girls he means. "Didn't the one with the short hair and the nose ring come to a meeting last year?"

"Uh-huh." Joy Marie slips two more chairs into place. "But she didn't come back."

"And who thought she would?" asks Clemens. "She slept through the whole thing."

"You were lucky," mutters Waneeda as they lift another desk. "She's a lot more fun asleep than awake."

"OK, but why did she come today if she's not really interested?" Clemens is looking at Joy Marie. "That's what I mean. What was she doing here?"

Joy Marie looks at Waneeda.

Waneeda is looking at the ceiling. If he figures it out for himself, fine. But if he doesn't, she's definitely not going to be the one to tell him why. He's in advanced math, for Pete's sake. He can add one and one and get two.

"Well, you know . . ." Apparently, it also isn't going to be Joy Marie who explains to Clemens why this particular dawn has broken and this miracle has occurred. This is not to protect Waneeda, of course, but the club. Clemens has so many principles that he might kick out all the new members if he discovers the truth. "People change."

"Mountains change faster," says Clemens. "And anyway, what about the other girl? The pink one?" Clemens, shuffling backward, looks over his shoulder. "Isn't that the girl who threatened me that time?"

Waneeda swallows the last morsel of caramel. "She's a witch. You're lucky she didn't turn you into a toad."

Joy Marie slams a chair down very close to Waneeda's feet. "Well, I guess she's changed, too," she says brightly. "That was last year. She must've matured."

Clemens looks doubtful. "Besides threatening me, she told me to stuff my campaign up my finite resources."

"I'd like to stuff *her* up a finite resource," mumbles Waneeda.

"You know, you two don't have to be so down on them," says Joy Marie. "They've joined — that's what's important. And they and all the other new ones seem pretty excited. Why can't you just leave it at that? We have a chance to start all over with these new members and really do some good."

Clemens smirks. "You mean if all these new members come back."

Joy Marie and Waneeda exchange a corner-of-the-eye look.

"Oh, they'll be back," says Waneeda.

You couldn't keep any of them away with dogs.

And that, of course, includes Waneeda.

Chapter Nineteen

Seen to be Green

Some girls might be daunted by the idea of changing from a fur-loving carnivore into a recycling vegetarian more or less overnight, but Sicilee saw no problem.

Kristin, Loretta, and Ash all thought she'd lost her mind.

"You mean you're going Green?" Kristin hadn't looked so horrified since her last bad haircut. "I know he's gorgeous and everything, Siss, but you can't be serious."

Loretta and Ash agreed. "Maybe if he was a big movie star or something," said Loretta.

"Or a prince," said Ash.

"Sweet Mary!" Sicilee moaned. "Do you guys read the words, or do you just look at the pictures? Watch my lips! I am not *really* going Green. I'm just going to act like I am." What could be easier? "You know, like wearing tinted lenses or a wig. It's only for show." She may look like an angel, but she thinks like a politician.

"So you're not *really* scarfing tofu and hugging trees?" checked Ash.

"Of course not. The only thing I want to hug is Cody, and I'm only meat-free when I'm at school. I'd rather give up water than give up meat."

Giving up water would probably be easier.

Sicilee decided that, since Cody always brings his lunch from home, she should bring hers, too—forging yet another link in the chain of love that will eventually join them. How could he *not* go out with a girl who carries her lunch from home in an eco-friendly insulated bag? Unfortunately, the Kewes's refrigerator contains a lot more to drink that isn't water than things to eat that didn't once walk, swim, or fly. Today, for example, the only vegetables Sicilee could find (unless you count the bean sprouts in the leftovers from last night's takeout) were some limp leaves of lettuce, a small tomato, and a carrot that had been in the crisper so long it could almost bend.

Having to put something together for lunch is one of the reasons that (unknowingly following the treacherous path forged by Maya Baraberra) Sicilee has been running late all week. The other is that, now that she's in competition with Maya, Sicilee has to look not only more perfect than she usually does (a fairly impossible task without major surgery), but more environmentally friendly as well. She spends at least an extra half hour on her makeup every morning, so that she looks completely natural and smells like something made by God rather than a lab. She spends even more time scouring her wardrobe for clothes with some kind of plant or animal motif to show that she cares about more than designer labels. Today, however, she's left the floral tops and cat socks at home and is wearing brown, the color of soil.

Her lunch bag artistically poking out of her backpack, Sicilee hurls herself from the Cadillac, slamming the door behind her. In fact, she's been running so late that Kristin, tired of hanging around waiting for her every morning, got a ride from her mother today. "You know, school's not just about classes," Kristin informed her. "I need to have some interactive time with my friends, too."

Oh, tell me something I don't know, thinks Sicilee. As if interactive time isn't just what she wants herself. Desperately. Interactive time with Cody Lightfoot. Hanging out in the hall before homeroom. Laughing and talking. Comparing notes on brussels sprouts. But getting Cody by himself is like trying to get an audience with the pope. If he isn't hanging out with a gang of boys, he's being escorted by a guard of grinning girls—Maya often just feet behind him, waiting for her moment to pounce.

Tomorrow, Sicilee suddenly decides, she'll wear all green. She doesn't know why she didn't think of this sooner. Then, when Cody looks her way, he will immediately think of forests and fields of tall grass waving in the

116

wind without even realizing it—and of how much she, like he, cares about saving and protecting the environment. Thinking about Cody as she hurries toward the entrance, she is practically on top of him before she sees him. And he's alone! He's totally alone! Sicilee glances over her shoulder, but for once Maya isn't in pursuit. The prize is hers! She trots the last few paces.

"Hi!" Sicilee falls into step beside him, smiling like a dozen suns. His answering "Hi" has a lot in common with a welcome sign—generic and not really welcoming, just there—but Sicilee is too excited to notice. "I am, like, so glad to run into you," she gushes. "I've been wanting to talk to you about the meeting on Monday. I was, like, so impressed by everything you said."

"Thanks." His smile sits on his face like a coat on a vacant chair. It's possible that he recognizes her. But it's also possible that he doesn't. Just as the sun shines down indiscriminately on city and village, and on rich and poor, with the same intensity, so Cody smiles on people he doesn't know with the same warmth he shows his best friends. "What's important is that everything I said is true."

"Oh, I know, I know." Sicilee leans a little closer. "I especially liked what you said about having fun and not alienating people?"

"Yeah . . . well . . . I hope I didn't make it sound too much like a party." Somehow, she never noticed the

117

dimples before. "Like I said, these are very serious issues we're dealing with."

"Oh, I know, I know." Her arm brushes against his. "It's just that, you know, before you came, the Environmental Club was about as much fun as—" As what? She doesn't want to say something like "as watching educational TV," which her friends would think is funny. She wants an image that will subtly show him that they're on exactly the same page.

"As an oil spill?" Cody offers.

"Exactly! That's exactly what I was going to say. As much fun as an oil spill." She gives him a conspiratorial look. "And as for alienating people—well, to be totally honest, and I know he's your friend and everything, but—"

"Clem's the man," says Cody. "Like I said at the meeting, if you need facts and statistics to back up your arguments, he's got all the dope."

Or is the dope.

"Oh, I know, I know. . . ." chitters Sicilee. "And I'm sure that could come in really handy . . . but don't you think that, besides always being so depressing, he can be a major bully, too? *Do this. . . . Don't do that. . . .* He even wanted to stop us all from drinking soda! Can you believe that?" She touches his arm. "Some people find it very off-putting."

"I don't," says Cody. "I admire his passion. He's a true man of principles." He half turns, smiling impishly.

"But even Clem'd tell you, he's about as diplomatic as a wounded bear."

They're still laughing as they step into the building.

Things are suddenly going so well that Sicilee can be forgiven for thinking that they are going to continue going so well.

But, of course, they aren't.

They're barely through the door when Maya Baraberra emerges from the blur of students like a shark from a shoal of minnows. Maya now dresses exclusively in clothes that have been previously worn by someone else and has added a new and fairly extensive range of buttons to her book bag.

"Cody! Sicilee!" Any passing stranger would think they were her two best friends.

"Hey," says Cody. He doesn't recognize Maya, either.

Sicilee merely maintains her usual smile.

"Whoowhee . . . get a look at you! Talk about being in touch with the Earth!" Maya, for a change, is not looking at Cody. Her eyes move from Sicilee's boots to the coat and finally stop as they meet Sicilee's eyes. "That's not *real* leather you're wearing, is it?" she asks doubtfully.

Trust the Barbarian not to be able to tell the difference between real leather and some cheap imitation. "Of course it is," purrs Sicilee. "It's Italian."

"Oh, wow. Really?" Maya scrunches up her face so

tightly that her nose ring seems to be looking at Sicilee, too. "It's just that . . . you know . . . I thought you said you were vegan—or at least a vegetarian."

As smoothly as she can, and still smiling, Sicilee attempts to climb out of the trap Maya has laid for her. "I'm not eating them, you know. I'm just wearing them."

"But still . . . you've got all that wasted land and water . . . and the carbon emissions during production . . . and the environmental degradation . . . and all the toxins of the dyes. I mean, it's good that they didn't come from China, with all the pollution and slave labor and everything, but *Italy* is still pretty far away."

Whereas Maya's clothes obviously came from a thrift store.

Sicilee smiles on. "I only just became a vegan. I can't throw out my entire wardrobe overnight."

"Oh, of course you can't. . . ." agrees Maya. "What are you supposed to do if you don't have any shoes or coats that aren't leather?"

"And what about you?" Sicilee glares down at the frayed and dirty shoes on Maya's feet. "Those aren't bedroom slippers you're wearing."

"No, they're not." There are few things that make a smile sweeter than triumph. "They're actually totally vegan. Like me." Maya swings one foot in the air so Sicilee can get a good look. "That'd be hemp and reclaimed tires, not dead cow."

120

Merciful Mother! Wearing somebody's old tires — it's like admitting you eat from the garbage.

"They look like you made them yourself," sneers Sicilee. And can only hope that she sounds as disgusted and unkind as she feels.

"Oy! Wait a minute. Pull back on the rope there."

They are so intent on insulting each other that Sicilee and Maya's attention misplaced Cody for a few seconds, but now they turn to find him grinning at them. Or at least grinning at Sicilee.

"I have that exact same pair of shoes."

Sicilee forces herself to laugh, too. "Well, I'm sure they look much better on you."

The day never improves after that. For once, Sicilee runs into Cody everywhere she goes. Now actively trying to avoid him, she has only to turn a corner or glance down a hallway to make him appear. And every time she sees him, she knows that he sees her leather boots, as conspicuous as a pair of alligators. The other person she sees constantly, of course, is Maya Baraberra. Maya, who normally tries to avoid Sicilee with the same thoroughness with which Sicilee tries to avoid her, gives her a big cheesy grin and calls out, "Hey, Sicilee, I really love your boots!"

No wonder Sicilee couldn't wait to go home.

And home is where she is now, standing on a stool to reach the top shelves.

Several blocks away, Kristin sits on her bed painting

121

her toenails while she talks to Sicilee on the phone. "Where are you?" asks Kristin. "You sound like you're in a cave or something."

"I'm in my closet."

Kristin dips the brush in the tiny bottle, carefully wiping off the excess on the rim. "Doing what, exactly?"

"I'm trying to find something to wear on my feet that isn't responsible for the horrible death of some stupid cow, what do you think?"

"Didn't I tell you it was going to be trickier than you thought?"

"Sweet Mary!" Sicilee wails. "What am I supposed to do? Go barefoot in the middle of winter?" She doesn't even want to think about handbags.

"You could always wear high-tops or something like that," suggests Kristin.

No, she couldn't.

"And look like the Barbarian? I'd rather wear paper bags on my feet."

"Well, what about that fake leather stuff vegetarians and vegans wear then?" tries Kristin.

Sicilee feels a new panic engulf her. "Vegetarians *and* vegans?" she repeats.

"Yeah, sure. They have lots of fake stuff. Cheese . . . mayonnaise . . . meat . . . milk. And leather. Jackets . . . shoes . . . boots . . . sneakers . . . bags. Whatever."

"That's not what I meant," says Sicilee. "I meant how

come you said vegetarians *and* vegans? You mean there's a difference?"

"Um, duh. . . . Yes." Kristin turns on the hairdryer and plays it across her toes. "Why? What did you say you are?"

"Vegan." Sicilee hears Maya Baraberra's ultra-irritating, super-cool voice saying, *I bet you don't even know what a vegan is.* "I thought they were the same thing."

"Oh, boy, have you gotten on the wrong bus!" This is the first time Sicilee ever noticed how witch-like Kristin's laugh can be. "Vegans are, like, really fanatical. Vegetarians are just a pain in the butt. You know, all vegans are vegetarians, but not all vegetarians are vegans."

Now she tells her.

"Merciful Mother!" Sicilee steps off the stool and sits down on the floor with a thud. "Fanatical like how?"

"Well . . . they won't touch anything that's ever been *near* an animal. And I mean *nothing.* No milk, no eggs, no butter, no cheese—"

"No cheese? You mean they don't eat pizza?"

"Not with cheese." Kristin wiggles her toes. "And no honey, either."

"Honey?" What does honey have to do with chopping up cows and putting them in a bun with ketchup? "Are you making this up?" demands Sicilee.

"Who could make this up?" asks Kristin.

"I don't believe it." She refuses to. "You have to be

wrong. No one could live like that. It's like punishing yourself just for being alive."

"It gets worse," Kristin assures her. "You know that sweater you were wearing today? And the blouse? They're out, too. No wool and no silk."

No wool and no silk? Is she supposed to go naked as well as barefoot?

"And your silver parka's out because it's filled with duck down."

"What am I supposed to do? Wrap myself in a blanket?"

"Not a wool one," says Kristin.

Sweet Mary! Is there no end to this?

"Which means that you should ditch all your mittens and gloves and scarves."

Kristin has never shown any sadistic tendencies before, but she has to be putting Sicilee on. She *has* to be. "How do you know all this stuff?" demands Sicilee.

"Don't you remember when my brother went through that post-punk, pissed-off-about-everything phase during his first year in college?"

"Vaguely," says Sicilee. "Didn't he have a pin through his eyebrow?"

"Yeah, but besides the pins and the tattoos and stuff, he went vegan. You wouldn't believe how torturous it was. You'd think he just got off the spaceship from Mars. He wouldn't touch anything until he'd read the label.

And can you believe it? He wanted to throw most of my makeup away! And my shampoos and conditioners and God knows what else. How sick is that? It drove my mom totally nuts. It was like living with the food police. And God forbid you ate an egg! He went into mega-meltdown, like you'd bitten the head off a live chicken."

Sicilee groans. Holy Mother! No wonder nobody likes these people. They want to wring every drop of joy out of life that they can.

"I have it! I have it! I know what you can do!" Kristin is so excited that a cotton ball falls from between her toes. "Just *say* you're wearing fake leather or fur or silk or whatever. Some of the stuff they make now is pretty cool. Nobody'll know the difference."

Gloom floods Sicilee's heart. "Maya will know."

"Maya?"

"Yes, *Maya*. Little Miss Oh-How-I-Love-Your-Boots. What do you think she's doing when she skulks past our table at lunch? Taking the scenic route? She's checking up on what I'm eating—that's what she's doing." No wonder she smirked at Sicilee the other day when she saw her eating a cheese sandwich. It's a miracle she didn't say something about it this morning. *Oh, wow. Sicilee, you're the only vegan I know who eats cheese* and *wears leather.*

"Oh, get real, Siss," says Kristin. "She can't rip your clothes off you to check the labels."

"I wouldn't put anything past her," says Sicilee.

125

Chapter Twenty

Juanita, Mary Jo, and What's-Her-Name

I can't help it—those two really push my buttons," Waneeda is saying. "It was bad enough at the meeting, when they wouldn't shut up even to breathe. All that blah-blah crap about how Green they are. It was enough to make you puke."

"I don't know. . . . I thought they were pretty funny." Joy Marie smiles over her sandwich. "It was like watching a game of verbal tennis. I kept expecting one of them to fall over the net."

If only . . .

"Oh, right. And I suppose you think it's hilarious the way they follow Cody around like tracker dogs." No wonder he always walks in groups of three or more; he needs the protection.

"Yes, I do," says Joy Marie. "Maya's usually so cool she wouldn't break a sweat in a sauna. And as for Sicilee . . ." Joy Marie grins. "Come on, Waneeda. It's like finding out that the Queen of England takes out her own garbage."

A smile pushes at Waneeda's mouth. "Yeah, well . . ." she concedes, if grudgingly. "I guess that is pretty funny. But it isn't funny the way they've been pouring it on ever since the meeting." Waneeda can't decide which of them irks her more: Sicilee strutting around looking as green as one of Robin Hood's Merry Men or Maya plastering her bag with all those new buttons (NO COAL . . . DAMS FOR THE DAMNED . . . BE A SOLUTION TO POLLUTION . . . WHERE WILL YOU BE WHEN THE OIL RUNS OUT? . . . WHERE DO YOU THINK THE ENVIRONMENT IS? and so forth, as Clemens might say), so that it's a miracle she can lift the damn thing. "It's not like they're fooling anyone."

Joy Marie allows herself a small smile. "You mean besides Clemens."

Clemens doesn't count. Expecting him to realize what Sicilee and Maya are doing would be like expecting an Amazonian native to tell you where to eat in New York.

"But don't you think they're outrageous?" insists Waneeda. "Are we all supposed to be stupid or something? You'd have to have the brains of a rock to believe that either of them gives a toothpick about the planet."

Joy Marie chews thoughtfully for a few seconds. "You mean unlike *you*?"

"Excuse me, but I don't drive around in a car as big as a bus. And I don't go shopping every single weekend, either," snaps Waneeda. "And as for all that malarkey about being vegetarians . . ."

Joy Marie is of the opinion that they have to give Maya the benefit of the doubt. "She does have a BE KIND TO ANIMALS—DON'T EAT THEM button on her book bag."

"OK, maybe Maya," says Waneeda. "Her crowd probably thinks red meat's really passé."

"Well, it's nice somebody does." Joy Marie glances at the plate of spaghetti and meatballs Waneeda is eating. "I've never noticed you avoiding it."

"But I've never claimed to be a vegetarian," argues Waneeda. "When did I say that? Never, that's when. But Sicilee did. *And* she has fur boots. And a fur coat! People who wear fur boots don't refuse to eat cows!" Waneeda jabs at a meatball with so much force that it jumps onto her tray. "You know as well as I do that the only reason either of them went to the meeting was Cody Lightfoot. They were all over him like flies on a corpse."

"At least they acted like they were interested in the environment and had something to say." Which, of course, is not something that can be said about Waneeda.

Trust Joy Marie not to let that go. "Can't you get off my case about that?" snaps Waneeda. "And, anyway, they were just trying to impress him."

"Maybe." Joy Marie looks down at her sandwich. "But I bet they know as much as you do about being Green. Maybe more."

Joy Marie is, in fact, being diplomatic. For the last year and a half, Waneeda has let everything Joy Marie's tried to tell her about the environment circle around her head and immediately vanish into the ether without the inconvenience of having to go in one ear and out the other first. And Joy Marie knows it. So does Waneeda.

Nonetheless, Waneeda is all set to defend herself— but isn't given the chance.

"You ladies aren't busy, are you?" asks an unexpected voice beside them. "You mind if I have a few minutes of your time?"

Waneeda and Joy Marie both look up in surprise, if not complete confusion. Having Cody Lightfoot suddenly appear beside you takes some getting used to even if he hasn't almost caught you talking about him.

Possibly because he's used to girls gaping silently at him, Cody doesn't wait for an answer but pulls out the chair next to Joy Marie and sits down. "Don't let me impinge." He waves one hand at Joy Marie's sandwich and Waneeda's plate of spaghetti. "I can talk while you eat." His other hand holds a plain brown folder, which he lays in front of him on the table.

Waneeda is so surprised that Cody wants to talk to them that she swallows half a meatball without chewing it first.

"Is it about the meeting?" asks Joy Marie. "Because if it's about the meeting, I haven't had time to type up the minutes yet. I usually do that over the weekend."

"The minutes?" He smiles as if she's said something

odd but adorable. "You mean all that old-fashioned so-and-so said this and so-and-so said that blah-de-blah?" He half turns in his seat and leans his elbows on the table, so that he is looking at both of them in an almost conspiratorial way. "I wouldn't worry about that, Mary Jo. You know, there was so much going on." Joy Marie is so unused to being smiled at like this by a boy that she makes no response to the fact that he still doesn't know her name. "It'd take you hours just to get down everything Clemens said." He gives her a mischievous wink. "All you really need to type up is the gist. You know, twelve new members . . . decision to have a big celebration for Earth Day this year . . . raising awareness—that kind of thing. Just for the record."

"They're minutes," says Joy Marie. "I wasn't planning to turn them into a term paper."

Cody laughs, but Waneeda is watching his fingers tap on the folder. The only boy who has ever spoken to either Joy Marie or her in a voluntary, friendly way and not because of some ulterior motive is Clemens. She wonders what Cody wants.

"So what is it you want to talk about?" ventures Waneeda. And then, when the Lightfoot smile falls on her like an especially brilliant beam of sunlight, she says, stumbling, "I mean . . . if it isn't about the meeting."

"It's Juanita, right?" But he gives her no chance either to agree or disagree with his innovative interpretation of her name. "I hear what you're saying, Juanita. Thing is, it kind of *is* about the meeting. It's linked. Connected." His smile somehow circles both of them. "Like a string to a balloon."

Waneeda and Joy Marie nod. Uncomprehendingly.

"See, the thing is . . . I don't know if Clem told you, but I got to have a few words with our great leader yesterday."

"Great leader?" repeats Waneeda. Has Cody been to Washington and back in only a day?

Cody doesn't realize that he's been asked a question. "Don't get me wrong: I comprendo that Clemens has had his bad scenes with Dr. Firestone—I've heard all about them. But the good doctor and I hit it off all right. He has that weird tie-thing going on, but he's not as unreasonable as Clem led me to believe. He absolutely heard what I was saying."

Dr. Firestone. Of course that's who he meant. Still not certain where this conversation is going, Joy Marie and Waneeda nod again.

"I'll announce it at the next meeting, of course, but the terrific news is that he's totally on board. And he really loves our slogan: Make them aware, and they will care. He was a little apprehensive that we might offend some people while we're trying to get them on board. You know, because there's been some precedence for that kind of negative thing? But I told him there was no need to worry. I said that the new Environmental Club is as user-friendly as a puppy now. And then I explained about the Earth Day gig and getting local businesses as well as the school involved and everything, and he was over the moon. He says he'll back us two hundred percent."

"That's great," says Joy Marie. "Dr. Firestone is usually in front of us, telling us to stop—not behind us." Suddenly aware that she's still holding half a cheese sandwich, Joy Marie takes a small bite.

"Clemens must be really thrilled," says Waneeda.

"Right. Of course he is." His eyes on them, Cody opens the folder. "And I knew I could count on your help. I knew straight off that you guys are real backbone types." He leans forward just a little bit more, as though he's about to confide some secret that may break their hearts. "Which kind of brings us back to those minutes you mentioned before, Mary Jo."

Waneeda lowers her fork. She knew he wanted something.

Dr. Firestone, who may wear wacky ties, but is still both a pedant and a bureaucrat, would like to see something in writing. No major document or anything like that, just a brief description of how they see the Earth Day gig working out, and some of the thoughts there have been on how to generate interest among the student body as well as among the good citizens of Clifton Springs. Something to show his people—the rest of the staff and the school board and the town council—so they know what's going down.

"I figured that since you're the lady who was taking notes . . ." Cody trails off as if he's waiting for Joy Marie to fill in the blank, but she is chewing rather automatically at this point and doesn't stop to speak. "I brought you this. It's what we used last year? In my old club? I figured you could use it as a model. Or even borrow from it liberally. It's just to get us started." Without much effort, his smile could disarm a large army. It makes Waneeda drop her fork. "Which should make it pretty easy for you to whip up a couple of pages and run off some copies for Dr. F." Now he seems to be trying to disarm not a large army but entire nations. "I know it's kind of short notice—I can't tell you how much I appreciate this; it is so awesome of you—and I'd offer to help with the typing, I really would, only I'm, like, all thumbs when it comes to stuff like that." He spreads his fingers in the air so that he seems to be smiling at them through a fence. "And I'm busy as a bird, really. But maybe Juanita here could give you a hand."

Juanita isn't so sure. She wants to *look* at Cody, not work for him.

But before either Joy Marie or Waneeda (or Mary Jo or Juanita, for that matter) can raise any objections to this plan, Maya Baraberra suddenly lands beside them, grinning and babbling and spilling her soup.

By the time Maya is on her way again, Waneeda and Joy Marie have forgotten what it was they were going to say.

"So we're all set, right?" Cody gets to his feet. "Dr. F would like those copies by Thursday, if you can see your way clear." He links his hands like bird wings and flaps them. *"Tempus fugit."* As he turns to leave, he nods at Maya, halfway down the aisle. "Who *was* that girl?" he asks.

Juanita might make Waneeda think of a girl who is sensual and exotic, but it's a lot better than having no name at all. Waneeda smiles.

Chapter Twenty-one

It isn't easy being Green

But did you see her? Did you see what she's wearing today?" Maya yanks open the door to the cafeteria as though it has personally offended her. "Green! She's all in green! Even her *eyes* are green! *Gott im Himmel,* she looks like the Jolly Green Giant's girlfriend!"

Alice, who has seen Sicilee several times this morning, says, "I just don't see what you're getting so worked up about." She picks up a tray and follows Maya to the lunch line. "I mean, really. So she's in green. Even if she suddenly sprouted leaves, Sicilee Kewe is still the human equivalent of a ten-million-gallon oil spill, for God's sake. How could she be any competition for *you?* I mean, Cody's not stupid, is he?"

"Of course he's not stupid." Maya reaches for a cheese sandwich but remembers just in time that she's a vegan now. "He's incredibly intelligent." She scans the day's offerings. Ham sandwich. Tuna sandwich. Chicken nuggets. Spaghetti with meatballs. Pea soup. Clearly, the cafeteria staff aren't aware of the crucial relationship between veganism and saving the Earth. "But you should have heard her at the meeting, Al. She made it sound like she invented conservation while she was washing her hair. She—"

"Yeah, I know." Not a day has gone by since the meeting that Alice hasn't heard about this. In detail. By now she feels as though she was there herself. "But she *didn't* invent conservation. She probably can't even spell it."

"It doesn't matter if she can spell it or not. She's determined to get a date with Cody. *Gott im Himmel*, Alice! She came to school with him yesterday!"

This is another episode in the life of Maya Baraberra that Alice has heard so much about she feels she must have witnessed it. "You don't know that. All you saw was them walking in together."

"They were laughing."

"And?"

"And he's never laughed with me, has he?"

Alice resists the temptation to bang her head against the chrome shelves. "But I thought you said that you humiliated her in front of him. He's going to know she's not much of an environmentalist after that."

"I said that I *tried* to humiliate her in front of him." Maya slaps a plate onto her tray. "But she just bounced right back. *I'm wearing them, not eating them. . . . Well, I'm sure they look better on you. . . ."* She isn't even sure that Cody was making fun of Sicilee when he told her that he had the same shoes as Maya. He could have been laughing *with* her, not *against* her. "The problem is that Sicilee has the ego of a Master of the Universe. *And* she's devious. She'll do anything to get what she wants. I bet that even her parents are afraid to turn their backs on her." Maya pays for the soup, two apples, and the roll she finally selected. "So let's just stroll by her table to make sure she really is eating vegetables."

"Oh, for God's sake . . ." Alice groans. "Again? Are we going to do this every day for the rest of our lives?"

"Only if we have to," answers Maya as she steps into the lunchroom. And stops so suddenly that Alice nearly walks into her.

There, right in front of them, and no more than a step or two away, sits Cody Lightfoot. It's a dream come true. He's alone. By himself. Or as good as. He's not with Sicilee Kewe, which is the important thing. He's with What's-Her-Name—the skinny one who looks like a librarian in an old movie—and her schlumpy friend. He isn't eating, but talking. Instead of his lunch, there are several pieces of paper in front of him.

Maya glides up to their table as if she's on wheels. "Hi, guys! How's it going?"

Waneeda and Joy Marie, who know very well that Maya isn't talking to them, don't even bother to nod.

137

Cody, in the middle of a sentence, breaks off to look at Maya. "Hi," he says. "How're you?"

"I'm fine." Maya's head bobs for emphasis. "I'm terrific."

Cody smiles as if he is really glad to hear this. "That's great." And looks down at the papers with a certain amount of longing.

"You know, I haven't had a chance to say how terrific the meeting was. Remember, I sat next to you? And I was the first person to talk about why I was joining the Environmental Club?" Just in case he has forgotten. She wasn't sure, yesterday, that he actually knew who she was. "I thought it was really *so* inspiring. *You* were." She sets her tray down on the table with a bang. "Oh, God. Sorry." Soup slops over the rim of her bowl and onto her tray.

Cody moves his folder out of the way. "Yeah," he says. "It was a good meeting. Fruitful."

"But I bet the next one'll be way better," enthuses Maya. She leans on the table, sending more soup over the edge and one of the apples rolling through the puddle. "Because if everybody's like me, I already have so many ideas. I—"

"What is that stuff?" Cody's looking at her soup as if it is toxic waste about to spread throughout the lunchroom and drown them all.

"Soup. Pea soup." Maya beams. "You know, because I'm vegan?"

Oh, of course, he's supposed to say. *You're the girl who shops in secondhand stores and rides her bike everywhere and is vegan—just like me.* But that isn't what he says.

"What makes you think it's vegan?" asks Cody.

Maya is still smiling, but not so happily now. She has the unpleasant feeling that she's watching victory (or at least a chance to score on Sicilee Kewe) being snatched from her grasp. "Because it's made of peas." Her laugh isn't particularly happy either.

"Yeah, but what else is in it?" asks Cody. "Usually they make it with a ham bone or even chicken stock."

This, of course, is news to Maya. Despite her belief that she's been a vegetarian for the past six months, it has never occurred to her to read the label on anything, except to check the calories per serving. Fortunately, she is no stranger to adjusting the truth on the spur of the moment. "Oh, this soup's not made like that," says Maya. And then, inspired by despair, adds, "I checked. I mean, we vegans can't be too careful, can we?"

"Dead right. That's why I always bring my lunch from home." Cody's eyes are still on the carnage on her tray. "I guess you checked the roll, too," he says.

Why can't he just flirt with me? Maya silently fumes. That's all she wanted, just a few minutes of harmless flirtation. Did he think she'd stopped so she could drown him in pea soup made with the blood of lambs? Did he think she'd gone over to him so he could give her a crash course in veganism for airheads?

"Oh, yeah," says Maya. "Of course I did."

It is only when she picks up her tray to beat a hasty retreat that she notices Sicilee, loitering a few feet away by the garbage cans. Sicilee's smile brightens as she mouths the word, "Touché!"

Chapter Twenty-two

Waneeda builds a plane

Humans tend to be creatures of habit, and Waneeda Huddlesfield is no exception. Every day for as long as anyone can remember, Waneeda came home from school, dumped her backpack on the sofa, grabbed a snack, and spent the rest of the afternoon watching TV. Then she sat at the dining-room table with her parents and shared a meal whose conversation was largely provided by the television set. After that, she watched some more TV (and snacked some more), until it was time to do her homework while she watched TV. (If she could have watched TV while she was sleeping, she probably would have.) If she got bored with TV, she played games on her computer instead.

But all that has changed.

Now Waneeda goes to her room as soon as she gets back from school and does her homework. She emerges only briefly, to eat with her parents in the glow of the television screen, and then she immediately goes back to her room, locking the door behind her (though the possibility of her mother getting off the couch and barging in on her is as remote as the return of the wood bison).

"What are you doing in there?" Waneeda's mother asks every night as Waneeda puts her plate in the sink. "That's what I'd like to know. What are you doing in there? Always in your room. Do you see your daughter, Oscar? She's always in her room. It isn't normal."

And every night, Waneeda says as she makes her escape, "What do you think I'm doing? I'm building a plane."

Obviously, it isn't true that Waneeda is spending her evenings constructing a light aircraft in her bedroom. It's much too small to hold even a glider.

What Waneeda does in her room is explore her new interest in the trials and tribulations of the third planet from the sun. As we know, Sicilee and Maya's new interest in the planet and its problems is due to love, but, although Waneeda did join the club because she wanted to be near Cody Lightfoot, her new interest owes much more to Sicilee and Maya than to him. And to Joy Marie's crack about Maya and Sicilee knowing more about being Green than Waneeda.

It was then that Waneeda made her decision. It was going to be bad enough to have to sit through meetings dominated by the Deadly Duo—the Cool Fool, with her dumb buttons like she's going to forget what she believes if it isn't written down, and the Living Barbie la-di-da-ing around like the rest of humanity only exists to feel bad that they aren't her—without knowing in her heart that they really do know more than she does—and every day probably know a little more.

And that is why, that night after supper, Waneeda sat down at her computer and typed in the words *global warming*. On the second site she visited, she took a quiz: *How much do you know about climate change?* The answer turned out to be less than even she would have guessed. The answer turned out to be: just about nothing. Waneeda stayed at her computer till one in the morning.

It was all pretty overwhelming. There were over five hundred million responses when she typed in *pollution*. Over eighty-six million for *carbon emissions*. Sixty-three million for *endangered species*. And nearly two million for *hole in ozone layer*. When you know nothing, Waneeda realized, you don't even know where to start. You have no idea what information might actually prove of some use, or what information is less useful than a golf ball to clear up an oil spill. The enormity of the task before you exhausts you before you begin. It was the kind of situation that would normally cause Waneeda to give up without a fight. But this time she couldn't. Not with the smug smiles of Sicilee and Maya burned into her brain. She knew that she needed help, but she couldn't very well ask Joy Marie—not after ignoring everything she's said for the last year and a half—so the next night she was up until one again, and up until one the night after that, too. Waneeda figured there was a real danger that her brain might implode.

But the following morning, she happened to emerge from her street at the same time that Clemens emerged from his. It was as if her guardian angel had suddenly shown up to answer her prayers. Clemens Reis—who better? Even Cody said that Clemens's knowledge is awesome—and there's nothing Clemens likes better than to share information. Besides which, although he is undeniably peculiar, Clemens has always been nice to Waneeda. Once, at the beach when they were little, she dropped her ice cream in the sand and Clemens immediately gave her his.

"Clemens!" screamed Waneeda. "Clemens, wait up!"

Unused to anyone actually *asking* him to explain things, Clemens, of course, was only too happy to help. He suggested books to read and loaned her documentaries on DVD. He gave her several pages listing websites that cover everything you ever wanted to know about environmental degradation but didn't know whom to ask—from air, ground, and water pollution to deforestation and plastics. Waneeda's been going through it systematically, making notes and asking Clemens the next day any questions that she has.

Tonight, Waneeda sits down at her computer and turns to the page headed: *Reasons not to eat meat.* There are several sites listed, but beneath them, underlined in red, Clemens has scrawled: *Watch that DVD I gave you. You will be tested!* Waneeda laughs. It's going to be another long night.

Chapter Twenty-three

Sicilee goes out with her friends

So, fairest Sicilee," says Rupert once they're all settled at a table at the back of Uncle Tony's. "What exciting, five-star, life-changing things have been happening in the wonderful world of Kewe lately?"

Sicilee looks over at Rupert. Up until this moment, she has been having a really good time. These days, she is usually in a state of at least mild stress at school and, when she hasn't drifted off into one of her lovelorn reveries, anxiety at home — always worried about what to wear and what to say (or what she's going to wear and going to say), but tonight, going to the movies with her friends, she's actually managed to forget about Cody Lightfoot for more than two consecutive hours. Which these days is a record. But there is something in the inane way Rupert's grinning at her that makes her think that brief idyll is about to end. Possibly in an ugly way.

"Nothing." She shrugs off her new parka (made from ethically sourced materials and trimmed in fur that has never been closer to an animal than Sicilee's head) and picks up her menu. "Same old, same old, really."

"That's not what we heard," says Abe.

"That's right," agrees Davis. Rupert's inane grin seems to be as contagious as measles. "We heard that you were boldly going where no one's boldly gone before."

"Risking isolation, destruction, and possible certain death," chips in Chris.

Sicilee clamps her teeth together to hold her smile in place. Somebody's told the boys about her new extra-curricular activity. Somebody with a mouth the size of Lake Michigan. Which one of them was it? She glances at Kristin, Loretta, and Ash, all of whom are gazing at their menus as if they haven't eaten enough pizza here to feed half of Sicily. She'll find out later.

"Well, you heard wrong."

Davis leans across Kristin to brush something from Sicilee's arm. "Oh, sorry." He might sound more sincere if his smile was less jubilant. "I thought there was some bark on your sleeve."

Loretta, Ash, and Kristin all bite back their smiles, but the boys laugh uproariously.

Following the example of her friends, Sicilee is gazing at her menu. "You know, I don't think I'll have any pizza tonight," she says, as though this thought has just occurred to her. "I think I'll just have a salad." There is no way she can eat pepperoni pizza in public. What if Maya Baraberra and her friends walk in? What if Cody does?

"Salad?" hoots Rupert. "But we always get pepperoni pizza with double cheese."

"And am I stopping you?" Sicilee speaks so sweetly that it might be wise for Rupert to remember that sugar kills. "But I'm having a salad. I don't want anything too heavy this late at night."

Chris leans toward her earnestly. "So what's the deal, Miss Kewe?" He waggles his eyebrows. "An eager world hangs on your every word. Is it true that all of a sudden you've decided to be born-again Green?"

Sicilee takes a sip of water. "If you're referring to the fact that I've joined the Environmental Club, Christopher," she says evenly, "no, it doesn't mean that I've been born-again Green. It just means I'm taking an interest in my country and in my planet." She sets her glass back on the table very carefully. "As all good citizens should."

"Well, it sounds to me like you've been born-again Green," says Chris. "I mean, look at you. You're dressed like you live in Arizona." Tonight, Sicilee is in muted earthy tones — beige and umber, sienna, ocher, and terra-cotta. "*And* you're eating salad."

"I eat salad a lot, Chris. It happens to be very good for you. I eat it all the time."

"Not by itself, you don't," says Rupert.

"Well, tonight I do." Sicilee's afraid to pick up her glass again, in case the temptation to throw its contents at Rupert proves too strong. "I told you: I want something light."

"Or maybe you've become a vegetarian," suggests Davis.

Merciful Mother, is there nothing the boys don't know? she thinks.

Sicilee's mouth is so rigid it could crush bones. There had better be one thing they haven't been told. "And what if I am?" It certainly beats being vegan. After what Kristin told her and what she overheard of Maya's conversation with Cody, Sicilee figured that given the choice between veganism and working fourteen hours a day gluing the soles on sneakers, she'd choose the sweatshop any day. "In case it's escaped your attention, Davis, vegetarianism's very popular nowadays."

"Sure it is," sniggers Davis. "Especially among rabbits."

Kristin, possibly to keep herself from laughing with the others, finally comes to Sicilee's aid. "Actually, a lot of really famous people are vegetarian," she says. "Isn't that true, Siss?"

"Yes, it is true," says Sicilee. Though she'd be hard put to name any of those famous people.

"You mean like Hitler?" asks Rupert.

"I don't think I could give up meat," says Loretta. "It's so, like, radical. Like having a stud put in your tongue."

Ash squiggles up her nose. "And it's so, you know, *meatless*. I mean, what do you eat if you don't eat meat?"

"Salad," says Abe.

Davis wants to know if this is the last time Sicilee will be hanging out with everyone socially.

"It's not a cult, Davis—it's a club," Sicilee explains. "I can hang out with anyone I want."

"I didn't mean that. I meant because it's going to kind of cramp everyone's style, isn't it? OK, you eat a bowl of lettuce when we come here, but what happens when we go bowling? No more deluxe nachos or hamburgers. And no more pool parties or barbecues when summer rolls around . . ." He pretends to wipe a tear from his eye. "What a shame, after all the fun we've had together, Siss. We're really going to miss you."

Sicilee's smile is as steady as the smile on a statue. "What a shame that I can't say the same about you."

"Ooooh . . ." crow Rupert and Chris.

"Ouch!" Davis shakes his hand as though he's burned it. "That really, really hurt, Sicilee. I think I may be traumatized for life."

Chris, having regained his composure, leans forward again as if he's about to say something important. "I have a question, Miss Kewe. I want to know, now that you're living on bean curd and recycling your toenail clippings, does that mean you're going to cut off your hair and wear combat boots from now on, too?"

Sicilee never realized before how little she really cares for Chris. He has the same laugh as Woody Woodpecker, but isn't nearly as amusing. Or as cute. *"Meaning?"*

"Meaning?" Chris splutters some more, looking at the other boys for backup and approval in an incredibly irritating and childish way. "Meaning that everybody knows the Green brigade is pretty much gay."

Sweet Mary, she's surrounded by fools. If smiles were punches, Sicilee would knock him out cold. "I'd rather be gay than an ignoramus like you."

Rupert—who apparently gets his information from a different source from Chris—wants to know if Sicilee is going to become a nudist. "You know, back to nature . . . running around in the moonlight worshipping the Corn God . . ." He gives her a smile that would be sleazy from anyone who looks less like a chipmunk. "That'd be cool."

Sicilee rolls her eyes. "That's only funny if you don't think you're joking."

Maybe she doesn't really care for any of them.

Except Abe. Abe hasn't cracked one juvenile joke or laughed so hard he nearly choked. In fact, Sicilee has always had a soft spot for Abe, who plays the saxophone and works in his father's nursery, and who suddenly says to her in total seriousness and with no trace of sarcasm,

"So, is that true, Sicilee? Are you really taking an interest in the planet and everything?"

"Of course it's true," says Sicilee. "You don't think I'm doing it for fun, do you?"

Abe shakes his head. "No, I guess not."

Sicilee returns his smile with a very nice smile of her own.

Chapter Twenty-four

Maya goes shopping

Get away from me!" shrieks Molly from the backseat. "Don't touch me!" She kicks her legs and hides the cereal bar she was opening behind her back.

"*Gott im Himmel,* don't be such a baby." Maya can only hope that the club has more success educating the student body than she's having educating the Baraberras. She pokes her head into the gap between the passenger's and the driver's seats. "I don't want your stupid bar, Molly. I just want to see it."

"Get your own!" screams Molly. "Mom! Mom! Make her leave me alone!"

Mrs. Baraberra's eyes stay on the road. "Leave Molly alone, Maya." From the tone of her voice it seems likely that she has probably given this command before.

Maya faces the front again, thumping and harrumphing. You'd think that her mother would be thanking her for giving up a Saturday morning to help her with the shopping. Really, why couldn't she have a family like

Cody's—aware, concerned, and principled—instead of the one she has—unaware, unconcerned, and with the principles of telemarketers? "I only wanted to see what's in it."

Molly kicks her seat. "Cereal's in it."

The car seems almost to sigh as they turn into the parking lot. "By now you'd think you'd know what's in it," says Mrs. Baraberra. For a woman known for her sunny disposition, she sounds a little bitter.

Maya's conversation with Cody about the hidden contents of pea soup and rolls may have convinced Sicilee that even pretending to be vegan was too much like hard work, but for Maya it was a moment of revelation. She had never given a thought to what was in the soup or the roll or anything else before. She'd assumed that if something wasn't dripping blood, it was meat-free. Now Maya reads all labels as if they are the Dead Sea Scrolls. She was surprised to discover just how many things that she assumed are vegetarian aren't. Cody is right: you can't be too careful. This is why Mrs. Baraberra sounds a little bitter. It's bad enough that Maya's suddenly decided to reject things she's always loved, like scrambled eggs and cheese and chicken casserole, but now she questions her mother about every single thing that comes into the house. *But does it have whey? Does it have lactose? Oleic acid? Keratin? Was it processed with lard? With animal charcoal? With isinglass? How much sugar's in it? How many additives?*

154

Is it carcinogenic? Toxic? Is it from a sustainable source? Was it flown thousands of miles, or is it locally sourced? Mrs. Baraberra is beginning to feel as if Maya's the Royal Inquisitor and she's the heretic.

"You are what you eat, you know," says Maya, though, in fact, she could assume that her mother does know this by now. "It's really important that we watch what we put into our bodies." Reading labels has proved to be not only addictive but informative as well. "Especially older people like you and Dad. Arthritis and heart disease are only a part of the fate that could await you if you don't have a healthy diet."

Mrs. Baraberra pulls into an empty space. "Your father and I appreciate your concern."

The bitterness, now tinged with sarcasm, in her mother's voice doesn't go unnoticed by Maya. "I'm only trying to help, you know."

"Don't." Mrs. Baraberra turns off the engine. "You just worry about you, and I'll take care of the rest of us."

Once inside the supermarket, Mrs. Baraberra and Molly go off to buy all the things that make Maya grimace and pretend to gag, and Maya goes to search for things that she can eat.

"We'll meet you by the frozen foods in half an hour," says Mrs. Baraberra.

But half an hour later, she and Molly stand in front of the freezers of ice cream by themselves.

Maya, as it happens, has gotten no farther than aisle B.

Her mother finally finds her scrutinizing the contents of a package of tortillas like Sherlock Holmes studying a pile of cigar ash. "For God's sake, Maya. What are you doing? They're just flour and water."

"I told you: you can't be too careful." Maya holds out the tortillas. "Look. They have milk in them."

Mrs. Baraberra doesn't look. "We don't have all day, Maya. We'll meet you by the bread in ten minutes."

Twenty minutes later, Molly is sent as a scout. Maya has made it out of aisle B and is reading her twelfth box of cereal with the avidity of a gambler checking the racing results.

"Mom's getting mad," announces Molly. "She says you'd better hurry up."

"Tell her that I need just five more minutes," says Maya. "No, make that ten. I'm almost done."

Twenty-five minutes later, Mrs. Baraberra marches down aisle E to tell Maya what time it is.

"But it's not my fault," argues Maya. "This store doesn't have any sugar that I can eat. It's—"

"So don't eat it. You're the one who's always telling us how bad it's supposed to be." Maya's mother thrusts some bills into her hands. "Molly and I will be in the car. If you're not out in fifteen minutes, we're going home without you."

It is possible that Maya has spent the longest amount of time selecting the smallest amount of goods in the history of Clifton Springs, but this isn't only because she's been hypnotized by the small print on wrappers, cans, and boxes. Maya got up this morning with one of her hunches. *I'm going to run into Cody Lightfoot today,* she thought as she rubbed the sleep from her eyes. She could feel it in her bones. And there would be no Sicilee Kewe to interfere; no Sicilee Kewe trailing behind him like toxic fumes. He'd be all by himself. It would be just her and Cody. The way it's meant to be.

So when Mrs. Baraberra suggested that she come shopping with her and pick out her own stuff, Maya immediately recognized the finger of Fate, stirring up the waters of her life. *Cody'll be in the supermarket,* Maya decided immediately. *Shopping with his dad.* She was ready to go before her mother had finished writing out her shopping list. And so she has lingered longer than she needed, giving Fate a chance to get Cody out of bed, out of the house, and, at least metaphorically, into her arms — thinking that at any minute she would look up to find him beside her and they'd laugh together over what was in that box of crackers or can of soup. On the other hand, it's a bitter winter's day and Maya doesn't want to have to walk home. She speeds through the last few aisles, grabbing things she already knows she can eat, and comes out in Baked Goods at the far side of the store.

She is checking the breads—pick one up and put it down, pick one up and put it down—when she becomes aware of someone behind her, so close that she can feel his breath against her cheek. Her heart flaps and flutters like a chicken surprised by a fox.

"What the hell are you doing, Maya? You look like you're the bread inspector."

She turns around. Fate has been toying with her again. She can hardly hide her disappointment.

"Just pick a loaf," says Jason. "They're all the same."

Maya explains that this isn't true. "Not if you're vegan."

"Vegan?" Usually, when he smiles like that, Maya thinks Jason looks really cute. Today, he just looks annoying. "You never told me about that."

"Well, you knew I was a vegetarian," says Maya. "It's not that big a difference really. I didn't feel it needed a public announcement."

"No, I guess it didn't." He laughs. "But isn't it kind of extreme?"

"Isn't the death of the planet kind of extreme?" Maya has been doing her homework. "It's not just about not eating meat, you know. The way we produce our meat doesn't just pollute the atmosphere; it pollutes the ground and water, too—and takes up tons of land that could be used in a more productive and sustainable way."

"Oh, right. I guess that slipped my mind." Jason

looks as if he's sorry he asked. "So how long has this been going on?"

She shrugs. "A while."

Up until now, Jason's expression has been perplexed but good-humored. Now it becomes thoughtful in a wait-a-minute kind of way. "You mean since you joined the Saviors of Planet Earth, right?"

Like Sicilee's friends, Maya's are pretty much unanimous in thinking that she's crazy for joining the Environmental Club. Mallory said that it was about as cool as wearing panty hose. Shayla said that it was more like wearing surgical stockings. Finn wanted to know if she'd lost a bet. Shelby said that he, for one, had better things to do than fish tin cans out of the Pascasett River. Brion said he could think of better things to hug than trees. But it's Jason who's been the most sarcastic and scathing. Jason who said that, if he didn't know better, he'd think she only joined because she had a crush on Clemens—and said it without any hint of a smile.

"Anybody who's serious about what's happening knows that going vegan is one of the best things you can do. Even the UN says so."

Jason nods. "So that means your friend Cody Light-foot's vegan, right?"

Maya can feel herself starting to blush. "Cody? What makes you say that?"

"Oh, I don't know. . . ." Jason gestures vaguely. "Maybe

the fact that every other sentence out of your mouth is: *Cody says this* or *Cody says that.* . . ."

"I'm really sorry, but I have to go," says Maya, already starting to push her cart. "My mother's waiting in the car."

Chapter Twenty-five

If you don't know the words, hum the tune

Sicilee's mother, though very fond of her, of course, has always been a little worried that her only child lacks a certain amount of depth. Or, as Sicilee's father put it after the fight about enlarging her closet, "The only thing she's really serious about is being superficial." Since the beginning of the new year, however, Sicilee has started to blossom in ways neither of her parents could have predicted. Mrs. Kewe can't get over the change.

"I certainly never expected *you* to join an environmental club," she admitted when she heard the news. "I never thought you had any interest in helping nature." Possibly because the only thing Sicilee has ever been known to do in the backyard is lie in a deck chair by the pool. "Or in stopping climate change," she added.

Sicilee hadn't planned to tell her mother about the club — when dealing with her parents, Sicilee believes that the less she says, the less she has to lie — but in the end she had no choice: it was that or starve.

"I've become aware of how precious and vulnerable our planet is, and have learned to care," said Sicilee, paraphrasing something Cody said at the first meeting. And then, continuing to paraphrase him, added, "I don't want to sit in the back of the world bus while pollution and overconsumption drive it over a cliff."

"Well, that really is something. You certainly are developing and maturing." Her mother beamed. "I can't tell you how proud and pleased I am."

"I'm only trying to be a responsible citizen," said Sicilee, paraphrasing herself.

"But what brought all this about?" asked her mother. "I can understand that you'd be concerned about global warming and melting glaciers—all of us are. But do you think there might be a little more to it than the zeitgeist? Perhaps it's realizing that you're growing up and that your future will be what you make it? Or perhaps you're beginning to come to grips with mortality."

Sicilee sighed.

This is an example of why she wasn't going to mention anything about saving the planet or eating vegetables to her mother. Margot Kewe, being a· psychoanalyst, is a thoughtful, questioning kind of person. It isn't enough for her to know *what* you did; she always wants to know *why* as well. As if the simplest action has some complex, hidden meaning. As if the fact that you left your cell phone out in the rain three times last summer must mean that you were tired of talking to your friends and not just that you forgot about it because your mind was on something else.

But Sicilee couldn't eat old lettuce and tomatoes and flexible carrots for lunch for the rest of the semester. Sweet Mary, she's a growing girl; she needs more sustenance than that. The problem was that if she told her mother that she wasn't eating meat at lunch—and only at lunch—her mother would have wanted to know why. Even if Sicilee could have come up with a plausible excuse, her mother would then have wanted to explore her motives even further. So she told her mother about the Environmental Club and that she'd decided to become a vegetarian and would need some suitable things for her lunches. Those salads they do at the gourmet deli, for instance. Or the vegetable sushi at the Japanese restaurant.

"You really are serious, aren't you?" Her mother shook her head as if she were the one who'd been asked a question. "You know, I've been reading a lot about vegetarianism lately. Apparently, meat production is one of the greatest contributors to global warming."

"That's right," agreed Sicilee, who, as luck would have it, had had a conversation with Cody only that morning that touched on this very topic. "It's responsible for more greenhouse gases than the transportation system of the whole world."

"Well, listen to you!" Her mother was obviously impressed. "You sound like an expert!"

"I'm working on it," said Sicilee.

Sicilee's mother, wanting to encourage her, decided to help Sicilee become an expert. The very next day she came home with the current issue of *VegNews*.

"Wow," said Sicilee. "I didn't know we had our own magazine."

And a day or two later, she presented Sicilee with three books that she thought Sicilee would like.

"I was only going to get the book about living with the Earth," her mother explained, "but they all looked so interesting. . . ."

"Gee . . ." said Sicilee. She smiled, but she smiled wanly. They are all very long books. "How can I ever thank you?"

Her mother said she didn't have to. Just seeing her push herself in new and selfless directions was thanks enough.

The new and selfless direction in which Sicilee has pushed herself at the moment is the corner of a sofa she is sharing with Cody Lightfoot, whose arm stretches casually along the back of the couch, coming so close to her that she would hardly have to move to lean forward and kiss his fingers. Cody is talking—warmly . . . passionately . . . intimately. And Sicilee, her eyes wide and expression intense, is listening as if memorizing his every word for the quiz that follows.

In fact, Sicilee has to concentrate just to hear him over the joyous thudding of her heart. She can't believe it's just the two of them. No klutzy boys noisily interrupting or chatter of girls surrounding him the way they usually do. No freaking Maya Baraberra waylaying Cody like some kind of environmental highwayman the way she always does—*Oh, Cody, I wanted to ask you . . . Oh, Cody, I thought you'd like to see this. . . . Cody, what do you think about that . . . ? Oh, I think so, too*—flashing her HELP THE EARTH FIGHT BACK and BE KIND TO ANIMALS—DON'T EAT THEM pins and acting like she was born with a carrot in her mouth.

This private moment, almost foot-to-foot and knee-to-knee, eyes staring into eyes, hearts beating as one, is like a dream come true. In fact, it is like several dreams come true. The ones that end with Cody taking her in his arms and Sicilee waking with a smile on her face. One of the big differences between those dreams and this moment, however, is that the dreams always take place in some secluded corner by candlelight or on a deserted, moonlit beach—not in the student lounge in the middle of the day.

"Then, after we made the bicycle-powered generator," Cody is saying, "in seventh grade, for our science project, my friend and I made this wind turbine." This would be another difference; in Sicilee's dreams they talk about love and how wonderful each thinks the other is, not the environmental movement. "We figured that it was way cooler because we didn't have to pedal. It wasn't big or very sophisticated, but it worked just dandy."

"A wind turbine! Wow. Really? That is so awesome."

Sicilee has had several small successes in the past weeks—walking with Cody, talking to Cody, once even making him laugh with a joke she heard on the radio about how many Green activists it takes to change a lightbulb (none; they use candles)—but this is the longest one-on-one Sicilee has ever had with him. It has ranged from endangered species to plastics to innovative solutions to our energy problems, but Sicilee's part in it has consisted largely of words like *wow, really,* and *awesome*—and a good deal of earnest head shaking. Which is not the way it's supposed to be. Indeed, to avoid this very situation, Sicilee has spent over a week sitting at home with only Lucy, her cat, for company, actually reading the books her mother bought her instead of hanging out with her friends and enjoying herself. The idea was that this would make it possible for her always to have something relevant to say to Cody or at least an intelligent question to ask. But instead, it has proved to be an endless, exhausting, and, apparently, futile task. There is just too much to know. And most of it, as far as Sicilee can tell, is terminally boring. Statistics. Facts. Pages of information with footnotes and references. Bibliographies. Things only someone like Clemens Reis would want to know. She often falls asleep after only a paragraph or two. Even if she rehearses a couple of relevant comments and intelligent questions, she forgets what they were the minute Cody opens his mouth.

"After that we made a bigger one that we put on the roof of the garage, and we powered the light over our workbench and a radio with that."

Sicilee's smile goes into rigor mortis as she frantically rummages through the files of her mind for something Greener and more savvy to say than "Wow!" Something to show how much she knows about alternative sources of energy. Which, as it turns out, is not all that much (and largely based on a rant of her father's about the cost of solar panels). "Obviously, it's, like, so totally worthwhile, but they must've been really expensive to build."

"Nah." Cody shakes his handsome head. "It was pennies—even the bigger one—a handful of Lincolns. Most of it we made from stuff we got from the dump or found on the street." He shakes his handsome head again, but this time in disappointment and disbelief. "It's, like, so totally amazing what people throw out. Perfectly good, usable stuff. You'd think they'd never heard the Green mantra."

This, of course, is Sicilee's cue, but instead of reciting

she simply smiles. She is smiling so much that her cheeks ache. It seems that, for all her reading, she has never heard the Green mantra, either.

"Reduce. Reuse. Recycle," says a voice right behind them.

Cody raises his head. "Exacto!" He grins, sticking up both his thumbs. "The Three Rs."

Sicilee's teeth clench in irritation. She might have known that it was too good to be true. Maya Baraberra is another thing that never happens in Sicilee's dreams. The girl must have him bugged.

Maya dumps her book bag between Cody and Sicilee and, with the agility and nonchalance of someone not wearing a tailored skirt, climbs over the back of the couch to join them.

"I'm so glad I ran into you two," says Maya, looking at Cody. "I saw this awesome show on the Discovery Channel last night? And it brought up so much stuff that I really need to talk to someone about." Now she looks at Sicilee with a smile like a dose of strychnine. "Someone who's really clued in, you know?"

That, of course, is the last time either Maya or Cody actually looks at Sicilee.

Cody saw the program, too. He's been dying to discuss it. It really blew him away. Words and phrases Sicilee has either never heard or doesn't remember hearing — *clear-cut . . . oil shale . . . resource substitution . . . biodiversity . . .*

the three faces of power . . . *primativists*—fall from his and Maya's lips like autumn leaves fall from the trees. Sicilee has no choice but to sit there and listen, looking fascinated and pretending to know what they're talking about.

How does Maya know all this stuff? How does she remember it? And then a new question occurs to Sicilee: Why bother? Proving that Joy Marie Lutz is right and every cloud does have a silver lining—even the one that brought Maya into the lounge today—it is in the second that she asks herself that question that Sicilee has her great idea. It is an idea both simple and touched with genius. An idea that will grab Cody Lightfoot's attention and shake it the way Lucy the cat pounces on and shakes her catnip mouse when she's feeling really playful. This idea will knock that so-cool-I-rule smile from Maya Baraberra's face for the next fifty years.

Sicilee is so happy she fairly shimmers. She's been going about this all wrong. It's like buying a new outfit. In order to buy a new outfit, you don't need to know how to design and sew a dress, cobble a pair of shoes, make socks, knit a sweater, or fashion glass and gold into an attractive necklace with matching bracelet. All you need is a credit card and a ride to the mall. Saving the planet is exactly the same.

Put another way, you don't have to know the words to be able to hum the tune.

Chapter Twenty-six

One great idea deserves another

Maya leans back in her chair, her legs casually stretched out in front of her (so that every time Sicilee glances at the floor, she will see Maya's environmentally friendly feet and be annoyed), and lets Cody's sweet, warm voice pour over her like sunshine over a verdant field. Her soul softens; her heart melts; her thoughts dissolve into stardust. Cody, standing in the center of the circle as usual, is talking about stalls and sponsorship and fund-raising, but that, though interesting in its way (and certainly relevant to the meeting), is not what Maya hears. Maya hears: *Baby, you know that I dig you.* Maya hears: *You're incredible — I've never known anyone like you.* Maya hears: *I'm begging you, just give me one more kiss.* Sighing softly, she feels rather than sees the drill-like eyes of Sicilee Kewe fall on her, and looks over to find Sicilee smiling superciliously across Cody's empty seat. *Enjoy yourself, you poor, dumb cow, because you won't be smiling for much longer,* thinks Maya, and returns her own eyes to the middle of the room without giving Sicilee the satisfaction of making any response.

Maya is feeling pretty pleased with herself. It has taken much longer than she expected, but, finally, she is making some real progress with Cody. And, once more illustrating the relationship between silver linings and clouds, she owes it all to the cafeteria's pea soup. Maya's study of vegan websites—and her new understanding of things like whey, sugar refining, the true meaning of *natural sources*, and the many uses of fat taken from the stomachs of pigs—has given her a new confidence and authority. Which, in turn, has made her conversations with Cody longer and more personal. They discuss what cookies they can eat and the barbaric slaughter of cattle. He swapped her half his nondairy cheese sandwich for half her nonmeat salami. He told her where to buy a non-toxic water bottle. She made him laugh with a joke about plastic bags. He recommended a shampoo. She gave him a recipe for vegan cupcakes. And yesterday, in a moment that will forever be held in her memory like a fly in amber, she balanced a notebook on her arm while Cody, leaning against her, his breath as soft as the stroke of a feather against her face, jotted down the names of some documentaries that he thinks she might be interested in. "I haven't had a chance to watch them all myself yet," said Cody, "but Clem says they're really good."

The business of the afternoon drifts around her. Usually Maya is tense and watchful through these meetings—waiting to see what Sicilee will say, trying to guess what Sicilee's next move will be, ready to pounce on any show of weakness and undermine any show of strength—but today Maya has more important things on her mind. She is about to make her move. As soon as she can get him alone, Maya is going to ask Cody if he wants to come over to her house one evening to watch one of the documentaries he recommended. How can he refuse?

Maya is now imagining herself and Cody in the Baraberras' living room, side by side on the sofa with a bowl of chips balanced on the narrow gap between their legs. The lights are out, the door is shut, and her family has gone to visit some suitably distant place like Norway and won't be back for hours. Totally engrossed in the movie, they are silent as they watch, but as soon as the credits begin to roll, Cody takes the chip bowl and puts it on the coffee table in a meaningful way. He turns to Maya, his arm slipping over the back of the couch, leaning toward her. "Maya," he whispers, his mouth almost touching her ear. "Maya . . . Maya, I—"

"I have an idea!"

Maya returns to Room 111 with a start.

Sicilee is on her feet, swinging her hair and rattling her bracelets as if she's about to announce that she's discovered the Meaning of Life. "I know we've been getting some really excellent feedback about Earth Day and everything," Sicilee is saying, "but I was thinking that maybe we've been concentrating too much on that. You know, not doing anything about educating people like we said we would? I think we need to make them aware so they'll care even before they get to the fair."

"Oh, great. Now she's a poet," mutters Maya, making a spare-me face.

But Sicilee, of course, is no longer looking at Maya. If her smile were sunshine, Cody would be burned to a crisp.

Cody, however, doesn't step into the shade. Maya watches in horror as he opens his arms to Sicilee the way he opens them to Maya in her fantasies, as though inviting the girl who isn't aware and doesn't care to step into them.

"Don't keep us in suspense —" pleads Cody. And he hesitates. Maya sits up straight, her bones locked. Why does he pause? Was he going to call her "baby"? Was he going to call her "Siss" the way her friends do? Sicilee is practically glowing; she has ideas about what he was going to call her, too. (In fact, Cody hesitates because the only thing he can remember about Sicilee's name is that it has something to do with pizza — but neither Maya nor Sicilee will ever know that, of course.) "Shine the light of knowledge on us. Tell us what your idea is."

Maya's smile is as gone as the woods that once covered Manhattan. Has she made a mistake? Was she so certain of victory that she dropped her guard? So sure of success that she moved her eyes from her opponent to the prize? She's definitely misjudged to what depths someone like Sicilee—someone not handicapped by scruples—is willing to sink.

"Well . . ." Sicilee shrugs as though she actually knows what *modestly* means. "It kind of hit me that a lot of people, you know, they want to do stuff to help the planet, but they really don't know what to do." She removes two sheets of paper the same shade of purple as her blouse from the purple folder in her hand. "So what I figured was that we could do a series of posters on, you know, basic things we all can do to make things better."

Of course, it's an embarrassingly simple idea—how could it not be when it comes from someone who thinks that an example of an existential question is: *What should I wear with these shoes?* But even Maya can see that it's not a bad idea.

Cody thinks it's a great idea. "Man," he says, "that's so close to being a stroke of genius, you couldn't tell them apart."

Maya sits a little straighter, raising her hand. "Excuse me," she says, smiling almost apologetically, "but I have a question."

Sicilee turns to her with the look a queen might give a cat. "Yes?"

"Well, I was just wondering if maybe it isn't a little antienvironmental to use brand-new paper that matches your clothes when you could write your notes about how to save the planet on the back of an old envelope or something like that?"

Sicilee's smile doesn't dim. There is no way the Barbarian is going to ruin this moment of triumph for her. She may be snide, sneaky, unprincipled, and treacherous, but this time she has met her match. "Well, obviously I would have, Maya. Sweet Mary, of course I would. But, unfortunately, we'd just taken *everything* to the recycling center, and there wasn't any scrap paper at all in the house." And then she sails on as though the only sound for the last few minutes has come from her. "So I already jotted down some suggestions. Just really easy things anybody can do. You know, like recycling and composting organic waste and cutting back on disposable items and using those energy-efficient lightbulbs? I figured that if we put up a list of maybe twelve different things every week or so, by Earth Day everybody will be, like, really with the program."

Maya can't believe her ears. Couldn't Sicilee think of anything more obvious? That's like telling people to open the door before they walk through it. She looks at Cody, expecting him, if not to laugh out loud, at least to stop smiling as if Sicilee just invented a car that runs on air.

But Cody says, "Hey, I like it! I really like it!" He thinks it's a great idea. He is jubilant. Exultant. If he stands any closer to Sicilee, he'll be past her. "Let's see what else you have there." He reaches out his hand to her.

This time, Maya doesn't bother raising hers. "Recycling and energy-efficient lightbulbs?" she asks. "Are you serious?" She says this in a kindly, helpful way. "I mean, I really don't think that there's anyone who isn't living in an igloo who doesn't already know about those things."

Cody disagrees. "No, she's flat-out right." Cody says you should always start with the really obvious stuff and work your way up. "A-B-C," says Cody. "That's how you teach." He touches Sicilee's fingers. He smiles at Sicilee in a way that he has never smiled at Maya. There are places in the world where the way Sicilee smiles back at him would get them both arrested. Maya shuts her mouth so tightly she can feel her teeth.

Things, however, are about to get even worse.

It may be a bitter moment for Maya, but for Sicilee it couldn't be sweeter if it were covered in honey. Cody is standing so near her you could barely slip a cell phone between them, and Maya is glaring at her as if she would turn Sicilee into a lizard if she hadn't left her cauldron and broomstick at home. "You know what?" says Sicilee. "I just had another idea." Luminous with victory, she grabs Cody's arm and purrs, "Wouldn't it be really cool if Maya did some of her cartoons to go with my lists?" She moves her head just enough so that she can look right into Maya's eyes. "You know, because she's so artistic."

The only reason Maya doesn't gasp out loud is that her mouth is clamped so tightly closed. The girl's completely delusional. Can she possibly think that Maya would work *for her*? Or is she just trying to jerk Maya's chain?

"That could be really awesome," says Cody, though not to Maya. "That could really float the boat."

Maya unclamps her mouth and gives Sicilee a look that could sink every ship in the navy. "Oh, what a shame," she says, managing to keep any trace of regret from her voice. "I'm afraid I can't help you, *Siss*." There is no trace of regret in her smile, either. "Because I already have a project. And it's pretty all-encompassing, if you know what I mean. It doesn't leave me any time to doodle pictures of lightbulbs." She rises from her seat, addressing the group at large. "Actually, I've been mulling it over for a couple of weeks now. You know, doing some preliminary sketches . . . getting my thoughts in order . . . sorting out my ideas?"

"Oh, really?" Sicilee brushes a long, golden hair from her sleeve. "And just what is this all-encompassing project, pray tell?"

Maya can only wish she knew. She forces herself to smile, her eyes darting around the room as though the idea that will save her is tucked into a corner or languishing on the window ledge. In fact, the idea that saves her is sitting on the lap of a girl named Daphne. It is a bottle of lemon-flavored water. Only a few days ago, Maya had a conversation with Cody about plastic. Cody said that the problem with plastic wasn't just that, instead of wonders of civilization like the pyramids, we're leaving our descendants mountains of plastic that won't rot away for a thousand years, but that we completely ignore the hidden costs of mass production. Maya's smile takes on a luminosity of its own. "I call it *Do You Know?*" she says, staring back into Sicilee's eyes — glacier-blue today to match her heart. "It'll be a series of illustrated information posters that say things like —" She pauses, as if searching for an example. "Like . . . do you know how many liters of water it takes to make one liter of Coca-Cola? And then I give the answer. You know, two and a half. That kind of thing."

Cody nods his head approvingly — as well he might, since this information came from him to begin with.

"I don't know what's rising or what's transiting, but the stars are righteously with us today," he says. "Two great ideas in one afternoon! How outlandishly cool is that? I tell you all, I'm as happy as a bear in salmon season." He looks over at Clemens. "What did I tell you, bro?" demands Cody. "We are going to be so gold we'll have to rename ourselves El Dorado."

Clemens says something and Cody walks toward him, while around them everyone else starts to talk.

Maya and Sicilee, standing facing each other now, are smiling at each other in a way that suggests pistols at dawn.

"So where are all these *preliminary sketches,* Baraberra?" Sicilee waves her purple folder in Maya's face. "We've all seen my ideas. Where are yours?"

"I didn't bring them today, did I?" Maya rests a hand on the back of an empty chair, leaning forward. "I didn't feel ready to show them yet."

"Oh, I'm sure." Sicilee leans toward her. "Like you even thought of this *all-encompassing* project of yours more than five minutes ago."

"I don't want to burst your little princess bubble, Sicilee, but in case nobody told you, drawings aren't like writing down 'turn out the lights' and 'recycle your fashion magazines' while you're straightening your hair. They actually take some time and effort."

"Let me tell you something, poor little worker bee." Sicilee tilts toward her. She even smells purple. "You have *so* bitten off more than you can chew this time. And I, for one, hope that you choke on it."

"Well, don't bet on it," counters Maya. "Because if you think you're going to change the world with your feeble lists, you're in for a big surprise." She moves so close, their noses almost touch. "In case this is something else no one bothered to tell you, a picture is worth a thousand words."

It is Sicilee who pulls back first. "Did you know that you're, like, a million times more irritating than a mosquito?"

"I'll take that as a compliment." Maya laughs.

"A mosquito can be crushed," says Sicilee.

"You'd better make sure it doesn't give you malaria first," says Maya.

Chapter Twenty-seven

Waneeda finally volunteers
for something

Waneeda, Joy Marie, and Clemens shut the door to Room 111 behind them and head down the stairs. Waneeda and Joy Marie are talking about the meeting. Which is to say that Waneeda is complaining that the meetings have turned into *The Maya and Sicilee Show* (or *Two Princesses in Pursuit of a Prince,* as Waneeda also calls it when she and Joy Marie are alone). They have more opinions than the Supreme Court and a psychotic need to share them with everyone else. Any time one of them volunteers to do something for Earth Day, the other will volunteer to do two things. Their exclamations of approval, agreement, and admiration follow everything Cody says like a particularly cheerful Greek chorus. The only consolation Waneeda has is that they obviously irritate each other even more than they irritate her. "I just don't understand how Cody doesn't notice," Waneeda grumbles as they reach the main doors.

From behind them, someone shouts out, "Hey, wait up!"

The three of them stop and turn around to see Cody, who has just stepped out of the office, trotting toward them.

"I'm really glad I caught up with you guys," he says as he follows them outside, "because we're going to need your help here, with the Things You Can Do and Did You Know? campaigns." Several steps behind Waneeda and Joy Marie, he nonetheless manages to give the impression that he has his arms around their shoulders. So there's no doubt which guys he means. "You know, laying out the posters and typing them up and copying them and everything? Dr. Firestone is really enthused about these ideas. He thinks we should get started pronto."

Here is another thing of which Cody is apparently unaware. Although Joy Marie was well disposed toward him to begin with because he was saving the club and Waneeda was well disposed toward him because of his breathtaking good looks, neither of them is feeling that well disposed toward him now. While the other girls volunteer for all the look-at-me Earth Day projects to win Cody's approval, it is Waneeda and Joy Marie whom Cody volunteers for all the boring scut work—typing and photocopying, e-mailing and gathering information, putting up notices and flyers—who keep everything going. Though not in what you could call a cheerful way.

"Don't look at me," says Joy Marie. "I have enough to do already."

"Why us?" asks Waneeda. "Why can't the geniuses do it themselves?"

"Well, you know, they have pretty full agendas already. They're both on a bunch of committees for Earth Day." He flashes a smile that is a heck of a lot less disarming now than it used to be. Now it always accompanies something Cody wants them to do. "Anyway, you ladies are so good at that stuff."

"Didn't you hear what I said?" asks Joy Marie. "I already have enough to do."

"Me too," lies Waneeda.

"There's no big hurry for it," Cody assures them. "Why don't you think about it? You can let me know later in the week." He falls into step beside Clemens.

Despite this slight setback, Cody is still as happy as a bear in salmon season—or, possibly, even two bears—talking excitedly about the awesome meeting and Sicilee's and Maya's mind-blowing ideas, while Clemens walks beside him, silent except for the occasional "yeah" or "um," and Waneeda and Joy Marie walk a few paces behind.

"Man, I can't believe that I didn't think of that stuff myself," Cody is saying as they reach the road. "I mean, it stands to reason, doesn't it? People can't know what they don't know. I mean, there are things you know you know—like how to make spaghetti—and there are things you know you don't know—like how to build a house—and then there's all the stuff you don't know you don't know—like—"

"What happens after we decimate every old-growth forest on the planet?" mutters Clemens.

Cody seems not to have heard him. "I guess that I've been so wrapped up in Earth Day, I totally shot past the exit," says Cody, more or less shooting past an exit again. "You know, I was concentrating on one tiny detail, and I missed the big picture." He laughs in his easy, good-natured way. "There's none so blind as he who will not see, right?"

You can say that again, thinks Waneeda.

But it is Clemens who says, "Yeah, tell me about it."

Cody raises an eyebrow. "What's wrong, Clem?" he asks. "You seem a trifle ponderous."

"I'm not ponderous," says Clemens. "I'm just agreeing with you. You're right: there's nobody as blind as someone who refuses to see."

"We're talking about me now, right?" Cody stops walking. "What is it I'm not seeing, bro? What've I missed?"

"What aren't you seeing?" Clemens stops as well. "The *trees,* Cody. There aren't any woods left around here, but you still don't see the trees. We were supposed to be trying to save the trees, remember? That was going to be our big push this year. But you've completely ditched them. All we talk about now is Earth Day."

184

"Man . . ." Cody sucks in his bottom lip. "Earth Day's important."

"So are the trees."

Waneeda and Joy Marie have also come to a stop, deliberately not looking at each other, but standing shoulder-to-shoulder just close enough not to miss anything.

"Look, I know you're irked that the trees are off the agenda." Cody makes an it's-not-my-fault gesture. "But I thought you understood that we have to focus. The trees aren't in our frame."

"Well, they're in *my* frame." Clemens stares at a point to the left of Cody's head. "We can't just abandon them. They need us. They're prisoners of time."

"Be reasonable, Clem. You've tried your best. You wrote all those letters. You gave your tree speech at Christmas. You spent a week trying to get people to sign your petition." This is true. Clemens and Joy Marie sat outside the office every morning and afternoon for two weeks, attracting the disapproval of Dr. Firestone, but little else. "And what did you get? Fifty signatures? Fifty signatures aren't going to persuade anybody."

"Then we have to try harder, not quit," insists Clemens. "We have to cut our losses, forget the school, and expand our efforts into the community."

"You don't get it, do you, bro?" Cody shakes his head sadly. "It's a done deal, Clem. The town council's OK'd it.

The planning permission's gone through. It's going to be the last word in sports excellence—the biggest facility in the state. Plus, the school gets a sports scholarship to make it even sweeter. There's nothing anybody can do."

"You're wrong," says Clemens. "Firestone and the developer railroaded it through. If we get enough signatures, we can stop them before they start. Launch an appeal. Let everybody in the town vote on whether the trees should go or not."

"And you'll still lose." Cody's voice has lost some of its usual lightness. "Get real, man. You can't stop progress."

"But we have to. That's the whole point of this. We can't just keep burying the planet in asphalt and concrete. We have to draw a line somewhere. Enough is enough. We're murdering the Earth, for God's sake. We don't need progress—we need sustainability."

"Clemens . . ." Cody's sigh is soft but heartfelt. "It's just a couple of trees. And they're going to plant *more* trees for the ones they cut down. Three times more. So where's the pain? Nobody thinks it's a big deal except you. We need to concentrate on things people can get really excited about."

Clemens pushes his glasses back into position. "Like using bags that say I AM NOT A PLASTIC BAG for shopping?"

"Why not? What's wrong with that?" Although seemingly unaware that he and Clemens aren't alone, Cody suddenly turns to Joy Marie and Waneeda. "Mary Jo!

Juanita!" He holds up his hands in mock despair. "Help me out here. What do you ladies think?"

"I wish you'd stop calling me Mary Jo," says Joy Marie. "My name's Joy Marie."

As if she just agreed with him, Cody shifts his charmingly imploring smile to Waneeda. "Juanita?" he prompts.

Waneeda's voice has yet to be heard this afternoon — or any other afternoon, for that matter. At the first meeting, when the other new members stood up to talk about themselves and their love of gorillas and tofu burgers and walking twenty miles a day, Waneeda stayed in her seat, chewing. At the next meeting, when everyone else was shouting out ideas for the Earth Day celebration, Waneeda unwrapped another candy. And so the weeks have passed, with the other new members all bursting with enthusiasm and bubbling with suggestions, and Waneeda eating and listening. Today, while just about every other girl in the room only had eyes for Cody, Waneeda found herself watching Clemens, slumped in his chair with his usual bad posture, fiddling with the paper clip on his glasses, not saying anything either. Like the last polar bear on the last ice floe, floating off into oblivion.

Waneeda looks over at Clemens. She feels sorry for him. "I'll help you with the trees if you want," she says.

Chapter Twenty-eight

How to lose friends and not influence people

I'm sorry I'm late." Sicilee puts her lunch bag on the table and slides into the empty chair next to Ash. "I left something in my locker, and I had to go all the way back for it."

"Oh, that's where you were." Kristin smiles over her slice of pizza. "We thought you were outside hugging a tree."

Ash and Loretta giggle in a way that has never irritated Sicilee when aimed at people who have a bad haircut or are wearing the wrong shoes but now that it always seems to be aimed at her, irritates her quite a lot.

"Oh, right." Sicilee's laugh is short but sharp. "And get bark all over a five-hundred-dollar jacket?"

No one laughs along with her.

"Or, you know," Kristin drawls on, "we thought that maybe you were just too awesomely busy to eat lunch with us today." Her smile is made no more endearing by the smudge of tomato sauce at the corner of her mouth.

This, of course, is a pointed remark. A dig at Sicilee who has been too awesomely busy for quite a few things in the past couple of weeks. Where before the four of them were inseparable—the teenage girl equivalent of the Four Horsemen of the Apocalypse, united by a single purpose—lately there have been only Three Horsemen making their rounds. Suddenly, Sicilee always has a meeting to go to or something vague and unspecified that she absolutely has to do. She's taken to spending a lot of time "studying stuff." But worst of all, and possibly beyond forgiveness, Sicilee has actually missed not just a couple of shopping expeditions but an important Diamonds meeting as well. Loretta, Ash, and even Kristin are justifiably skeptical and suspicious. What's up with that? They used to be what she was busy with, and now she's too busy for them. They would very much like to know what's going on. What happened to the part where she was only *pretending* to join the geeks' club? When did Sicilee Kewe start worrying about schoolwork? When did she become casual about shopping? When was there something more important than her friends? Exactly what planet are they supposed to be on?

"Sweet Mary, what's wrong with you guys? Excuse me, but the last time I missed lunch was months ago, when I got a run in my tights and I had to go home and change." Because now they always make her feel defensive, Sicilee gives them all a generous smile. "I'm only late because I

189

wanted you to see this." Her eyes widen with sincerity. "You know, because you're my closest friends and I value your opinions?" She pulls a green folder from her backpack and puts it on the table. "It's my own idea." Her smile brightens. "To make people aware."

Loretta shows all the enthusiasm of someone presented with a piece of cold toast. "Aware of what?"

Sicilee sighs. Merciful Mother, what does she think? Aware of the spaceship sitting out in the parking lot? "You know . . . Aware of how easy it is to be Green." She turns the folder around so Loretta can see the words written across the front.

Loretta reads as if this is a skill she has just acquired, "'Twelve Easy Ways You Can Save the Planet.'" She looks at Sicilee. "Is this what you've been doing instead of hanging out with us? Writing a self-help book?" To accompany the irritating laugh, she's developed an irritating grimace. "I thought you're supposed to be getting a date with Cody Lightfoot, not a degree in environmental studies."

"Um, duh, Loretta . . . That's what I'm trying to do, isn't it? Get a date. I mean, I'm obviously not doing all this for my health, am I?"

"Well, I'm sure I wouldn't know, would I?" Loretta snaps back. "Since we hardly ever see you long enough to have an actual conversation anymore. You know, because you're always *so* busy."

Sicilee's mother says that the best way to avoid an argument is simply to refuse to engage in it. Don't bite the bait. Don't reply. Just step away. So, although Sicilee rarely follows her mother's advice, instead of sniping back, she removes two sheets of paper from the folder and continues as if Loretta hasn't spoken. "Everybody in the club thought it was a great idea." She also ignores the sour, *ooh-everybody-in-the-club* looks on their faces. "You know, except for Maya the Barbarian. So now I feel that I need some feedback from the general public." She hands one page across the table to Kristin and Loretta, and the other to Ash who is sitting beside her. "I'd really like to know what you guys think."

Kristin stares at the paper with her mouth all screwed up as though it shows something gross and revolting—one of Clemens Reis's photographs of tortured animals, for example. "What is this thing?"

What Kristin is glowering at is not Sicilee's beginner's guide to going Green, but page 110 of the annual report of the company Sicilee's father runs.

"'Revitalizing the existing infrastructure . . .'" Loretta reads over Kristin's shoulder. She looks over at Sicilee as if she must have lost her mind. "What the hell is that supposed to mean?"

"Oh, Sweet Mary, not that side." Sicilee snatches the page from Kristin and turns it over. "You should always use both sides of a sheet and the backs of envelopes and stuff like that," she explains. "You know, so you don't waste so much paper?"

"Oh, of course," mutters Kristin. "How environmentally incorrect of me not to realize that."

"I don't think this side is much better," grumbles Loretta.

Kristin seems to agree. "My God, Siss," she groans, "you don't really expect people to do all this stuff, do you? There are, like, millions of things on this list."

"Twelve." Sicilee leans across the table, pointing at the heading on the page in Kristin's hand. "See?" Sicilee can't pinpoint the exact moment when Kristin started being so critical of her, but it's already getting very old. "That's why it says 'Twelve Easy Ways You Can Save the Planet' at the top."

"Twelve's a dozen, Sicilee." Kristin is speaking very slowly and distinctly. "And that's a lot, if you want to know what *I* think."

"Well, I *do* want to know what you think." Sicilee is starting to realize that she may have made a big mistake. "That's why I'm showing it to you."

"You know, it's really not *that* bad," says Ash. "I can do this stuff. Turn lights off when you leave a room. . . . Don't let the water run when you're brushing your teeth. . . . Recycle plastic bottles. . . ."

"You see?" Sicilee gives Ash a pleased nudge. "I told you it's easy."

Loretta, however, has begun reading farther down the list. "'Ditch the car—it's not that far'?" squeaks Loretta. "'For those short trips to town or school or to visit your friends, leave the car at home.'" She turns to Sicilee, her eyes so wide you'd think she was putting on her mascara. "Are you for real? You expect us to walk everywhere?" She splutters with laughter. "Sicilee, God gave us cars so we don't have to walk."

"Oh, really?" Sicilee's smile is far more pleasant than she feels. "Then what did he give you feet for, just so you'd have someplace to put your shoes?"

Loretta leans back, folding her arms across her chest. "And what about you, Sicilee? I haven't noticed you wearing any holes in your shoes."

Feeling as if she has turned down a deserted road by herself on a dark night in a bad neighborhood, Sicilee sits up a little straighter. "I am going to be walking, Loretta," she says very clearly. "I just haven't started yet."

Loretta gives her a bottle-of-vinegar-and-a-bag-of-lemons smile. "Yeah, sure you are. As soon as summer vacation starts."

"Well, you can count me out," says Ash. "I'm not walking anywhere. In case you haven't noticed, it's winter out there. Didn't you see the snow on Sunday, Sicilee?

193

What did you think it was? Global dandruff? I do not walk in the snow. Do you know what snow would do to my *boots* and my *skin*?"

Kristin taps a foot softly but restlessly against the floor, watching Sicilee as though she has never really seen her before. And maybe she hasn't. Not this Sicilee, all in Southwest tones again (brown and beige and terracotta) with her crunchy-granola list of things *she's* decided *they* should do. Kristin feels betrayed. All of a sudden, she, Ash, and Loretta are in the wrong? Who does Sicilee think she is, telling them what they should do, like God's gone on vacation and left her in charge? It wasn't all that long ago that Sicilee would have been as likely to suggest to her friends that they walk to school as she would have been to suggest that they swap their lives with teenagers living in the slums of Lima, but now she's changing into someone alien and unfamiliar right before Kristin's eyes. If you were to tell Kristin that Sicilee thinks it's Kristin who's become critical, she'd laugh hollowly. It is Sicilee who has become critical. Critical and judgmental. Sicilee's always pointing out that they're doing something wrong. Sitting there every lunch hour with her organic salads and fake chicken sandwiches like she's better than the rest of them. Just who does she think she is?

"Maybe Sicilee means that you should take the school bus," suggests Kristin.

"Oh, yeah. Right!" Ash squeals. "The school bus!

That's a great idea!" The sparkly pink hearts dangling from her ears swing wildly as she laughs. "Are you serious? You think *I'm* going to take the school bus? Like some little kid? Are you nuts?" The idea of joining the poor unfortunates on the bus whose parents won't buy them cars or drive them to school makes Ash laugh so much she knocks her bottle of water off the table.

"That's another thing you have to give up," says Kristin. "Don't drink bottled water. That's number seven."

"And drink what?" Ash wants to know. "Water from the tap? You mean, sewage? Water with everybody's pills and crapola in it? Why don't I just lap it up from the gutter like a stray dog?"

"Don't be ridiculous," Sicilee begins. "The point is—"

"Holy Mother of God," says Loretta. "What is *this*? Wear it more than *once*? Wear *what* more than once?"

"Well, what do you think? Heavy armor?" By now, Sicilee has not even thought of smiling for at least two minutes. "Clothes, Loretta. Wear your clothes more than once."

"Are you sick?" Loretta makes a series of strangled, hacking sounds. It is either ironic laughter or an attempt to cough up a piece of tuna salad that has gone down the wrong way. "Wear the same thing *two days in a row*? What's that supposed to do for the planet? Make it die laughing?"

"Sweet Mary, why are you all being so difficult?" At

the moment, it looks as though Sicilee may never smile again. "It doesn't mean wear the same thing on Tuesday that you wore on Monday, for God's sake. It just means don't wash everything after you've only worn it once. You know, so you save on energy and water and everything."

"Even if you've got mustard on it? Or *dirt*?" Ash's face makes it clear to anyone who might be interested that you don't have to be threatened by killer mummies armed with Uzis and machetes to know what true horror is. "Oh, I don't think so, Sicilee. Some of us have standards."

"Here's another interesting item," says Kristin with what can only be described as demented glee. "Don't dry-clean." She looks over at Sicilee. "What are you supposed to do instead? Beat your clothes on rocks?"

"Waitwaitwaitwaitwait, this is even more gross!" screeches Loretta. *"Buy used!"* Apparently, Loretta, too, has discovered the essence of true horror. "Buy used what? *Clothes?* Are you saying that I should wear somebody's smelly, cast-off clothes? Then what are all the poor people in the Third World supposed to wear?"

"Are you all being deliberately dense?" asks Sicilee.

"Well, excuse us for breathing," says Ash.

Sicilee snatches up the unwanted pages of advice. "And excuse me for trying to educate you." Her unsmile moves from Ash to Kristin to Loretta. "I'm obviously wasting my time."

Kristin, Ash, and Loretta all stare back at her with looks like barbed-wire fences.

"Just where do you get the nerve to tell *us* what to do?" Loretta would like to know. "Not only do you *not* walk to school, you are *not* wearing somebody else's clothes. You are wearing *your* clothes. We were with you when you bought that outfit."

"And let's be totally honest here." Kristin leans forward, in the earnest I'm-only-saying-this-for-your-own-good way of a very best friend. "You're not even really a vegetarian or a vegan or whatever you told that dumb club you are. You came to my house last week and ate steak. Rare." She kicks Sicilee's foot under the table. "And your boots aren't vegan leather, either — they're the ones you bought in November."

"Sweet Mary," Sicilee cries in exasperation. "I can't just throw out a hundred pairs of shoes, Kristin. We're supposed to be living in a waste-not, want-not kind of way."

"You don't have to throw them out," says Loretta with a smile. "You can give them away."

Chapter Twenty-nine

Late but not late enough

It's Saturday, and on Saturday afternoons Maya and her friends always meet at Mojo's coffee bar, a dimly lit and brick-walled room, where they sit at worn wooden tables, eat paninis and bagels, drink espressos, and listen to jazz and Latin funk. Hood up, head down, Maya hurries through the falling snow, watching her breath float in front of her in tiny, frozen clouds. Late again. Interestingly enough, however, the main thought in Maya's mind isn't that she's late again, but that if, by some sadistic twist of fate, she should run into Cody Lightfoot, she will have no choice but to join a cloistered convent and spend the rest of her life behind a high brick wall. She could never face him again if he saw her like this.

The bell tinkles as Maya bursts through the door, stopping to shake the snow off her boots onto the newspapers spread across the entrance. She throws back her hood and squints into the room, adjusting her eyes to the atmospheric gloom after the brightness of the day outside.

The others are all gathered around their favorite table in the corner, already eating their lunches.

"Yo!" Maya calls as she sidles through the packed room. "I'm sorry I'm late."

"Better late than never." Jason waves a fry in greeting. "Which makes a nice change."

Alice pats the seat beside her on the bench. "We were afraid you weren't coming because of the weather."

Maya sighs inwardly. *Why didn't she think of that?* It's not only a good excuse—it would have been more or less true.

"It's damn cold out there," says Finn. "I wouldn't have come myself, only I knew my dad would volunteer me to shovel the driveway when the snow stops, so I decided to take my chances with frostbite."

Maya slips out of her coat and hangs it on one of the hooks on the wall, throwing herself onto the bench next to Alice so quickly and with so much force that Alice drops her fork. But not quite quickly enough.

"What the hell are you wearing?" Mallory leans around the table for a better view. "Are those your little sister's clothes?"

"Of course they're not Molly's," says Maya. "I was late, so I just put on the first thing I found."

Which is true in the sense that she is wearing all she

could find. What Maya is wearing are clothes she schleps around the house in that haven't seen daylight in at least a year. Uncool clothes. Clothes she wouldn't want to be buried in at night on an uninhabited island in the middle of the Atlantic.

"But those pants are way too small for you." Mallory is now peering under the table. "They don't even reach the top of your socks."

"And that shirt!" Shayla's face bunches up with distaste. "What's all over it? Is that *blood*?"

"Of course it's not blood. It's henna." Maya grabs a menu from the middle of the table, even though she has been here enough times to know that there are only three things on it that she can eat. "I had a little clothes crisis — that's all."

"What happened?" asks Alice. "The washing machine broke?"

Maya shakes her head.

"The dryer?" guesses Mallory.

"Not exactly."

What exactly happened was that, having done her bimonthly, environmentally friendly load of laundry yesterday, Maya was then filled with such a sense of goodwill toward every living thing on the planet that she decided she would hang her clothes on the line and dry them the way that Nature intended. She didn't take the weather into consideration.

"They froze!" Shelby chokes on his coffee. "Are you serious? Your clothes *froze*?"

Maya glares at him. "And how was I supposed to know the temperature was going to drop?"

"It's winter, Maya," says Shayla. "What did you think the temperature would do? Hit ninety?"

"I guess the snow didn't help, either." Brion laughs.

Jason, sitting across from Maya, leans his arms on the table. Maya's outfit isn't what's bothering him. "So what's your excuse for missing the movie last night? You were making your own bean curd and you forgot?"

"Oh, you are *so* droll." Maya looks around for the waiter, but he is busy with another table. "I just had stuff to do, that's all."

"More important than Friday night at the multiplex?" Jason's lopsided grin isn't always as attractive as Maya sometimes thinks. "What stuff? Were you out wrapping blankets around trees with your pal Cody?"

Maya gives him a withering look. Lately, Jason has become almost as annoying as Sicilee Kewe.

"You didn't miss much," says Alice. "The movie wasn't that great."

"Bo-riiing!" agrees Mallory.

Shelby, whose choice it was, laughs. "Oh, come on. It wasn't that bad. Nobody fell asleep, did they?"

"I did," says Finn. "But you couldn't tell because I can sleep with my eyes open."

Jason is still leaning toward Maya. "So what were you doing this time?" he persists. "What did you have to do that was more important than hanging out with your friends?" It isn't even a smile, really. It's more of a smirk. "Or were you just afraid that if you saw everybody else eating double-cheese pizza you'd cave in and renounce your holy vegan vows?"

Jason has become so annoying not only because he's always making snide remarks about Cody Lightfoot, but also because he's always on Maya's case about something. He sniped at her for missing a couple of lunches. He rode her for not going skating last week. And today it would seem that he's irritated because she's not eating cheese.

"You can gorge yourself on double-cheese pizza till your eyes fall out for all I care," Maya informs him with a sugary smile. "It doesn't affect me at all." She reaches into her backpack and pulls out a manila envelope. "But since you're so incredibly interested, here's what I was doing last night. It's my own special project to get ready for Earth Day. It's about what's in all the stuff we use all the time. You know, the hidden stuff." She puts the envelope down on the table. "There are four copies in there. You guys can look it over while I get a coffee. See what you think."

"Nerd Nation strikes again," says Finn.

Jason reaches for the envelope. "I know that I speak for everyone here when I say that we can't wait."

Despite her outfit, Maya's in a good enough mood to laugh with the others. She's worked hard, and she's pretty pleased with her efforts. There was a time, not so long ago, when Maya thought she was Green enough. She knew about climate change, recycling, and eco-friendly lightbulbs. She cared about pigs, polar bears, and whales. It never occurred to her that she should put some extra effort into learning about the environment. Why learn what you already know? Only now that she has been putting in some extra effort she realizes that she didn't know half as much as she thought. She was like someone adrift on a dark, cold sea, thinking the tips she could see were all there was of the icebergs.

But there are even more icebergs on this dark, cold sea than perhaps Maya thought.

As she returns to the table with her black coffee and plain, dry bagel, she can't help noticing that the boys all wear grins as they read through her project, and Mallory and Shayla are laughing out loud. Alice, too loyal to laugh, just looks bewildered.

"Whoowhee!" whoops Brion. "Geekdom rules!"

"Is this the kind of thing they talk about at their meetings?" asks Shelby.

"That must be why you joined," mutters Jason. "The stimulating conversation."

Mallory and Shayla are the last to look up.

"I don't know how you can spend more than two

minutes with them. Look at this stuff!" Cream cheese drops from Mallory's bagel onto the page in front of her. "They're all out of their tiny minds. I mean, talk about conspiracy theories—this bunch makes those guys who think we never walked on the moon seem sane."

"Are you going to publish this in the school paper?" asks Shayla.

Maya sits down. "Publish it?"

"Well, yeah . . ." Shayla glances at Mallory. "It's a satire, right? Of the nerds' club?"

"It's not a satire." Maya half smiles, in case Shayla is just pulling her leg. "It's my project? To get everybody ready for Earth Day? I'm just stating a couple of facts." The book Maya got from the library is full of facts.

"Facts?" hoots Mallory. "Are you saying that you think this stuff's true? That, like, pretty much everything we use is destroying us and the planet?"

"Not *everything,*" Maya explains. "But those are the facts. Petrochemicals are in practically everything. Even our—"

"Oh, dig you," teases Finn. "*Petrochemicals are in practically everything.* A couple of days ago you wouldn't have known the difference between a petrochemical and a candy bar!"

"You are joking, aren't you?" Shelby looks around the table, grinning. "I mean, yeah, we all know some things are pretty toxic. Pesticides and stuff like that. But deodorants? Talcum powder? *Food?*"

"I'm not joking," says Maya. "Everything in there is true."

Shelby's grin seems to have gotten stuck. "But this makes it sound like we're taking our lives in our hands just mopping the floor."

"You know, you really should've come with us last night," says Jason. "You've been spending way too much time with the lunatic fringe."

"But it's all true," Maya says yet again. "There's a lot of stuff that you don't want to swallow or breathe in or put on your skin. Even our—"

"Oh, come on, Maya." Alice is giving her a hopeful, if not actually encouraging, smile. "Are you saying that my shampoo, soap, shower gel, makeup, and body spray are all really bad for me and the environment? How is that possible?"

"Well, they are if—"

"So, what are we supposed to do?" asks Mallory. "Stink like a pair of old gym socks? Go around with our teeth falling out and our faces all naked?"

Shayla would like to know what they're supposed to wear. "You're saying that all my clothes are made from *oil*? And dyed with poisons? So what's the big solution, Maya? Should I wrap myself in leaves?"

"I don't see what the big deal is," says Maya. "I mean, you guys are already Green. I'm just—"

"Stating a couple of facts that make us look as evil as baby-seal killers," says Shayla.

Alice says loyally, "Oh, come on. Maya isn't blaming us."

"Of course I'm not," agrees Maya. "That would be blaming the victim."

Shelby clutches his heart. "Oh, now we're victims!"

Alice sets down her cup, looking hopefully at Maya. "But don't you think that maybe you're getting a little carried away? I mean, all these things . . ." She gestures at the pages of Maya's project. "The manufacturers and the government and everybody, they wouldn't let us buy that stuff if they thought it was doing so much damage."

Maya opens her mouth to say that, as far as she can tell, they *are* letting us buy that stuff, but Mallory doesn't give her a chance.

Mallory holds up one hand. "Let's just back up the truck here." She looks at Maya. "What about *you,* Maya? You drink bottled water. You wear clothes and makeup. You use soap and shampoo."

"That's right!" Shayla slaps the table. "You used to eat fish and chicken all the time! And you ride around in a car throwing toxic emissions into the atmosphere just like everybody else!"

"I never said that I was perfect," protests Maya.

"No, only Cody Lightfoot's perfect," mutters Jason.

But Maya doesn't hear him because the others are all laughing so much.

Chapter Thirty

Sicilee loses an argument with her mother

Kristin said that Sicilee was bluffing.

"Yeah, sure you are. . . ." Kristin laughed as though she'd never heard anything funnier. "We have met, you know, Sicilee. There is no way *you're* going to start walking to school. I mean, my God, if the sedan chair was still around, you'd be carried into homeroom."

"Oh, really?" In contrast, Sicilee wasn't laughing at all.

Kristin made one of her most childish faces—the one where her mouth goes all lopsided and sarcastic and her eyes roll back. "I know you, Sicilee. The only way you're walking to school is in your dreams. You're going to get your mother to drop you off a couple of blocks away and pretend that you hiked from home."

"You're being really unfair, Kristin." Sicilee pouted. "It just so happens that when I said that I'm going to walk to school, I meant that I'm going to walk every step of the way. You know, *on my feet?* Left, right, left, right? That kind of thing?"

"As if . . ." said Loretta. "And I bet that at night you're going to do your homework by candlelight and knit yourself a sweater."

"No, I know what she's going to do after that," chimed in Ash. "She's going to start wearing other people's old clothes!"

Sicilee's expression soured. Is it possible that her friends have always been so cynical and sarcastic, and she just never noticed?

"I *should* bet you." Sicilee swung her hair over her shoulder. "We'll just see who laughs last."

Kristin, Loretta, and Ash were, of course, totally right to be skeptical. Sicilee had every intention of getting her mother to drive her to some secluded road near the school and then stroll down to join the other intrepid walkers like Cody as if she really were a committed environmentalist on a carbon-free journey.

Life, however, is full of unforeseen complications, and the unforeseen complication in this case proved to be Dr. Margot Kewe.

"But I heard you tell your friends that you're walking to school from now on," said Sicilee's mother. "I didn't have the impression that you meant just a couple of blocks. I thought you told them that you'd be walking all the way."

The woman has the hearing of a bat and the memory of an elephant.

"Yeah, I did say that—and of course I'm going to walk all the way," explained Sicilee. "Eventually. But I meant when the weather's better and it's not so cold. For now, I figure that if you could just drive me to, like, the top of Vanzander—"

Her mother frowned. "But you're going to tell the girls that you walked from home?"

"Only for a week or two." Sicilee hesitated, chewing on her bottom lip and rocking in place as if torn between honesty and loyalty. With a tortured sigh, honesty won. "The truth is, they've been giving me a really hard time lately, Mom. You know, about being Green? They think it's all a major big joke. And way uncool. You should hear the things they say to me."

"They probably feel a little jealous and resentful." Dr. Kewe nodded sagely. "That often happens when one member of a group does something different. Separates herself. It makes the others feel threatened."

Sicilee stifled another tortured sigh. "Yeah, Mom, I know. But—"

"I'm sure they'll get over it," her mother reassured her. "Surely what's much more important is that you're doing the right thing. And your father and I certainly don't think it's a joke. We're very proud of you and all the positive things you've been doing since you joined your club." The posters. The lights turned off when she leaves a room. The water not left running for hours while Sicilee brushes her teeth and puts on her makeup. The hardly worn clothes stuffed into bags and hauled to the car for the thrift store. The interminably long baths replaced with short showers. The new willingness to wear something two—even three—times before putting it in the laundry. "And didn't you say just the other night that the environment is more important than comfort or convenience?"

Sicilee blinked. "I was just quo—"

"No, honey, I'm very sorry, but no can do. It's a shame your friends don't understand how serious you are and won't support you, but I think it would be extremely irresponsible of me to do what you're suggesting." Her mother didn't sound all that sorry. "I can't possibly undermine your commitment by enabling you to cheat."

"Yes, you can," said Sicilee. "And anyway, it wouldn't really be cheating. It'd be being flexible. And it'd just be for a little while. I swear as soon as it gets warmer—"

"I'm not going to lie for you, Sicilee. What if Kristin's mother says something to me about how wonderful it is that you're walking to school?"

Hearing of a bat, memory of an elephant, and mind of a criminal lawyer.

"Mrs. Shepl?" Sicilee squawked. "Who's going to tell *her*?"

"You don't think she might notice that you're not sharing rides to school with Kristin anymore?" Sicilee hadn't thought of that, of course. "And naturally I've told her all about you and your club. She's very impressed at how socially responsible you've become."

Merciful Mother. No wonder Kristin's been acting so strange. Mrs. Shepl nags the way other women breathe.

"Besides, it's not really that far, honey. It can't be much more than a mile." Margot gave her a motherly hug. "The exercise will do you good."

And so it is that, on this crisp winter morning, with Jack Frost nipping at her nose, Sicilee Kewe finds herself walking all the way to school, just like she said she was going to do.

"Not that far, my old socks . . ." she mutters, trudging past sparkling hedges and lawns.

Distance traveled by foot, she has already discovered, is different from that same distance traveled by car. When you're in a car, time and the scenery all fly by, and you move as quickly up a hill as along a flat road. The journey to school — just long enough to touch up your makeup or compare your homework answers with Kristin's if you're in the Escalade — is now so long that it seems possible the road is actually growing in front of her. The only things that fly by are birds. And as far as her mother's optimistic *"It can't be much more than a mile"* is concerned, Sicilee has come several miles already, and she's still nowhere near the school, and may be dead by the time she does get there. She might as well be on a treadmill at the gym: step-step-step-step-step-step-step, over and over and over again and always staying in the same place. Except that, on the treadmill in the gym, she isn't carrying a handbag and a backpack with the combined weight of a sleeping bear cub. And she isn't wearing boots with heels or a heavy coat. And she has someone to talk to or can listen to her iPod (which, she's discovered, you can only do when you're hiking through the sidewalkless suburbs if you don't mind being suddenly beeped at, nearly run off the road, or jumped on by some lunatic dog with filthy, wet paws). And in the gym she can stop the stupid machine whenever she wants and take a break.

A car speeds past her, churning up a fine spray of slush that Sicilee isn't quick enough to avoid. "I hope you break down in the desert and your phone's not working!" she shouts after it. "It would serve you right!"

Having no running machine to stop, Sicilee comes to a stop herself. So far, the exercise isn't doing her much good at all. Her legs ache, her boots and coat look like she's been hiking through mud, and there's a blister starting on her left heel. She's pretty sure that, despite the Arctic temperature, she's sweating. She would very much like to cry. Having already learned that you don't want to lean against a car in this cold unless you want your skin ripped off, she leans against a large tree. She looks around.

She has no idea where she is. Has she ever been on this road before? Does she recognize anything? The houses do look familiar, but mainly because they look like houses — with doors, windows, chimneys, mailboxes, driveways, garages, and snow-covered lawns. If you've seen one tree or shrub, you've seen them all. Fences are fences. Cars are cars. Lampposts are lampposts. So many people have a cute little wheelbarrow or some other ornament out front, or a wind sock hanging from the porch, that it's impossible to tell them apart. What about the statues of meerkats stuck in the lawn on the other side of the street? Surely she'd remember if she'd seen *them* before?

But although Sicilee has, in fact, passed these meerkats hundreds, even thousands, of times, she has never actually seen them. Just as she has never seen the tree she's leaning against, or the cat who always sits in the living-room window of the house behind her, or any of the other things that only exist on this particular road — no matter how similar its windows, doors, lawns, and wind socks may seem.

There is only one thing to do. She'll have to call her mother. Surely her mother will be reasonable. After all, she is not a heartless, mean-spirited woman. She gives to charities and sponsors a boy in a village in Africa. Sweet Mary, the woman technically works in the healing professions. It's her job to help people and ease suffering — not cause it. Her only child is lost in the wilds of suburbia, probably suffering from frostbite and hypothermia. She can't possibly refuse to come to her aid.

"Oh, for heaven's sake, Sicilee," huffs Margot Kewe. "You were born in Clifton Springs. How can you not know the way to school?"

"But things look different in a car from how they look when you're right in them." At least indignation has so far prevented Sicilee from bursting into tears. "I think I must've taken a wrong turn or something."

"What street are you on? What's the nearest road that crosses it?"

"Wait a minute." Sicilee steps away from the tree to read the signs. "I'm on Burr, and the next street's Streb." Near weeping a few minutes ago, now Sicilee wants to laugh. Didn't she say that her mother wouldn't let her down? "How long will it take you to get here?"

"Oh, I'm not coming to get you," says her mother. "I'm going to tell you how to go from there."

"But, Mom!" A tear now slides down Sicilee's cheek. She brushes it off before it can freeze. "You can't—"

"Sicilee! Hey, Sicilee!"

She turns around.

Abe is trotting toward her across a yard. He looks almost as happy to see her as she is to see him.

"I'll talk to you later," she says to her mother, and snaps the phone shut. To Abe she says, "What are you doing here?"

"I live here." And now she knows where she is. Abe lives around the corner. Merciful Mother, she's only a couple of blocks from school. "My God, I don't believe it!" Abe laughs. "Kristin said you were walking to school from now on, but I thought she was pulling my leg."

"Really?" Sicilee picks up her things. "Why would you think that? Haven't you seen my Twelve Easy Ways You Can Save the Planet posters?"

"Yeah, sure I have," says Abe as Sicilee falls into step beside him, suddenly neither cold nor tired anymore. "I've been meaning to tell you that I really like them. You make some good points. They make you think."

No one has ever accused Sicilee Kewe of making them think before. She swings her handbag, light as a bucket of popcorn, and smiles.

Chapter Thirty-one

Waneeda and Clemens agree on several things

In the end, of course, Waneeda and Joy Marie gave Cody the help he'd asked for with the Things You Can Do and Did You Know? campaigns. He said there was no one else who could do it. "I'm telling you, everybody's already tied up with committees and stuff," he pleaded in front of Ms. Kimodo. "You know I'd do it myself, but I'm running all over the place trying to drum up support for Earth Day."

"We're tied up, too," bleated Joy Marie and Waneeda.

"But you're so good at this stuff," Cody persisted. "You could do it blindfolded."

Ms. Kimodo sighed wistfully.

Cody threw himself onto his knees, clasping his hands. "Please," he begged. "You have to help. Dr. Firestone's breathing down my neck."

The sighs of Waneeda and Joy Marie were more resigned than wistful.

Today, however, there is a slight change in the cast of Environmental Club drudges. Joy Marie is thirty miles away, rehearsing with the county orchestra, and so it is Clemens who is helping Waneeda print the latest batch of flyers and put them up around the school.

Mrs. Skwill greeted him like a long-lost friend, albeit one with whom she has some issues.

"Clemens Reis!" cried Mrs. Skwill. "You haven't darkened my door in weeks. It's usually your friend Cody who comes in to see Dr. Firestone these days." Normally a woman of few words (many of them "no"), Mrs. Skwill paused only long enough for Clemens to open his mouth. "I guess he's your public relations person now, being so personable." She stretched her lips into a straight line and nodded at Clemens. *Unlike you* . . . "So enthusiastic and inspiring." *Also unlike you* . . . "You must bless the day he came to Clifton Springs. He does so much for your club, doesn't he? Always talking about what your plans are and what you're hoping to achieve. . . . I can't tell you how much we've all learned about the environment and all its problems from him." It was also rare to see Mrs. Skwill (whose default setting is "cautious") almost gleeful. "This Earth Day party of yours is really going to be something. Bigger even than the one we had when the town turned three hundred."

It was Waneeda who interrupted the administrative assistant's enthusiastic monologue. "Do you think we could use a photocopier?" she asked. "We have some more flyers we need to run off."

Mrs. Skwill glanced at Clemens. "Are you sure you want him with you?" she asked Waneeda. "You know he's going to go on and on about all the health risks of photocopy machines and laser printers, don't you?"

Waneeda said that she knew.

"He's a very nice boy," Mrs. Skwill continued, as though Clemens had either gone deaf or left the room, "but he's very depressing. Don't breathe this . . . and don't touch that. . . . He never stops. I don't know how you can stand it."

Waneeda pulled on her hair and smiled.

Mrs. Skwill would undoubtedly be surprised to learn that Waneeda doesn't find Clemens depressing at all. Since she has been spending so much time with him, slouching through Clifton Springs with a clipboard and a stack of Save Our Trees petitions, Waneeda has discovered that there is more to Clemens Reis than saddle shoes and doom.

"I really appreciate this," Waneeda tells him now as they start on their rounds. "It'd take me forever to do it by myself."

"Fair's fair. You help me." Clemens gives her a conspiratorial wink. "At least no one's going to slam the door in our faces doing this." Which is something that happens fairly often when you're asking people to save ancient trees.

"I guess Joy Marie's right." Waneeda laughs. "Every cloud does have a silver lining."

Clemens holds the flyers against the wall and Waneeda does the taping. And all the time they work, they chat as though there was never a time when the only words they ever exchanged were "hello" and "good-bye." As though it was always obvious that they were meant to be friends.

"It's funny about Maya, isn't it?" says Waneeda as they start on the first floor. "I used to think she was as deep as a puddle. But now I'm kind of changing my mind." Waneeda slaps tape over the cartoon they're putting up of a woman pouring the contents of her mop bucket down the sink, where it travels through the pipes and drains and ends up in a river full of dead fish. "Some of these are really good."

Clemens shrugs. "They're all right."

"All right?" Waneeda's eyebrows rise skeptically. "Hey, I know you weren't too enthusiastic about the cartoon concept to begin with, but you have to admit that they're better than just 'all right.'"

"OK," Clemens concedes, "so maybe I was wrong about her trivializing serious issues. Most of her cartoons are pretty right on." He gives Waneeda a poke with his elbow. "But then you have to take back what you said about Sicilee." What Waneeda said was that Sicilee telling people how to be Green was like the blind leading the blind—straight over a cliff. "She had a good idea, too."

He aligns the latest installment of Twelve Easy Ways You Can Save the Planet next to the cartoon. "There aren't as many dust-your-lightbulb type of suggestions as I expected."

"OK, some of it's not bad," says Waneeda. "But can you actually see Princess Kewe following her own advice?"

"Well . . ." Clemens smiles mischievously. "Maybe not all of it, but she does walk to school now." Indeed, she sometimes walks the last block with them. "And I can see her reading labels—I don't think she'd have a problem with that. And she probably takes a shower now and then instead of long baths. And even turns off lights."

"OK, but can you see her swanning into the Salvation Army thrift store?" demands Waneeda. "The only things she'd wear that belonged to someone else would have to be made out of diamonds or gold."

"The Salvation Army?" Clemens looks as though he is trying very hard to picture this unlikely event. "Sicilee in the Salvation Army . . ." It isn't an easy image to call up: Sicilee strolling into the Salvation Army in one of her tailored suits and a string of pearls, looking for something to wear for a weekend on somebody's yacht.

"Excuse me, my good woman, but do you work here?" mimics Waneeda in a high, gushy voice. "Can you tell me where you keep the Juicy Couture?"

Their laughter echoes down the empty corridor.

They are still laughing when they return to the lobby.

Night has fallen over Clifton Springs. Outside, the snow that still remains on the lawn sparkles in the lights that line the drive, but the sky itself sparkles with stars. They stand by the glass doors, putting on their coats.

"It's funny—I never really used to look at the sky before," says Waneeda. "But now I look for the moon and the stars every night."

"Me too," says Clemens. "I'm always relieved they're still there." He opens the door and holds it for Waneeda. "You didn't used to wear your hair down much, did you?" he asks as she walks past him.

"No." Waneeda shrugs. "But . . . you know . . . it's been so cold."

"It looks nice," says Clemens, and he follows her out.

Chapter Thirty-two

Maya wins an argument with her mother

The lyricist Chuck Berry famously wrote that "you never can tell." He was talking about teenagers. Teenagers, Mr. Berry suggested, can really surprise you. Mr. Berry never met Sicilee Kewe, but if he had, he would have been tempted to point to her in her puffy, hooded coat and the sensible, flat-soled boots she's been wearing to school lately and say, "See? That's exactly what I meant!"

Previously walking no farther than the length of the mall, Sicilee has amazed everyone. No matter how cold and blustery the day, Sicilee — cheeks rosy from more than her usual blusher — has been seen striding onto the campus, looking as though she was born on the hoof and has no memory of ever sitting in a plush and heated Cadillac, plugged into her iPod, a caffe latte in the cup holder beside her. And no one has been more amazed by this new development than Maya Baraberra. To make it even worse, Sicilee sometimes arrives with Cody

Lightfoot (and Clemens, Waneeda, and Joy Marie, but Maya, of course, barely notices them), gliding up the drive like a swan down a river.

"Look at her!" Maya raged. "Acting like she's the first primate to climb down from the trees and walk around on her hind legs! It's not just sickening; it's physically impossible. That girl wouldn't walk to the bathroom if she could drive there. She must be getting a ride from her mother to somewhere nearby."

But Alice, who (to be honest) is as tired of hearing about Sicilee Kewe as she is of hearing about tofu and Cody Lightfoot, is less emotionally involved and therefore able to be more objective. "I don't think so," said Alice. "Haven't you noticed her coat or the state of her boots? If she's getting a ride, it's in the back of a pickup."

Which, of course, left Maya with no choice. If she had to endure even one more day of watching Sicilee sashay up the drive—with Cody or without him—or one more meeting in which Sicilee says, loudly, "Well, those of us who walk . . ." or "Well, when you walk, like I do . . ." Maya might have to move in with her aunt in Spokane or risk losing her mind.

It took Maya several days to find her abandoned bicycle, buried at the back of the cellar, flat on the floor with an old toy chest and several boxes on top of it, and even longer to clean it and pump up the tires, but today is the day of its maiden voyage.

Maya's mother glances nervously out the kitchen window at the dark, cloud-crowded sky and the backyard trees bending in the icy wind. "Why don't you let me drive you?" she asks. "I don't think this is very good weather for biking to school. It looks to me like it's going to snow again."

"That's one of the big problems with our society," says Maya. "We fear nature when we should embrace it. We want to control everything . . . to manipulate the moon and stars . . . to have things all our own way."

Mrs. Baraberra sighs. "I'm not trying to manipulate anything, Maya. I just don't want you to get caught in a storm."

"Um, duh . . . In case you haven't noticed, Mom, snow is a natural phenomenon. We should celebrate it, not hide from it. It's cars that aren't natural. Why aren't you worried about all the carbon dioxide we're pouring into the air and *my* lungs?"

Rather than get into long explanations about why she shows so little concern about the degradation of the atmosphere and her daughter's lungs by the burning of fossil fuels, Mrs. Baraberra says, "Fine. Take the bike."

It's a testament to the strength and depth of female friendship that Alice, hunkered into a plaid hunting jacket and matching bomber hat, is actually waiting for Maya at the end of the street, her mittened hands gripped so tightly around the handlebars of her own bicycle that it's difficult to tell if she's holding it up or if it's holding up her.

Alice squints into the morning glare as Maya walks toward her, pushing her bike. "What is *that*?"

"It's a portable missile launcher. What does it look like?"

"But it has a fringe, and it's pink and, like, sky blue," says Alice, whose own bike is a mature and tasteful silver. She narrows her eyes even more. "What's that on the handlebars? Is it a cow?"

"It's the horn."

"When was the last time you rode this thing?" Alice looks as though she thinks the bike may bite her.

Maya stamps her feet with impatience as much as cold. "I told you. A couple of years ago?"

Alice is less than reassured by this information. "But you've given it a test-drive, right?" She leans her head to one side, judging. "It looks a little small."

"Of course I tested it." It didn't occur to Maya even to ride it up and down the driveway. And then, because lies like company as much as people do, adds, "The size is fine." It's at least two inches too small.

"You know, it's not too late to change our minds," says Alice. "My mom said she'll take us." She shivers to emphasize how cold she feels already. "She thinks we're totally nuts biking to school in weather like this. She says we could get really sick."

"She's wrong." Maya watches her breath float in front of her like tiny clouds. "This is the sane and healthy thing to do. I even read that scientific research has proved that the car culture not only contributes significantly to climate change, but also to obesity, heart disease, alienation, and crime."

"My mom *is* wrong," says Alice. "Only one of us is totally nuts." There are no points for guessing which one she means.

Maya laughs.

"I'm not kidding. I think all that tofu's affecting your brain."

"No it isn't. It—" Maya breaks off and, like Alice, looks up at the sky. Tiny crystals of frozen water are suddenly hurtling toward them so thickly that it looks as if someone's dropping a curtain over their heads.

Alice looks over at Maya. "Did you know it was going to snow today, or are we just really lucky?"

Maya sighs. Obviously, the only luck she's having this morning is that the snow isn't accompanied by gale-force winds. "It's no big deal," she declares with a confidence she doesn't feel. "We'll be there before it starts to stick."

"Well, I definitely will." Alice pulls her phone from her pocket. The strength and depth of female friendship only goes so far. "I'm calling my mom."

"Alice, please," pleads Maya. "It's not like we're crossing the Alps. We're just riding to school. And I'll make it up to you, I promise. Anything. My original '77 Led Zep T-shirt. My firstborn. Anything. If you need someone to ride down the Mississippi with you on a raft, all you have to do is ask."

Alice hits the number for *Home* on her phone. "All I want is a ride to school in a car."

"What happened to the pioneer spirit that made this country great?" asks Maya.

"My ancestors never left Manhattan," says Alice.

"Well, mine did!" cries Maya, and she sets off into the falling snow.

As a matter of fact, Maya's ancestors, though they did leave Manhattan, didn't go any farther than Brooklyn. Which is a lot farther than Maya is ever likely to get today. The road is wet and slippery and filled with large vehicles that drive too fast and far too close, so Maya pedals slowly and cautiously. Maybe she should have listened to Alice. She hasn't gone more than a couple of blocks when she realizes how incorrect the phrase "just riding to school" is—making it sound as easy as strolling into the kitchen for a snack as opposed to, for example, crossing a significant mountain range on an old bicycle that is two inches too small for you. The bike is even more difficult to maneuver than she remembers. It wobbles and emits strange sounds that make her worry that something is about to fall off. Her legs ache after only a block or two. She is afraid to go too fast in case she skids. Maybe, besides listening to Alice, Maya should have listened to her mother, and waited for a day when it isn't snowing for her first ride. Maybe she should have taken a spin around the block once or twice for practice. Perhaps she should have worn ski goggles so she could actually see where she's going.

Maya would be happy to get off and walk, but of course she can't. This is a popular road, used by a lot of people she knows. Cars pass, beeping their horns; familiar faces laugh and shout things she would be happy *not* to be able to hear. Someone throws an empty Styrofoam cup at her as they hurtle by. Someone else shouts out, "Hey, Maya! Get a husky!" Ms. Kimodo waves. For Maya, to be seen pushing her pink-and-blue bike through the snow would be even more humiliating.

She may have frostbite. Her lungs hurt. She's lost all feeling in her toes. She's lost all sense of time. But still Maya pedals on. It will be worth it when she sees the looks on the faces of her friends. It'll be worth it to see the look on Sicilee's face as she glides onto campus, gloating, calling out, "You see, I told you I'd fix the flat!" And with any luck she will pass Cody, slouching along with Clemens, and shout out, "Hi!" and toot her cow horn.

Maya pedals up Schuyler, the last road before the school, gasping but triumphant. Usually Schuyler is full of students who live nearby, but today there is not one single person trudging through the snow, hood up, head down. Maya doesn't wonder why. Nor does she wonder why it's been some time since the last car honked at her as it passed. She thinks it just shows you how soft everyone is. Mollycoddled. Spoiled. So afraid of a little weather that they beg their parents to drive them just a couple of blocks because of the snow.

When she reaches the top of the hill, she stops to catch her breath. She gazes down the other side. The dark shapes of cars move steadily if slowly along the road that runs at the bottom of Schuyler like bison through a winter storm. The sidewalk should also be teeming with students, but except for two figures huddled into their parkas just stepping off the curb, it, too, is empty. Maya pushes off.

Maya is fortunate in three things this morning, and unfortunate in one. Her first piece of luck is that the hill is not a steep one. The second is that the two figures huddled into their parkas are Clemens and Waneeda, who are late because they've been standing at the gas station half a mile away with their petitions for the last hour. The unfortunate thing is that, halfway down Schuyler, her brakes fail.

"Look out!" screams Maya, sounding her horn. "Get out of the way!" And she tries not to look as the pink-and-blue bike coasts straight into traffic.

The two figures turn, but only one of them steps out of the way. The other one runs toward her.

"Jump! Jump!" shouts Clemens, lunging for her and pulling her free from the bike, which — and this is Maya's third piece of good fortune — clatters to a stop before it reaches the end of Schuyler.

"Are you all right?" Clemens helps her up.

Maya nods.

"Are you crazy?" asks Clemens. "You could've been killed."

"I know." Maya smiles at Clemens with no hint of mockery for the very first time. "You probably saved my life."

The three of them walk the rest of the way together, Maya pushing the bike. As they turn into the school, Cody passes them in his father's car. He turns in his seat and waves.

Chapter Thirty-three

Waneeda and her mother have an argument that neither loses or wins

Waneeda's mother wants to know what's wrong with the chicken.

This is a moment Waneeda's been dreading. She scoops up a forkful of peas. But it was as inevitable as it was dreaded. There was no way she could keep this a secret. Not without moving in with someone else. "Nothing's wrong with it."

Mrs. Huddlesfield glowers at the untouched leg on one side of Waneeda's plate. Mrs. Huddlesfield looks as if she's about to spit bullets. "Then why aren't you eating it?"

Waneeda shrugs, but doesn't raise her head to catch her mother's accusing, gimlet eye. "Because I don't feel like it."

"Don't feel like it?" Mrs. Huddlesfield's voice rises indignantly. "What do you mean, you don't feel like it? You love chicken."

Maybe more than Mrs. Huddlesfield thinks.

"What's the big deal?" Waneeda reaches for the bowl of salad, risking an innocent glance in her mother's direction. "I'm eating everything else."

"What's the big deal?" parrots her mother. "What's the big deal? Is that the thanks I get for working all day and racing back here to make a nice home-cooked meal for you? *What's the big deal?* You think this food just walks out of the refrigerator and puts itself on the table?" Her fork, a piece of white meat pinned to it, hovers in the air. "You think everybody gets a nice home-cooked meal like you do?"

Waneeda spears a slice of tomato. "Everyone who owns a microwave and a can opener does," she mumbles.

The fork clatters against Mrs. Huddlesfield's plate. "You can cook your own meals from now on if you think you're so funny."

"I wasn't trying to be funny." The chicken leg pushed to the far side of Waneeda's plate has tiny veins buried in the flesh. "I just don't feel like eating the chicken — that's all."

"What is this? Another one of your diets?" Mrs. Huddlesfield doesn't ask this in the kindly, affectionate way of a mother who is worried about her child's health. She asks it as a mother who knows that no diet Waneeda has ever been on has lasted more than a few days and who automatically expects her child to fail.

"Kind of." Waneeda has recently watched a documentary with Clemens on, among other things, factory farming (in fact, the same documentary that so efficiently emptied the auditorium last year), and now knows that, if it is true that "you are what you eat," she is a tortured, drugged, and septic pool of misery. "I've kind of decided to stop eating meat for a while."

"You what?" Mrs. Huddlesfield laughs the way you might if you discovered a two-headed possum in your bed—in amazement, horror, and disbelief. "And why in the name of all that is right and holy would you want to do a thing like that?" Waneeda's mother looks over at Waneeda's father, whose attention (up until now) has been fully absorbed by what's happening on the television screen. "Oscar!" she bellows. "Oscar! Did you hear that? Now she isn't eating meat!"

"What?" Waneeda's father tears his eyes from the real police chase taking place only a few feet away in the living room. "Who isn't eating meat?"

"*She* isn't." Mrs. Huddlesfield points to the only other person at the table, to clarify this statement and end any possible confusion. "*Your* daughter is refusing to eat meat!"

"Really?" Mr. Huddlesfield snaps a chicken wing in two. "What are you going to eat if you don't eat meat?"

"Well, you know . . ." says Waneeda. "I guess I'll just have to make do with the millions of other things there are to eat besides meat." She takes a deep breath. "I'm going to be a vegetarian."

234

From the look on her father's face, you'd think Waneeda had just announced her intention to become a mercenary.

"I've never heard such nonsense." Waneeda's father is so appalled that he has actually forgotten about the hysterical chase on the California highway. "Don't you know that if we didn't eat them, there'd be no cows or pigs or sheep? We're doing them a favor. Without us they'd die."

"And *with us* they die," counters his daughter. "Which puts them in a no-win situation."

"Don't be a wise guy." Mrs. Huddlesfield has retrieved her fork and is pointing it at her daughter. "You know what your father means. That's what animals are for. For us to eat."

"Really?" Even the leaf of lettuce on the end of Waneeda's fork looks skeptical. "Then how come, in nature, the chicken Dad's breaking into pieces will talk to her chicks when they're still in their eggs? And they'll talk back? How do you explain that? You think she's telling them they only have seven weeks to live and then they're supper?"

"So they talk to each other." Mr. Huddlesfield waves half a wing at her. "What's that prove, Waneeda? That instead of eating them we should send them all to Harvard?"

"Didn't I say she's been acting strange, Oscar?" interrupts Waneeda's mother. "Have you noticed how she's stopped flushing the toilet? Did you know she threw out all my air fresheners? Even that mountain pine you like so much? And she did something with the bleach. It's disappeared into thin air." It's just as well she hasn't been looking for the toilet cleaner in the last few days. "Didn't I say that I don't know what's come over her?" Although her questions seem to be directed to him, Mrs. Huddlesfield isn't looking at her husband. She is looking at her only child — thoughtfully, trying to figure out what's come over Waneeda that she can't see. And then all the lights go on in the house that is Mrs. Huddlesfield's brain. "It's that club, isn't it?" This is in no way a question. "It's that Clemens Reis! Isn't he a vegetarian? I'll bet he is. Look at those glasses of his. And that hat! He's put you up to this, hasn't he?" These aren't questions, either.

Although you wouldn't expect Waneeda's mother to forget that Clemens once catapulted a large toy piano into her backyard, it has to be said that she has also never forgiven him for that event. From the moment the piano leg bounced against the back door and made her drop the pitcher of juice she was holding, Mrs. Huddlesfield has thought of Clemens as an extremely peculiar boy. Trouble. Not normal. Not unless you live in another world. The kind of boy you want to keep your eye on — so that, years later, when he's arrested for doing something outrageous and the reporters gather around the house and ask her what he was like as a child, Mrs. Huddlesfield will be able to say, *Oh, I always knew he was odd.*

"It has nothing to do with Clemens," says Waneeda. "I've never even talked about it with him. I made up my own mind."

This would be a good example of wasting your breath.

"I should've known!" cries her mother. "When he came over the other morning like that, I should've known something was going on."

Mrs. Huddlesfield is referring to the first day Waneeda went door-to-door with the oak-tree petition with Clemens. He came to get her by climbing over the fence and knocking on the back door. To Mrs. Huddlesfield, of course, this was just another example of how peculiar Clemens is. In her retellings of this story, Clemens came over the fence like a burglar. Waneeda's mother wanted to know why he couldn't come to the front of the house like anybody else would. And Clemens, sitting down at the table as though he'd been invited, said that he did it because it was quicker.

"Oh, for Pete's sake," sighs Waneeda. "Nothing's going on."

Waneeda's mother isn't listening. Conversation is largely a solitary occupation for her. "I don't know why we can't have neighbors who have normal children," she continues. "I wouldn't mind if you were seeing a football player. Or a basketball star."

"I'm not seeing anyone," says Waneeda.

"Personally, I'm surprised he could get over the fence," muses Mr. Huddlesfield, who has yet to return to his television show. "He's not what you'd call athletic, is he? Not exactly All-American material."

"You wouldn't say that if you'd seen him the other day," says Waneeda. Surprising herself, she relates the story of Maya's runaway bicycle and Clemens Reis's quick thinking and acting. "It was like he was some kind of superhero. He just jumped for her and pulled her off the bike."

"A superhero who doesn't eat meat?" Waneeda's father gives a short, sharp laugh. "That'll be the day."

Mrs. Huddlesfield continues with her alternative conversation. "He's not a good influence on you," she says. "What's next? That's what I want to know. Are you going to protest outside McDonald's? Are you going to go on demonstrations dressed in a tutu? Is that what you're going to do?"

As if giving up meat is the first step on the road to anarchy and chaos.

"I'm not sure." Waneeda nibbles on her lettuce. "Maybe I'll plant some stuff in the backyard."

"Plant stuff?" Neither Mrs. nor Mr. Huddlesfield ever goes in the backyard because they're afraid of catching Lyme disease. "Plant what?"

"Plants," says Waneeda. "You know, flowers—and maybe a tree or two. Maybe I'll even grow some vegetables."

"Did you hear that, Oscar?" shrieks Mrs. Huddlesfield. "She's going to plant vegetables."

"That's exactly what you'd expect from a vegetarian," says Mr. Huddlesfield.

Chapter Thirty-four

It seems that Sicilee's changed her mind about more than one thing

As Ms. Kimodo has been heard to comment to friends and colleagues, Cody Lightfoot should be in the foreign service, not in high school. His ambassadorial skills are such that support among the students and faculty for Earth Day has grown steadily over the weeks—even to the point where the recycling bins Clemens fought to have put in the cafeteria are overflowing and teachers are sharing rides to school. He's a born diplomat, a gifted schmoozer. Innately charming, Cody has persuaded every department in the school to make some kind of contribution to the event—from the bicycle-powered generator being built by the Science Club to the workshop on preparing vegetarian food promised by consumer sciences. Effortlessly charismatic, he has so inspired the other members of the Environmental Club that donations and workers are pouring in for the many activities and stalls that have been planned.

But nothing is without its problems, is it? For, despite all of this and the crates of used goods already locked up in the school's storeroom, the project is still short on funds. Volunteers have been sent out carrying leaflets and wearing Earth Day buttons to ask for donations from local businesses and the community at large, but except for Cody convincing the electric company to be an official sponsor (which owes something to the fact that Cody's father knows the CEO), the response has been less than overwhelming.

"It's like we've built it, but nobody knows it's here," said Cody. "What we need is someone with a serious kick-butt sense of salesmanship to go out there and talk these birds right out of their trees. Someone who really knows how to get people to part with their dough."

Two hands were waving in the air before he'd finished speaking.

"I think it's terrific that you're giving up another Saturday at the mall to raise money for the Earth Day fair," says Mrs. Kewe. On Saturdays, of course—unless there's a big game, a flu epidemic, or a major weather event that closes roads and shuts off power—Sicilee, Kristin, Ash, and Loretta always go to the mall. At least they used to. Before Sicilee had so many other things to do. "That's what I call real dedication."

Sicilee smiles. "Oh, I'm dedicated, all right."

Her hand beat Maya's into the air by at least a half of a

nanosecond. There was no way she was going to let Maya raise hundreds of dollars single-handedly and get all the glory and praise.

"What about a ride into town, then?" asks her mother. "I think you can risk a tiny carbon toeprint for such a good cause."

"That's OK." Sicilee's smile is serene. "I'd rather walk."

Which, strangely enough, is true. Although Sicilee used to feel the same way about walking as the emperors of Europe and Asia felt about work (all right for some, but not for them), over the weeks of walking to school she has actually begun to enjoy it. She no longer counts the blocks or groans with boredom or wishes she was in one of the cars that race past her, talking about what this season's colors will be or listening to her latest download. She notices things that before would have passed her by like clouds — not just the meerkats on Burr, but that pond with ducks on Millett Lane and the wild parrots on the north side of town and the old barn that sits at the edge of one of the newer, anonymous housing developments like a ghost. She looks forward to seeing the Jack Russell who always runs out to greet her from the pink house with the swing on the front porch, and to passing the old man walking his dachshund who always wishes her "top of the morning," and to meeting up with Abe for the last leg of her journey. These things make her days more interesting, very much in the way that cloth-covered buttons or a necklace of glass beads will set off a plain dress.

Breakfast over, Mrs. Kewe stands on the front porch, waving good-bye. It's a beautiful day. Cold, but bright and sunny. If you look closely, as Sicilee now does, you can see the first buds appearing on the trees, the first flowers poking up through the ground. Winter is winding down.

Sicilee strides along, her hair blowing behind her, smiling with confidence, imagining Cody and her strolling through the Earth Day celebration arm-in-arm. She has no doubt that she will succeed in getting donations where others have failed. After all, if there's one thing Sicilee is very good at, it's getting money from people who don't necessarily want to give it. She's been practicing on her parents since she was two. Like the carrot dangled on the end of a stick in front of the poor donkey, Cody has stayed just out of Sicilee's reach for all these months. Yes, they are friendly. Yes, she has found herself standing so close to him that she can see the weave in his organic cotton shirt. Yes, he sometimes smiles at her in a way that makes her feel as if she's been punched in the stomach, sometimes looks into her eyes in a way that makes her forget where she is. He has even flirted with her now and then. But the promise she sees in his melt-your-heart smiles and soulful looks has never been fulfilled. Not even close.

The truth is that he's friendly with everyone, smiles at everyone, even flirts with Ms. Kimodo and Mrs. Sotomayor. The fact that he heaps praise on her Easy Ways to Save the Planet campaign doesn't count for anything, either. He heaps praise on Maya's Do You Know? posters with just as much enthusiasm. Indeed, he pretty much praises any idea that comes up—no matter what it is or who suggests it—as though it's the biggest thing since penicillin. It's no exaggeration to say that, *That's awesome, man, that's truly awesome!* and *That is, like, fantástico! You knock me back!* are phrases that come out of Cody Lightfoot the way hot air comes out of an air-conditioning vent. And, to make matters worse, lately Cody is so completely focused on Earth Day that those precious moments when she would walk the last block to school or the first block from school with him no longer happen. He's always either late or leaves early, running off to give newspaper and radio interviews; to talk to church and civic groups; to convince the bowling league, the American Legion, and the Historical Society that they all have a part to play in saving the Earth.

But this—at last—could be the thing that finally makes Cody take her seriously. Looks, popularity, and a passion for vegetables may all be ignored, but money is always guaranteed to attract attention.

Marching into town like an invading army, Sicilee

stops just outside the square to assemble her troops. Although the historic village of Clifton Springs has spread out over the centuries since it was founded and is now surrounded by several shopping centers and acres of housing developments, the heart of the village is still only four blocks of quaint wooden houses and small brick buildings around a large green where sheep once grazed. In the middle of the green, surrounded by oak trees and silver birches, there is a clapboard church (rebuilt 1820), a monument to the Civil War dead on one side and a sign pointing to the basement that says SAINT PAUL'S CHURCH THRIFT STORE on the other. She will start on the east side and work her way around.

Sicilee glances at the clock on the church tower.

Unlike Mrs. Kewe, Kristin, Ash, and Loretta were far from delighted by Sicilee's new sense of dedication.

"What, you're going to miss *another* Saturday?" Loretta made it sound as if Sicilee had missed those Saturdays on a whim when, in fact, one was canceled by the weather and Sicilee couldn't make the other because, as chairman of the music committee, she was auditioning bands. "Are you too good for shopping now?"

"Of course not." Sicilee laughed. "I just have a lot to do for Earth Day."

"Again?" asked Kristin. "Are you rebuilding the planet all by yourself?"

Sicilee laughed once more. "If only, right?"

"You mean you'd rather do that stuff than come with us?" demanded Ash.

Sicilee said that of course she wouldn't. "But you know how it is. Duty calls."

"It seems more like it's pulling your strings," said Loretta.

Ash was looking at her in a weird kind of way. "You know, you look the same, but you're different," she said. "It's like nerds have taken over your body."

"Don't be ridiculous. I just like to do what I say I'll do — that's all." Sicilee promised she'd meet them for lunch. "It's not going to take me very long. Save me a seat," she ordered. "I'll be there by one."

No problem, thinks Sicilee as she sets off to circle the green. As her father has said (more than once), she could talk a turtle out of its shell and it would thank *her.* She'll be finished by noon.

Unfortunately, Sicilee's belief that getting people to contribute to the Earth Day celebration is going to be as easy as getting a couple of hundred dollars from her mother suffers its first setback in Small World: Klothes for Kids, which also happens to be the first store she tries.

Bright and bubbly, Sicilee explains that she is from the Clifton Springs High School Environmental Club, that they are planning a major celebration for Earth Day, and that she is asking for either donations of money or suitable objects for the grand raffle. Her hand is ready to reach over the basket of socks next to the register for the check.

"Don't waste your breath," advises the manager, Mrs. Costa. "I told the girls who came the other day that I'm not interested. Earth Day, Smurfday, that's what I say. It's just another excuse to get money out of people."

"Oh, no, Mrs. Costa. That's, like, so untrue." Sweet Mary, she's not asking for money to buy new pom-poms for the cheerleaders; she's trying to save the planet. "Earth Day is like Mother's Day. You know, when you show your mom you really do appreciate all the stuff she does for you even if you don't always say so? Only this is for Mother Earth, not your own mom. And instead of giving her flowers we'll plant some."

"So you say," snaps Mrs. Costa. "But I never heard of no Earth Day before. How do I know you're not making it up?"

"Because it's been going on for years." Sicilee's smile doesn't flicker or dim. "You can check it on the Web. Years and years and years. All over the country. And all over the world, too. It's our recognition of how much we owe our planet." Since Sicilee's attention was focused on Cody Lightfoot when he explained the origins of Earth Day and not on what he was actually saying, she can only hope that this is true. "And our celebration's going to be really great." She lays a flyer detailing the day's events on the counter. "Just look at all the stuff we're doing to help everyone shrink their carbon footprints."

"I don't have a carbon footprint," Mrs. Costa informs her. "I've never been on a plane."

Sicilee's smile takes on an almost angelic quality. "Maybe not, but I bet a lot of the clothes you sell have flown here. They couldn't all have come by mule train."

"That doesn't count," says Mrs. Costa. "That's business. I'm talking about personally."

Someone less accustomed to getting her own way might retreat under so much pigheaded opposition, but Sicilee is undaunted. "Well, that's fantastic then, isn't it? If you, personally, have no carbon footprint, then you're already on our team!"

Mrs. Costa, however, is on no one's team. "What's this?" she wants to know, her finger tapping on something halfway down the flyer. "Secondhand clothes? You'll be selling secondhand clothes?" She looks up, her smile as thin as a snowflake and just as cold. "Business hasn't been so good lately. Do you seriously expect me to donate money to something that could affect my business? Isn't it bad enough that I've got that thrift store across the street?"

It should be mentioned here that Mrs. Costa is nothing like Mr. Kewe (who has never been known to use makeup, dye his hair blond, or wear frilly blouses with big bows at the neck), and yet, at this moment, she reminds Sicilee so much of her father that they might be twins. Mrs. Costa is being illogical in exactly the same way that Mr. Kewe is when he says things like, *Do you realize, Sicilee, that there are girls in the world who don't have any shoes?*—as if those girls will be somehow better off if Sicilee never buys another pair.

Sicilee makes the same earnest face she uses against her father's irrationality. "Oh, of course not, Mrs. Costa. That would be ridiculous." Sicilee knows that people respond better to self-interest than to self-sacrifice. She shifts from side to side, tossing her hair over her shoulder, looking vulnerable and corn-syrup sweet. "That's why I know you'll want to help us, right? Because we're not trying to put you out of business. It's global warming that'll do that." Sicilee leans toward the counter as if she's about to pat the manager's shoulder. "I mean, let's be honest here. If we don't save the planet, there won't be any children left to wear your clothes, will there?"

Emboldened by her success with Mrs. Costa (who finally coughs up one hundred dollars), Sicilee storms around the square, handing out her flyers and smiling her I-know-you-want-to-help-*really* smile, overcoming the most obdurate and irrational arguments with sincerity and common sense. We buy too much. We waste too much. We depend too much on resources that are running out and can't be replaced. Sicilee is unflappable, unstoppable. "Less is more," she explains. "If you buy a year's worth of groceries, you don't eat it all on the first day, do you? Yet that's pretty much what we've done with our finite resources," she says. "When half the world's a desert and the other half's under water, nobody's going to care if they can send e-mails on their cell phone or not," she warns. Realtors, lawyers, the jeweler, the toy store, the boutique, the deli, the market, the gift shop, the soda fountain, the candy store, the bike store, the hardware store, and the sports store all put up a fight but are defeated in the end by the rolling thunder of Sicilee's perseverance and persuasion. She amazes herself with how much she knows. She puts the checks in a green envelope and slips it into her cotton bag.

Sicilee is so involved in her task that it isn't until she comes around to where she started that she looks up at the clock on the church tower again. How time flies when you're saving the world. The only way she'd make lunch at the mall is if she'd left two hours ago.

It is then that her eyes fall on the sign by the door that leads to the basement of the church: Saint Paul's Thrift Store. Sicilee's had a successful morning. She's in a good mood. And perhaps the merchants of Clifton Springs aren't the only ones who have been moved by her arguments. *Why not?* she thinks. Swinging her bag over her shoulder, she strolls up the path and disappears inside without even bothering to check that no one's watching her.

Chapter Thirty-five

Plastic girl in a plastic world

The Birch Grove Shopping Center is part of the suburban sprawl that surrounds the historic village of Clifton Springs. Unlike the historic village itself, there is nothing either quaint or attractive about the shopping center — and no grove of birch trees, either. It's simply a row of boxlike concrete buildings with the supermarket at one end and a small parking lot dotted with litter and weeds in front. There are similar — if not actually identical — shopping centers in every direction. What distinguishes Birch Grove (at least today) is the presence of Maya Baraberra outside the entrance to the supermarket, dressed in a skirt covered with dozens of plastic bottles and a jacket and hat made of plastic bags. Ah, the things a girl will do for love.

Following a pattern that is now well established, Alice refused to come with her. "Even if I wasn't going to my grandma's for the weekend, I wouldn't come," Alice declared. "I'm not really good at exposing myself to ridicule." She didn't think Maya should go, either. "It's kind of, you know, *uncool,* begging for money," said Alice. "Like those geeks who try to get you to sign petitions you know nobody's ever going to read?" And it's doubly uncool if you're dressed as the town dump. "You know, I've seen guys dressed as rabbits and clowns and stuff like that," said Alice, "but I've never seen anyone dressed like garbage before. Everybody's going to laugh at you." Alice didn't understand why, if Maya had to beg, she couldn't wear regular clothes to do it. "It's not like you're advertising anything," Alice reasoned. "You're just asking for money." So are all those Santas at Christmas, argued Maya. Alice said that that was different because it's seasonal. Maya, however, wouldn't be persuaded. She wanted to make an impact. "You mean that you want to raise more money than Sicilee Kewe, so you can impress Cody," said Alice.

Which, of course, is true. If it weren't for Sicilee shooting her hand into the air as if it was on a spring and boasting about how easy it is to get people to donate when you're doing it for such a good cause, right now Maya would be hanging out with her friends at Mojo's, drinking coffee and listening to jazz like on any other Saturday afternoon. "It's not *just* that," lied Maya. "I actually am advertising something, you know. I'm advertising environmental ruin and the end of life as we know it if we don't stop using so much plastic." There won't be any more Santas at Christmas then, because there won't be any seasons. "I want to make people stand up and take notice."

Well, she's certainly doing that.

Maya began the day with the enthusiasm of a crusader. Let Sicilee go from store to store in the village like a double-glazing salesman. Maya would do something memorable and eye-catching. Something artistic. She wasn't going to just ask for money like Sicilee, which any fool can do. Maya was going to make a statement — create an event. Maya would be living, breathing conceptual art. She wouldn't be surprised if the town paper sent a photographer around and did a story on her: "Local Girl Set to Save the World."

But that was at the beginning of the day, long before those schoolgirls strutted by shouting out, "Ohmygod, it's the Incredible Bulk!"—their giggling sounding like a swarm of locusts. Before those younger schoolboys pulled off some of her bottles and lobbed them at her, shrieking with glee. And long before the droves of Saturday shoppers arrived, pretending not to see her and shoving their carts past her so quickly you'd think they were giving things away inside. Maya's been standing at the entrance to the supermarket since it opened and by now is feeling less like an installation in the Museum of Modern Art than someone dressed as a chicken to advertise a new fast-food restaurant. She is uncomfortable and constricted. Every so often she walks a few feet to the left or to the right, but movement is difficult and she can only see straight in front of her, so she never goes too far. She had given no thought to the fact that she might need to go to the bathroom. She had given no thought to the possibility that she might see someone she knows. The last thing she wants at this point in time is her picture splashed across the front of the *Clifton Springs Observer.*

Smiling gamely and holding out a bucket that says CSHS ENVIRONMENTAL CLUB EARTH DAY FUND, Maya stares out at the rows of cars, the busy road beyond them, and the small huddle of concrete buildings on the other side. It's not much of a view, and after looking at it for so long, Maya's mind has started meandering—the way minds do when you stare at a blank wall. A woman and a small child in a teddy-bear snowsuit wander by, and Maya's mind turns not to Cody Lightfoot, as it usually does, but to the unusual thought that this may be the first time a bear has been seen around here since long before the birch grove disappeared. Diverted, Maya's mind ambles back to a history project they did in eighth grade. The bottles clacking and the bags rustling every time she shifts or someone runs by her, Maya tries to imagine ancient, deep forests; to see black bears fishing in the river, wolves moving in the shadows; to hear the cracking of twigs as deer step warily through the trees.

Blinking in the reflection of sunlight off the roofs

of cars, Maya is failing miserably in this act of extreme imagination when the child in the teddy-bear snowsuit sees her.

"No, Mommy! No, Mommy!" he shrieks, leaning backward and tugging on his mother's hand. "It's a monster! It's a monster!"

The mother laughs, dragging him forward. "It's not a monster, honey. It's just a girl dressed up like a plastic bottle."

Earlier—when she was full of optimism and hope and hadn't yet been publicly humiliated—Maya would have laughed, too. By now she is lucky to be able to smile.

"I'm not really a plastic bottle," she explains as the mother and child come nearer. "I represent the billions of plastic bags and bottles we throw out every year. And that's just in America."

The mother smiles back in a placating, stay-away-from-me way, tightening her grip on her son's hand.

Hoping to make them stop or at least slow down, Maya talks faster and louder. "That's bags and bottles that are produced squandering precious resources. Bags and bottles that are used once and then spend the next thousand years in a landfill." She carefully stretches out the arm that holds the collection bucket to block them. "Think of it! The only thing with a longer life span is depleted uranium!"

"I'm afraid we're only visiting here," says the mother, darting past her with the bear in tow.

"What? Visiting the planet?" Maya calls after them. "Where did you park the spaceship?"

While Maya is temporarily distracted, another small child comes up to her. This one signals her presence not by screaming hysterically but by pulling on Maya's skirt.

Maya looks down.

The little girl is gazing at her earnestly and eating a candy bar, her mouth smudged with chocolate.

Maya's stomach growls. Lunch is another thing she didn't plan for.

"Yes?" Maya gives her a friendly, nonmonster smile.

The little girl chews slowly, almost meditatively, as though deciding exactly how to word her question, which is obviously an important one. "How come you're dressed like that?" she asks at last.

Maya has approached scores of people this morning to tell them about the Environmental Club and the Earth Day celebration, but this is the first time anyone has approached her. Maya responds with enthusiasm. She explains about climate change, plastic bags, and plastic bottles. She explains about the Earth Day celebration and all the fun things that are going to be there. "We're even having a contest to see who can make the best sculpture out of junk," she finishes. "Do you think you'd like to enter?"

The little girl shrugs. "I just wanted to know why you're dressed like that," she repeats. "You know, because you look so dumb." She runs after her mother (a woman who doesn't look as if she's ever turned a light off in her life), and Maya turns back to the parking lot with a sigh.

How much longer should she stay here, gazing out at nothing? She looks into her bucket. At the rate she's going, another week might not be long enough.

The project they did in the eighth grade was called Where I Live Now, and it was all about the animals that used to live in the area, before Jeroboam Clifton colonized it in the name of the English queen. Not just bears, wolves, and deer, but muskrats, otters, opossums, raccoons, skunks, beavers, wild ducks, and turkeys, and a sky full of birds. And there was a Lenape village near the river—the same river that no one wanted to help Clemens clean last year. When the Lenape lived there, the river would have been filled with fish, not garbage. Maya sighs again. There would have been a lot more to see then—and a lot more to hear than traffic and stereos and car doors slamming and shopping carts rattling over the asphalt.

Suddenly something catches Maya's eye that makes the Birch Grove Shopping Center look a lot more interesting than it did a few minutes ago—though not in a good way. A fire-engine red minivan has just turned into the far entrance.

Maya feels herself go as rigid as concrete. There is only one minivan that color in Clifton Springs, and it belongs to Brion Tovar's parents. She squints into the distance. Mr.

Tovar is driving, and beside him is Brion. Behind Brion are Shelby, Jason, and Finn. *Gott im Himmel,* what are *they* doing here? It's Saturday afternoon. They're supposed to be at Mojo's, eating bagels. But for some reason, they aren't. They're cruising through the parking lot, searching for an empty space. And in less time than it takes to throw an empty potato-chip bag into the gutter, they are going to find one and be jumping out of the car.

She can't let them see her. Maya has weathered the teasing, ridicule, and mockery with patience, if not actual good humor, but riding the pink-and-blue bike (now equipped with brakes) to school, always asking what's in the soup or sauce, or telling them what's in that cookie or that body spray, and often being seen with her new friends Clemens and Waneeda are nothing next to this. If they see her dressed like this, with her bucket, she'll never live it down. Uninvited, Alice's voice echoes through Maya's head. *It's really uncool. . . . Everybody's going to laugh at you.* Well, if they're not laughing now, they will be very soon. And the hip image she's worked so hard to build since the beginning of high school — and already dented — will never recover.

The normal response to danger is, of course, either to stay and bravely fight or to run away as fast as you can. There is no time for Maya to get out of her costume — and no way she's going to be standing here looking like the Scourge of the Landfill when Brion, Finn, Jason, and

Shelby stroll by. Especially Jason. The only question is in which direction she's going to flee.

The parking lot's too dangerous. The alley down the side of the supermarket's too far. Maya turns as sharply as a girl enveloped in plastic bags and bottles can, and rustling and clacking, heads for the supermarket's automatic doors. The opening is narrow for her costume, but by twisting her body she manages to squeeze through without knocking anything off the displays dotted around the entrance. With all the grace and ease of a robot made of tin cans, Maya moves into the produce section. It's unlikely that the boys are coming into Foodarama. Probably they're going to the pizza place or the taqueria at the other end. But if some evil star does guide them into Foodarama, it's even more unlikely that they'll be looking for vegetables or fruit. They'll cut straight across to the snack aisle.

Paying no attention to the people staring at her in open-mouthed amazement, holding aloft an apple or an avocado or a box of croutons that has been forgotten in surprise, Maya lumbers over to a revolving tower of salad condiments and stands beside it, ready to bury her face in the shelf of Thousand Island dressing and Italian vinaigrette if Brion, Shelby, Jason, and Finn do suddenly appear.

The same shoppers who would have pelted past her outside Foodarama show no fear or surprise at her presence beside the salad dressings. They come and go, testing the tomatoes and sniffing at the oranges—and looking over at Maya with indulgent smiles and mild curiosity. Several people ask her what she's promoting, and if she has samples. "What are you supposed to be, honey?" asks one woman. "Plastic Girl?" There hasn't been this much laughter in Foodarama since the pigeons got in last summer.

Word of the presence of Plastic Girl in Fruit and Vegetables moves through the store. Something's about to happen. There will probably be giveaways. A small crowd starts to gather, watching as if they expect her to start singing and dancing. Maya does, in fact, recognize some familiar faces—friends of her parents, a woman from her block, Shayla's mother—but for some reason this no longer bothers her. The panic that drove her through the electronic doors has vanished as completely as the Labrador duck. This, Maya realizes, is her great opportunity. She has an audience. An audience that is waiting to hear what she's going to say.

"Hi, everybody!" says Maya. "I'm Plastic Girl. And I'm here to tell you what's happening to the Earth."

She is still talking when there is a call over the loudspeaker for security guards to go immediately to the produce department.

Chapter Thirty-six

Truly great reasons not to save the trees

Clemens and Waneeda have spent the morning, as they have spent most weekend mornings for the last couple of months, trudging up and down the streets, roads, crescents, drives, and dead ends of Clifton Springs with their petition to save the old-growth oaks from being turned into firewood. Clemens has his jacket open so his *Trees Don't Grow on Money* T-shirt is visible. Waneeda's jacket is also open to reveal the T-shirt Clemens made for her (a picture of a tree being felled and the caption *Chainsaw Massacre*). Her hair, in keeping with the arboreal theme of the afternoon, surrounds Waneeda's head like a bush.

They stop at a blue ranch house whose front window is filled with china rabbits.

"Rabbits are a good sign," Waneeda decides. "It means they like animals. At least that's a start."

"Or maybe all it means is that they like buying figurines," says Clemens. Maya isn't the only one who's had a long morning. He slips a coin from his pocket. "Your call. Heads or tails?"

"Heads, you do the spiel," says Waneeda. "Tails, I do it."

In the world of petitioning (as in most worlds) some days are better than others. This one has been a fairly demoralizing one. The people who eagerly snatch the pen from their hands have been very few and very far between. Although many of the good folk of Clifton Springs have been courteous and even polite, if only vaguely interested, it would be misleading to suggest that Waneeda and Clemens have been universally greeted with warmth and support. Very often, curtains have twitched, but no one has answered their knock. Just as often, someone has answered the door and then shut it in their faces. Dogs have run after them. Small children have jeered at them. Adults have been unpleasant and rude.

"Heads, damn it." Clemens ruefully shakes his head. "I swear you have to be psychic."

"Just lucky." Waneeda tugs on a strand of hair. "Anyway, you're better at talking than I am."

Clemens pushes his glasses back up his nose. "Yeah, but people like you more." He sighs. "Everybody thinks I'm weird."

"You're not weird." She gives him an encouraging

smile. Today, Clemens is wearing an old black beret and one of his grandmother's many knitting projects, a scarf patterned with pine trees. "You're just different."

This time, the door is opened by a middle-aged man who listens patiently to Clemens's plea, but when he's finished says, "You don't think maybe the town needs a new sports center more than it needs a couple of trees? We've got plenty of trees, you know, but we don't have plenty of sports centers."

"But these aren't just any trees," argues Clemens. "Sports centers can be built anywhere, but these trees can never be replaced. They were here way before the white man. They're the living past and have witnessed hundreds of years of history. They've seen whole peoples come and go and the sky black with passenger pigeons. If these trees could talk they—"

"Yeah, but they can't talk, can they?" interrupts the man. "They're just trees." He grins in an I'm-laughing-at-you-not-with-you way. "And do you know what another name for trees is? Do you know what else they're called?"

Clemens and Waneeda glance at each other, but neither answers.

"Wood!" shouts the man. "That's the other name for trees! Wood!"

They can still hear him laughing after he's shut the door.

"I think it's time to take up our post at the village square for a while." Clemens slips his clipboard into his backpack. "This neighborhood's got some kind of juju curse on it."

"At least that last guy was original," says Waneeda as they head back to town. "That's the first time we've heard that one. I think that should go on the list. Which makes . . . what? Five or six for today?"

Truly Great Reasons Not to Save the Trees is the game Clemens invented to keep them from getting too depressed.

"Well, let's see." He frowns, thinking. "The first three were: *I can't find the ferret*, *It's too early*, and *I once fell out of a tree and broke my leg*. So that guy who said, *Son, you just don't get it, do you? The thing about trees is they grow back* was number four."

Waneeda laughs. "*You know what would happen if we didn't chop down trees? We wouldn't be able to get our cars out of the garages* was five."

"Well, what about the lady in the sweatsuit and the shower cap? What was it she said?"

"*Trees cause pollution.*"

Clemens looks as if he can't decide whether to laugh or cry. "And even when I said that they only cause pollution when you cut them down, she still wouldn't sign the petition."

They turn into the historic town of Clifton Springs.

"Oh, wait a minute, wait a minute." Waneeda pulls on Clemens's arm as if she's literally trying to slow him down. "What about that man with the funny-looking dog? The one who said that if I had to rake up the leaves I wouldn't be so eager not to cut down trees? He's number seven."

Clemens takes her elbow and guides her across the road to the square. "And how about Mr. Where-Would-We-Be-If-the-Pioneers-Had-Felt-Like-That?"

"And you said that we wouldn't be shopping in Walmart, that's for sure," gasps Waneeda. "And he slammed the door in your face. Just like the woman with the Yorkshire terrier that time. Remember her?"

"Remember her? Even if she hadn't had that dumb dog up her sleeve, I'd never forget her," says Clemens. "She shut that door so hard, she would've broken my foot if I hadn't been wearing my steel-toed boots."

"Well, at least you know that if you don't become some kind of environmentalist, you can always get a job as a door-to-door salesman," says Waneeda. "You're pretty good with that sticking-your-foot-in-the-door routine."

Clemens leans against the old cast-iron railings that surround the churchyard, solemnly shaking his head. "I couldn't take the constant rejection. It's soul destroying."

"We haven't had *total* rejection, though," argues Waneeda. "We've got at least twenty signatures so far today. That's not so bad."

Clemens sighs. "Except that I bet we would've made a lot more than twenty sales if we were Avon ladies selling makeup and not just students trying to save the environment."

"I doubt it," says Waneeda. "I think that the sight of you in drag would make them slam their doors even harder."

They are still laughing when Waneeda, who is facing the church, grabs his arm. "I think I must be hallucinating, Clemens. I could swear I see Sicilee Kewe coming out of the thrift store. With bags."

Clemens turns around. "Well, shuck my corn." He gives a low whistle. "It's either her or her twin sister."

"Hey! Clemens! Waneeda!" Sicilee comes hurrying toward them. "Look at all this cool stuff I got for, like, absolutely nothing." She starts pulling things from one of the bags. "Can you believe it? They've hardly even been worn!"

On the other side of the road, Mr. Huddlesfield, on his way to the hardware store for a washer to fix the leaking faucet in the bathroom (an environmental act inspired by his daughter, who taped a note on the bathroom mirror stating exactly how many gallons of water are dripping away every week), happens to glance over and see that very same daughter standing in front of the village square with Clemens Reis and a girl who definitely isn't Joy Marie Lutz. Mr. Huddlesfield rarely sees his only child out of the house or from any distance, and for a few seconds he doesn't recognize her. This is partly because he still isn't used to seeing her with her hair down and partly because she is animated and smiling (which is another way her father rarely sees her), talking and laughing with her friends. Mr. Huddlesfield changes direction and goes over to see what's going on.

"Well, maybe you'd like to sign our petition." Clemens thrusts his clipboard into Mr. Huddlesfield's hands.

"You can't fight city hall, you know," says Mr. Huddlesfield as he takes hold of the pen.

"That's number nine," says Waneeda.

Chapter Thirty-seven

Shop and drop

A light rain falls over the concrete sprawl that is Wildwood Mall, making the parking lot shine. There are no budding trees or early blooms outside the mall to herald the start of a new season, but to make up for that, the windows are brightly dressed for spring: pastel outfits and paper flowers; fluffy bunnies and baskets of colored eggs; floral rubber boots and bright umbrellas under cellophane showers. You can almost hear Gene Autry singing "Here Comes Peter Cottontail."

To complete the picture, Sicilee, Kristin, Loretta, and Ash, dressed as gaily as a May garden, climb out of the Shepls' minivan and scurry through the drizzle to the southeast entrance. The doors open silently as they approach, and bright lights and potted trees welcome them inside to where it is always a dry and pleasant day with background music and plenty of benches.

Ash waves her hand at the concourse that stretches invitingly ahead of them. "It's really hard to imagine life before they invented malls, isn't it?" The walk from the car, though brief, has apparently put Ash in a reflective mood. "I mean, it must've been just *gross* back then. You'd have to go all over the place just to put a decent outfit together."

Loretta thinks she may have stepped in a puddle and is examining her feet. "And you'd be out in the snow and rain the whole time, trudging from one store to another," she says. "My God, if you didn't get pneumonia or destroy your hair, your shoes would be totally ruined."

"And what did you do in the summer?" asks Kristin. "Just think of it—lugging all those bags around in the heat. . . ." She wrinkles her nose and shivers with distaste. "I mean, who'd want to shop *outside* when it's ninety degrees and just breathing makes you sweat? You wouldn't be able to go more than a block without having to change."

Were he here, Clemens Reis would point out that people used to shop only when they actually needed something. That they replaced things when they were worn out, not when they got tired of the color or fashion changed or they had nothing else to do but go to the stores. Clemens, of course, is not here—but Sicilee is, and Sicilee has now walked that last block to school with him and the others long enough to know that that is what he would say—and even to think of saying it herself. She catches herself just in time.

Today she is making up for not showing up for lunch last week, for the other Saturdays she's bailed on, for the Diamonds meeting she missed, and for trying to make them aware so that they'd care. She doesn't want them to think that she's changed. Though that, of course, is not the only reason.

Lately, Sicilee's begun to wonder if nerds really have taken over her body. She no longer sneaks a burger or piece of chicken or BLT whenever she has the chance. She's pretending that her shoes are made of vegetarian leather when they actually are. She went into a thrift shop without being dragged in by a team of wild horses. She bought stuff. She'd thought that buying secondhand clothes would make her feel like some charity case, but it made her feel kind of smart. And then, when she could still have gone to the mall for the rest of the afternoon if she'd really wanted to, she hung out with Waneeda and Clemens instead. They're not cool — merciful Mother, no one would ever call either of them cool — but they're OK. Their conversations can be pretty interesting. They laugh a lot. She had a good time. What's happening to her? Which, of course, is the other reason Sicilee is here today: to prove to herself that she hasn't changed.

So rather than make a remark that will only cause her friends to look at her as though she's dyed her hair green and stuck a safety pin through her nose, Sicilee says, "And plus, there'd be nowhere to sit down and no place to get a halfway decent latte. I mean, just think about that."

Arms linked and laughing, they set off down the concourse, as they have done so many times before.

The first couple of hours are fairly happy ones.

Chatting and joking, the girls go from store to store, from department to department, searching through the racks and piles of clothes like professional poultry sorters looking for defective chicks. Sicilee doesn't say that she doesn't really need to buy anything new, because not very long ago she went on something of a spending spree in the church thrift store (and she certainly doesn't mention that everything she bought used to belong to her and that her parents have yet to stop laughing). She doesn't mention the concept of need over greed or repeat the Green mantra — Reduce, Reuse, Recycle — either. Nor does she dare to suggest that liking a shirt doesn't mean that you need to have it in five different colors. She pushes such thoughts to the farthest corner of her mind, and as the morning passes, they fade as if they were part of a dream. She is back in the fold, and she is having fun.

They get on Loretta's case for having to try on everything twice. They tease Ash for always buying something pink. They joke about how long it takes Kristin to make up her mind.

"Maybe you should buy two or three new pairs of

boots," Loretta says to Sicilee. "You know, now that you do so much walking!"

They all crack up.

The colored plastic bags hang from their hands like party balloons. Sicilee, who now knows exactly how toxic the production of plastic is and exactly how long it takes a plastic bag to biodegrade, swings them as she walks and says nothing.

Shoulder to shoulder, Sicilee, Ash, Loretta, and Kristin all gather around the mall directory, choosing where they'll go for lunch. Burgers? Pizza? Thai? Mexican?

"Maybe Sicilee wants to go to that vegetarian place and eat bean sprouts," says Loretta. They all giggle, leaning against each other, bags bouncing.

They go to the gourmet burger bar for lunch. Although she has no desire for meat, Sicilee keeps smiling and orders the day's special, rare, served with salad and fries, like everybody else. Only she can't eat the burger. She has no trouble with the salad or the fries or even the bun, but every time she bites into the patty, she thinks of some poor cow, terrified out of its mind, being prodded with electric shocks. What if even just *some* of the things she's been told about industrialized farming are true? What if only *one* is? Which one would Sicilee want it to be? The gross overcrowding? The mutilations? The disease? It isn't a choice she wants to make. Loretta tells a story about the time her sister's head swelled up from her hair dye that is so funny that tears are streaming from their eyes, and Sicilee is doubled up over her plate, gasping for air. While everyone is shrieking and laughing, Sicilee slips the burger from its bun and into her napkin, and slips that into the pocket of her jacket.

It is after lunch—in the cosmetics section of the biggest department store in the mall—that things take a sharp turn for the worse.

Loretta and Ash fool around with the perfumes, while Kristin and Sicilee wander through the counters of makeup. Kristin wants a new lipstick. And maybe some new blush. And maybe something that will really bring out the color of her eyes. Sicilee, however, is showing none of the girlish enthusiasm she usually exhibits in the cosmetics department. Instead she looks almost nervous, as if what she's entered isn't a temple of beauty but a haunted house.

Kristin picks up a lipstick called Blood Wedding and puts some on the back of her hand. "What do you think of this?" she asks.

Sicilee picks up a lipstick, too, and reads the box. *Blood* seems to be the operative word. *What could make that vivid shade of red?* she wonders.

"Well . . ." says Sicilee.

Kristin tilts her head, considering. "Too dark?" She holds her hand to the side of her face and turns to the mirror. "Maybe you're right. It's practically spring. Maybe

I should go for something lighter. You know, a more natural shade."

Just because it says that something is natural on the label doesn't mean that it is.

"Well . . ." says Sicilee.

"Not pink, though." Kristin lowers her voice so Ash won't hear her. "Pink is too babyish. I want something more sophisticated." This time, the tube she picks up is Key West Sunset. "What about this one?"

Just because something is named after something good doesn't mean that it is.

"Well . . ."

"I don't know . . ." Kristin is studying her face in the mirror. "Do you think my mouth's too thin?" she asks. She pouts. She smiles. She sucks in her cheeks. "Maybe I should get a lip plumper. That girl Lisette in my gym class? She said they really work."

Cosmetics are made of chemicals, not magic.

"Did she say how?" asks Sicilee.

Kristin turns around as quick as a gunslinger hearing a noise behind her. "What do you mean *how*?"

"You know . . . I mean . . . the thing is . . . well, you know . . . they don't really make your lips fuller, do they? So how do they make them puff up?"

Kristin frowns. "What are you talking about? They do make them fuller. That's the whole point."

"Yeah, but they can't really change the way your lips

274

are." Which is the point Kristin should be paying attention to. "So I just wondered if Lisette told you exactly *how* they work." She puts Blood Wedding back in the display.

"What's that?" Kristin's frown deepens with suspicion, her eyes on the box. "What are you up to? Why were you looking at that?"

"I'm not up to anything," says Sicilee. "I was just checking out the ingredients in that lipstick you were looking at — that's all."

"Oh, really?" Kristin slaps Key West Sunset down on the counter. "And why were you doing that?"

"Why do you think? I wanted to see what's in it."

"It's makeup," says Kristin. "Makeup's what's in it."

"Yeah, but what's makeup made of?"

Makeup is one thing no one had to tell Sicilee about. She looked it up herself. Not because she thought it could be loaded with anything dangerous or bad, but, ironically enough, because of Kristin's comment that not all toiletries and makeup are vegan. Sicilee looked at all the tubes, jars, and compacts spread across her dressing table, and she was curious. It had never before occurred to her to wonder what was actually in the things she rubbed into her skin and smeared over her face. How was it possible that her lipstick or shampoo wasn't vegan? Was there animal fat in her foundation? Milk in her eye shadow? Ground-up chicken feet in her mother's night cream? Did the sweetness of her lipstick come from honey? The sweetness of her lipstick turned out not to come from anything as benign as honey. Chicken feet were the least of the problems.

Kristin is now standing with a hand on one hip and her head to one side as though she has a chip of wood on her shoulder and is waiting for Sicilee to knock it off. "So what's in the lipstick?"

"To tell you the truth, I don't really know." The list of ingredients on the box is a long one, consisting mainly of things whose names are unpronounceable and unknown unless you have a degree in advanced chemistry. "But most of this stuff is made from petrochemicals, and lots of them have toxins and carcinogens and preservatives and—"

"You're telling me that I'm going to get cancer from my lipstick."

Sicilee laughs. "Of course not. All I'm saying is—"

"What's going on?" asks Loretta as she and Ash come to a stop between them.

"Oh, you guys'll want to hear this," says Kristin. "Sicilee was just telling me how all our makeup's poisonous."

Sicilee sighs and rolls her eyes. "I didn't say that. All I said was—"

"I thought we were here to have fun." Ash looks accusingly at Sicilee. "I thought you were dropping all

276

that never-washing-your-clothes-and-eating-bean-sprouts garbage."

"Talk about born-again Green," says Loretta. "You people can't leave anything alone, can you? You're fanatical. You always have to convert everybody."

"I'm not trying to convert anybody." Sicilee practically yelps with exasperation. "I'm just trying to—"

"Educate us?" asks Kristin.

"No. I'm just trying to say that if we're putting this stuff on our skin and everything, we should know what's in it. I don't see what the big crime is in that." Three very unsmiling, hard-eyed faces, swathed in petrochemicals and irritation, stare back at Sicilee. This should tell her that it's time to stop talking, but for some reason it just makes her talk more. "I mean, chemicals get into our food from plastics, right? So it just makes sense that they must get into us from makeup and stuff."

"You know, you really are losing the plot," says Ash. "You're like one of those conspiracy-theory freaks. Next thing you know, you'll be telling us that the world's ruled by giant lizards. I mean, you can't really think that these mega-companies are going to *poison* people? How sick is that?"

"Well, they—"

"You know everything, don't you?" Loretta sneers. "It's really pretty awesome how much smarter than us you are."

"In fact, I'm amazed you can stand to be seen with us, we're so stupid." Kristin picks up her bags. "Why don't you do us all a favor and go home by yourself, Sicilee?"

"But I came with you guys," protests Sicilee. "How am I supposed to get home?"

"Well, you're the big walker," says Loretta.

"Or even better," says Ash, "you can take the bus."

Sicilee does both. She takes the bus back to town, and then she stomps home from there. The rain has stopped, and the sun has broken through the clouds. Though not the cloud that hovers over Sicilee, of course. Why do her friends keep getting mad at her like that? What did she say? No, really. What did she say? That makeup's made with petrochemicals? Sweet Mary, she's not the one who put the petrochemicals in the lipstick or the eye shadow. Or in anything else. You'd think they'd thank her. You'd think they'd say, "Hey, thanks, Siss. We don't want to suck carcinogens into our bodies." Not tell her to walk home from the mall. Not get all snotty and attitudinal. It isn't fair. Why should she be punished for telling them the truth?

Sicilee's mind echoes with the bratty voices of her friends as she marches down the leafy, pleasant streets of Clifton Springs. *Go home by yourself. . . . You're the big walker. . . . Take the bus. Go home by yourself. . . . You're the big walker. . . . Take the bus.* Sicilee isn't sure whether she's more hurt than angry, or more angry than hurt. She refuses to cry. She's not going to give them the satisfaction. So involved is Sicilee in reliving the scene in the cosmetics department and in not crying that she doesn't realize that she isn't alone until something cold and wet suddenly touches her hand.

Sicilee jumps and screams. Behind her—though not far enough behind her—is a very large dog, drool dripping from his half-open mouth, looking at her as if he's deciding which part of her he wants to bite first. How long has he been walking with her? Since she left the village? Was there something beside her while she waited at that last set of traffic lights on Boyer? Something big enough to be ridden by a small child?

"Nice doggy." Sicilee smiles. "Good boy."

The dog's bark is like a small explosion.

"Stay!" Sicilee doesn't point—she doesn't want to give him an easy target like a finger—but her voice is the stern one she uses when her cat, Lucy, does something she shouldn't, like climb into the washing machine. "Stay!" She turns and starts walking again. The stern voice doesn't work on Lucy, either. The dog follows, his nose nudging toward her, his head so close she can feel his breath—warm, moist, and surrounded by teeth. Sicilee's heart beats faster. *Oh, great,* she thinks. *The perfect end to a really lousy day.*

"Go home," she orders. "Shoo."

She walks a little faster. The dog lopes behind her.

They turn a corner, and the Kewes' house is now in sight. The only time anyone has ever seen Sicilee run since she was ten is in gym class, where she is given no choice, but Sicilee starts to run now. The dog starts to run, too. Past Mr. Kreple in his driveway, vacuuming his car. Past the Larkins' little girl, blowing bubbles in their front yard. Past Mrs. Novatny, reading on her porch. Sicilee runs faster, and the dog bounds after her, barking excitedly, now in full pursuit. Does he think it's a game, or is he coming in for the kill?

Their next-door neighbor stops on her stoop when she sees Sicilee galloping toward her. "Hi there, Sicilee!" she calls. "Tell your mother—"

If Sicilee were capable of thinking, her thought would be *Tell her yourself!* but both thought and speech are beyond her at the moment. She speeds by without a glance and races up the path, wedging herself between the storm door and the front door for protection while she desperately rings the bell. The dog jumps up and down beside her as if he's confused himself with a performing dolphin. Her mother's not home! Sicilee digs into her pocket for her keys and pulls out the soggy napkin wrapped around her Hamburger of the Day from her soggy pocket. Sweet Mary! The dog didn't want to eat her; he wanted to eat her lunch! Someday, this story will make even Sicilee laugh, but right now all she feels is weak with relief. She hurls the hamburger onto the grass, and the dog joyously follows.

Thankful now that her mother isn't home to want to know what happened and make her talk about it, Sicilee goes to her room and throws herself onto her bed. Lucy immediately leaves her seat by the window and jumps up beside her, purring warmly, sprawling across her lap as if she has no bones. Sicilee rubs Lucy under her chin and behind her ears the way she likes best. Lucy closes her eyes and smiles, and Sicilee's pulse rate starts to return to normal; her fear and anger begin to fade.

It is Lucy who has loved Sicilee unconditionally since the day they brought her home from the animal shelter when Sicilee was six, Lucy who can make Sicilee smile no matter how blue she's feeling, Lucy who always comforts Sicilee when she's low, Lucy who trusts Sicilee without question, Lucy who would never hurt her. She's not just a cat. She's not even just a pet. She is Lucy Kewe, who loves to play with Sicilee's shoelace and eat corn on the cob. It is Lucy, Sicilee realizes—and not Kristin, Loretta, or Ash—who is her best friend. And in that moment of realization, Sicilee suddenly understands what Clemens has been trying to tell them all along. Not everything that's important is human. Not everything that's valuable can be bought.

It is now that Sicilee finally starts to cry.

Chapter Thirty-eight

The last person to leave doesn't have to turn out the lights

Maya slides a tray of soy nuggets into the oven and shuts the door. "OK," she mumbles to herself, "they'll be done in ten minutes. . . . I already put out the chips and pretzels. . . . I'll stick the nachos in the oven when everybody gets here."

She straightens up and looks around the kitchen with a satisfied smile. Normally, the Baraberras' kitchen looks pretty much like the kitchen of everyone else Maya knows—pleasant in a functional, here's-where-you-peel-the-potatoes kind of way. But right now it looks more like a wizard's den. Maya gives herself an excited hug. This has got to be one of the best ideas she's ever had.

On Saturday nights the gang always gets together, and tonight, because Mr. and Mrs. Baraberra and Molly have gone out, they are coming here. But Maya has planned something different from the usual. Instead of watching movies and putting on some music, tonight they will play board games and talk. Maya has decided that tonight is Be Kind to Our Planet Night, when the use of electricity is more or less restricted to the fridge. Instead of having virtually every light in the house on, Maya has put dozens of candles all over the living room and kitchen—tea lights in glass holders at the windows, *botánica* candles in jars decorated with pictures of saints, and more candles stuck in candlesticks and bottles over the counters, shelves, and tables. Which is why she's smiling like a girl who's reinvented cool. Maya thinks the candlelight is beyond beautiful—romantic, mystical, and mysterious, transforming the boring old kitchen and the boring old living room into places of timeless magic. But then her eyes fall on Alice, and she stops smiling. "Alice! Alice, what are you doing?"

What Alice is doing is kneeling on the floor by the open fridge, stirring salad-dressing mix into a bowl of tofu sour cream.

"I'm making the dip like you told me to. What do you think I'm doing?" Alice's patience is as exhausted as she is. If proof were necessary (which, to be honest, Alice never thought it was), she now knows for sure that it's a lot easier to flip a switch than it is to light thirty-nine-and-a-half candles.

"But you can't leave the door open like that," argues Maya. "You're wasting electricity." *Gott im Himmel,* the whole point of this evening is to *save* it. "Go back to the counter."

Alice, however, is obviously not as enthusiastic about tonight as Maya. Alice likes watching movies and being able to walk around without bumping into things. And she certainly doesn't think that she's in a place of romance, mystery, or magic. Alice thinks she's in a dim, gloomy room filled with shadows and threatening shapes where making a simple dip is a major challenge.

"But I can't *see* at the counter," she grumbles. "I wouldn't even recognize my own hand if it wasn't attached to my arm."

"Of course you ca—" Maya breaks off as someone, finally realizing that the doorbell isn't working, starts banging forcefully on the front door. "They're here!" She picks up the Santa candle left over from Christmas. "Get off the floor," she orders. "You put the nachos in the oven. I'll let everybody in."

Shelby, Mallory, and Finn start talking loudly to Maya as soon as they hear her bump into the hall table.

"Why don't you turn on the porch light?" grumbles Mallory. "I nearly broke my neck on the steps."

"You know your bell's not working?" asks Finn. "I've been ringing it for ages."

"Oh, my dears, please step in. . . ." Shelby intones as the door opens to reveal that there is little more light inside than outside. "Welcome to the House of Baraberra. You may enter, but of course you may never leave. . . . Hahahahahaha . . ."

"What's with the candles?" Finn squints into the darkness of the hallway. "You practicing witchcraft again?"

"They must've blown a fuse," says Mallory. "How many appliances are you running? Are you using the microwave? My mom always blows a fuse if she has, like, the dishwasher and the washing machine going and she uses the microwave."

"It's not a fuse," says Maya. Behind them, she can just make out Jason, Brion, and Shayla getting out of Mr. Tovar's car at the curb.

"Well, it's not a blackout," says Shelby, craning his head backward. "It's only your house. The rest of the street's OK."

"Could we just go in?" Mallory gives him a shove. "It's freezing out here." She looks at Maya. "You do have heat, right?"

"Sure, we have heat." Maya gestures them inside with Santa, spilling wax onto the carpet (though it is too dark for her to notice that, of course). "Come on in."

It takes them a few seconds to find the coat hooks, bumping into each other and treading on each other's toes.

"Darn!" Mallory stumbles on the step down into the living room. "I'm going to be lucky to get out of here alive. Why the hell don't you turn the lights on, Maya? Are you sure it's not a fuse?"

"Wow. A major fire hazard," says Shelby as he steps

into the romantic, mysterious, and magical flickering glow of the living room. "Your folks aren't going to be thrilled if you burn the house down while they're out."

"We should've brought some marshmallows," jokes Jason as he, Brion, and Shayla grope their way past Maya.

"Actually, I think it looks pretty cool," says Shayla. "Very beat, you know? Like, way out, man."

"You want me to change the fuse?" asks Mallory.

"There's nothing wrong with the fu—"

"Maya!" Alice shouts from the kitchen. "Maya! The timer! I can't find the pot holders!"

"I'll be right back." Maya trips over one of her sister's abandoned shoes as she hurries down the hall.

Brion is standing near the TV, holding a handful of DVDs, when Maya returns carrying the drinks, a plate of nuggets, and the bowl of dip.

"Which should we start with?" he's asking.

"How would I know? I can't see what they are," complains Mallory. "Why can't we turn on a light?"

"You didn't bring *Poltergeist,* did you?" Finn laughs. "Or that one about the guy who tries to burn down the whole town?"

Maya sets the tray on the coffee table so carefully that she only knocks over one candle, which Shelby, who has very quick reflexes, manages to catch before it hits the rug.

"You know, I was only kidding about the fire hazard."

Shelby peels wax from his hand. "But maybe we should put on the lights just in case."

"No." Maya sits down on the floor, shaking her head. "I thought it'd be fun if tonight we did without any extra electricity. You know, no lights, no TV, no stereo . . ." She can only hope that they can all see her warm, encouraging smile. "And no movies."

"You thought it'd be fun?" Shayla's frown defies the flickering shadows. "Why would you think that?"

"Because I want us to really consider the planet—just for one night. Earth Day's coming up, and—"

"For Pete's sake," groans Brion. "What is this, Revenge of the Geeks? Why didn't you tell us this before?"

"I thought it'd be a nice surprise."

"Maya," says Shayla, "a nice surprise is when someone buys you a present, not when someone invites you over to sit in a dark room doing nothing all night."

Brion wants to know where the napkins are. "You can't really eat chicken nuggets without napkins, you know."

Maya—who, of course, also isn't using single-use paper products tonight—tosses him the dish towel she's decided to use instead.

"Are you saying we're not watching movies?" Shelby picks up a nugget. "I mean, no napkins is one thing, but no movies? We always watch movies. What are we supposed to do if we don't watch movies?"

Slowly and unsurely, Alice comes in with the rest of

287

the snacks. "We're going to play games," she says with all the enthusiasm of someone announcing that it's time to count the paper clips in that five-gallon jar. Realizing that her tone doesn't sound quite as supportive or enthusiastic as she intended, she adds, "Or just talk."

"But we talk all the time at school," protests Jason.

"Games?" Finn sounds like a cat coughing up a hair ball. "Assuming that you don't mean night basketball, what kind of games do you have in mind?"

"There are tons of games we can play," says Maya. "Charades . . . Pictionary . . . dominoes . . ."

"Don't we have to be able to *see* to play games?" asks Mallory.

"These nachos aren't bad," says Brion. "What's the cheese? That's not that stuff in the jar, is it?"

"No," says Maya.

Jason bites into a nacho. "Hey, this *is* pretty good. What is the cheese? Jack?"

Alice stuffs some chips into her mouth.

"It's kind of like cheddar," says Maya.

Mallory sniffs at a nacho, taking a tentative nibble. "It doesn't smell like cheddar."

"I said *kind of*." Maya pours herself some soda.

"Kind of how?" asks Shelby.

Maya raises her glass to her lips. "Kind of like vegan cheddar."

Everyone looks at Maya in the dim, shadowy light.

"Vegan?" repeats Mallory. "You mean like it's not really cheese? What's it made from? Bean sprouts?"

"Ew . . ." Brion spits his sixth nacho into the dish towel. "I knew it tasted funny."

"And what about this?" Shelby is looking at his nugget as if it's about to bite him. "Has this ever had a beak?"

Maya shakes her head.

"And the dip?" asks Finn. "Is that sour cream?"

"The dip's vegan, too," admits Maya. "I told you, it's Be Kind to Our Planet Night. Vegan is much better for the planet than dairy or meat because—"

"So what *is* in this stuff?" Brion looks like he still wants to spit.

"Tofu."

"Brother, it's going to be a really long night," says Shelby.

As it turns out, the night isn't long at all. The candlelight proves to be inadequate for playing either Monopoly or Pictionary, so because everyone seems to feel that they need the stimulus of a movie they've seen before to have anything to talk about, they end up playing charades. After only one round the chip bowls are empty—though the abandoned nachos have solidified and the nuggets are cold—and Maya goes off to refill them. When she finally comes back, having unearthed a jar of salsa as well, the light in the entrance hall is on and everyone is getting ready to leave.

"Where are you guys going?" Maya holds out the jar of salsa like an offering. "Look, I found this."

"We're going over to my house," says Shayla. "You know, where we can actually see each other and can turn on the TV?"

Maya finally notices that Alice has also put on her coat. "You too?"

"I'm really sorry, Maya," says Alice, looking at the wax spill on the carpet. "But if I don't go with them, I won't get a ride, either. And my mother sai—"

"Yeah, right." Maya sighs. "You have to get home." She turns to Shayla. "I don't get it. I thought you said that the candles were cool. You know, beat. Way out, man."

"They are. It's very atmospheric." Shayla shrugs. "But not for *hours*. And only if you're listening to music or somebody reading poetry or something like that."

"Not for more than ten or fifteen minutes, if you want to know what I think." Jason gives Maya a wink. "Unless you're making out. That'd be different."

"I think ten or fifteen minutes is my limit, too," agrees Brion. "This sitting around in the dark is pretty dead. Especially when you can't see what you're eating."

"In this case, that's probably an advantage," says Finn.

Maya, however, is still having trouble taking in what's happening.

"But—but I thought we were having fun. We were all laughing. We were having a good time." No one responds.

Maya looks from one face to another but it is difficult to tell whether the blank expressions are due to lack of interest or poor lighting. "Weren't we having fun?"

"Yeah, sure we were," says Jason. "But, you know, Mr. Tovar's giving me a ride."

Followed by Finn saying, "And I really have to get something to eat. Something real." Finn's face is screwed up as though what he's eaten is something rotten. "I've got this yucky taste in my mouth."

"But I have plenty of chips." Maya waves the jar of salsa. "And this. Look! Regular salsa." She doesn't mention that, of course, it's vegan.

"You know we love you, Maya," says Mallory, "but you're really starting to wander off the road."

"You've just gone so bizarro," chimes in Shayla. "I mean, I wasn't going to say anything. . . ." Maya can tell from the way eyes are shifting that what Shayla means is that she wasn't going to say anything *to her*—she's already told everyone else. "But my mother said she saw you in Foodarama dressed as a plastic bag."

"I wasn't dressed as a plastic bag," explains Maya. "I represented the billions of bags and bottles that are thrown into landfills every year. I—"

Shayla shakes her head, sadly. "You used to be so cool."

"The curse of Clemens," says Finn.

"Or someone," mutters Jason.

You can lead your friends to tofu, but you can't make them eat, thinks Maya as she watches them drive away. She feels more deflated than angry. More disappointed than hurt. Though, really, there is no one to blame but herself. Shayla was right. She should have told them what she'd planned. But, of course, she didn't do that because she knew if she did that they wouldn't have come.

Maya sits in the living room, watching the shadows move across the room as if they're dancing. Maya is rarely completely alone, without the TV on or music playing, or the computer calling to her from its corner in her room. But tonight she is alone, and undistracted — the house is so silent.

Moonlight spills across the wooden floor. Maya's never seen moonlight in the house before. Getting to her feet, she leaves the living room and steps out on the front porch. It's a clear, cold night, the moon bright white. She walks out on the lawn, standing in the moonshine, looking up at the spangled sky.

Maya had a hard time with her eighth-grade project on what Clifton Springs was like before white people arrived. She could imagine the woods and the animals because she's seen them in wildlife programs. She drew some pretty good pictures of otters, skunks, beavers, deer, bears, and opossums, and even one of the river when it was full of salmon rather than beer and soda cans. But she had a lot of trouble with the Lenni Lenape themselves. She stared out the window of her classroom, trying to picture a hunting party or group of wood gatherers, but all she saw was the football field. She sat on the riverbank, trying to picture the village—the children playing, the women gathering reeds and grasses, a canoe gliding on the water, silent as a dragonfly—but all she saw was the highway behind the river, the smokestacks of the electric plant on the other side. Even she knew that the one drawing she managed of a Lenape owed a lot to a picture book about Hiawatha that she had when she was little.

But tonight she can see them. The houses fade; the road disappears; the sky grows glassy with stars. And it is as if the people who were part of this land walk through the night, soft-footed, laughing to themselves, whispering stories as they go.

Maya leans against the tree in the middle of the lawn, ears sharp, eyes open.

And time loses itself in thoughts and dreams that may, in fact, be memories.

Chapter Thirty-nine

Joy Marie drinks flowers, and Waneeda plants them

Joy Marie is sitting on Waneeda's bedroom floor, reading over the final list they've made of the Earth Day activities and events. She looks up as Waneeda backs in through the door, carrying a tray.

"It's incredible how everything's coming together," Joy Marie says. "Do you know that we have nearly fifty different things happening? Fifty! Half the town's participating. This really has to be the biggest thing the school's ever done."

Waneeda's smile has a little more acidity in it than you might expect. "So I guess the club's safe for the rest of the year."

"Are you kidding? Dr. Firestone couldn't shut us down now even if he still wanted to. Which he doesn't." Joy Marie leans back against the bed. "Ms. Kimodo says that Dr. Firestone says that the school's going to recommend us for an Environmental Youth Award. How good would that look on our college applications?"

Waneeda sets down the tray next to Joy Marie. "You mean that it'll look good on Cody Lightfoot's college applications. He's the one Firestone always makes the big deal over."

Joy Marie puts a hand to one ear and cocks her head as if listening. "Hark!" she cries. "Is that a note of bitterness I hear?"

Waneeda plops down across from her. "It's you and Clemens who should be bitter. You're the ones who did all the work getting the club started, and now Cody's getting all the credit."

"Get out!" Joy Marie laughs. "If it wasn't for Cody, you would never have joined in the first place."

Waneeda squashes her mouth together and shrugs. "I might have."

"Yeah, sure you would've. You and all the others."

"OK," concedes Waneeda, "so maybe it would have taken me a little longer. . . ."

"And anyway, that's not the point, is it?" There are two mugs on the tray. Joy Marie moves the nearer one closer. "The point is that Cody completely turned the club around. You can't deny that."

"That doesn't make it right that Cody's become the spokesperson for the club, though, does it?" Waneeda picks up the second mug. "Everything's all about *him*. Cody this and Cody that. *What does Cody think? What does Cody say?* Like he's the only one who says or does anything important. Like nothing counts unless Cody says so or it was his idea."

"We're talking about the trees again, aren't we?" says Joy Marie.

"Yes, we are." Waneeda plunks her cup back on the tray. "We're talking about the trees." While Cody Lightfoot's been getting his picture in the paper and being patted on the back by Dr. Firestone, Clemens and Waneeda (through sheer stubbornness) have gotten enough signatures on the petition to postpone the clearing of the oaks until May, when their fate will be decided by a second, public vote. "But no one says anything about that, do they? Nobody cares that we've actually managed to stop them from going ahead."

"And you're surprised?" Joy Marie makes a face. *And where have you been for the last sixteen years?* "You have to be realistic, Waneeda. The Earth Day celebration has a way bigger profile. People just don't get excited about a handful of trees."

"But it isn't fair."

"Fair, schmair." Joy Marie lifts her cup. "Cody's the driving force behind Earth Day, so that makes him high profile, too."

Indeed, just as Clifton Springs has started to emerge from the dark and bare-branched days of winter, Cody has emerged from being the new kid in school to being a campus star. Cody has only to be seen bringing his own ceramic cup to the coffee bar to have half the school doing the same. If his profile were any higher, he wouldn't be able to leave his house without a bodyguard.

Joy Marie sniffs her tea. "What is this? It smells like flowers."

"It *is* flowers. It's chamomile."

"Chamomile?" Joy Marie's smile is bemused. "I thought you were addicted to Coke. When did you start drinking herbal tea?"

Unblinking and unsmiling, Waneeda gazes back at her as if this is an unreasonable question. "Since I found out about the dangers of sugar and artificial sweeteners."

Rather graciously, Joy Marie doesn't point out that Waneeda could have made this discovery a year ago if she had ever listened to a word that Joy Marie said.

"Anyway, it's Cody who's done all the schmoozing, isn't it? Getting Dr. Firestone on our side and buttering up the faculty and getting all the big sponsors on board and everything." Joy Marie takes a sip. It is definitely chamomile tea. "It stands to reason that he'd get most of the credit."

Schmoozing, like delegating, is one of Cody's great talents. If Sicilee is someone who could talk a turtle out of its shell, Cody could probably talk it out of its skin and into a soup pot. Not only has he persuaded the local radio station to plug the Earth Day celebration every hour for the next two weeks, but he is also going to be interviewed about the club on *The Morning Show,* the most popular breakfast radio show in the county.

"While everybody else does all the real work," grumbles Waneeda. "Let's be honest here. It's all the girls who joined because of him who are making Earth Day happen. Like Sicilee and Maya with their popular supergirl powers—look how much money and donations they've raised! Half the workshops are their doing." And most amazing of all, they've stayed in the club, even though they must have figured out by now that Cody has no real interest in either of them. "I just don't think it's right," persists Waneeda. "Clemens is the president. And you're the vice president. You're both really smart and dedicated. And you're the ones who did all the hard stuff. How come you and Clemens aren't being interviewed?"

"You know I don't want to be interviewed. It's my idea of hell," says Joy Marie. "And nobody in their right mind would want to interview Clemens. You never know what he's going to say. Besides, Clemens looks like a geek, and Cody looks like a movie star."

"Um . . . duh, Joy Marie," says Waneeda. "It's *radio.*"

"OK . . ." Joy Marie smiles. "Then maybe they've heard about Clemens's speech last Earth Day, and they don't want to risk alienating their entire audience."

"Oh, ha ha ha." Waneeda scowls over her mug.

"The thing is that Cody's really charismatic." Joy Marie peers at the bowl on the tray. It seems to be filled with nuts and raisins. Was every store in Clifton Springs out of candy? "He'll probably grow up to be president."

"So I guess that means Clemens will be his entire cabinet," says Waneeda.

Joy Marie chews thoughtfully on a cashew. "He'll probably be vice president *and* secretary of state, too."

It isn't until she's getting ready to go that Joy Marie notices the egg cartons covered with plastic on top of the bookcase by the bedroom window. "What is that?"

"It's my nursery."

Joy Marie isn't sure whether this is a joke or not, so she only smiles with half her mouth. "Your nursery? You're hatching chicks?"

"Yeah. And next I'm going to get some burger boxes and grow cows." Waneeda peels back the plastic from one of the crates so Joy Marie can see the tiny seedlings underneath. "See?" She points to each box in line. "I have basil, corn, beans, zucchini, cucumbers, peppers, and tomatoes." She beams like a proud mother. "I've started a garden in the backyard. These'll be ready to go outside pretty soon. And then I'm going to plant some pumpkins. And some flowers, too. I already put some bulbs by the fence."

"You? You're growing vegetables and flowers?" Although by now she is certain that Waneeda isn't joking, Joy Marie laughs. "Waneeda, you've never grown anything in your life. Not even your nails."

"Well, now I am." She points out of the window. "Look! See, I've dug up the beds! And I've already planted the onions and potatoes. See there where I have those stakes in the ground?"

Joy Marie looks down at the freshly made beds where the grass used to grow. "You got down on your knees and dug all that up? Waneeda, you didn't used to *eat* vegetables, let alone grow them."

"It's very meditative," says Waneeda. "Plus, my parents are afraid of nature, so I get a lot of peace and quiet."

"What's happened to you?"

"I don't know." She doesn't. "But this growing thing is really incredible." Waneeda picks up an open packet from the bookcase and shakes a few seeds into her hand. She points at one of them. "Look at that, Joy Marie. That's going to be a tomato plant. Can you believe it? That tiny little dot is going to be a tomato plant. Don't you think that's amazing?"

Joy Marie's eyes move from Waneeda's hair, fluffed out around her head like a cloud, to the original Clemens Reis T-shirt she's wearing and, instead of her usual sweatpants, the long, floral skirt. "It's not the only thing that's amazing," says Joy Marie.

Chapter Forty

Spring brings more than bugs, buds, and birds

J oy Marie is out sick today, so Clemens and Waneeda are on their own for the walk to school.

Waneeda smiles into the shower of blossoms falling down on them like confetti as they near the school. "You know, I really love this time of year," she says. "Everything looks so pretty."

Everything looks so pretty, indeed. Spring has officially arrived, humming and buzzing, and dressed in blue skies and sunshine and swaths of green and bursts of blossoms. Even here, deep in the suburbs, where the roads are all paved and the houses trail one another up and down and back and forth like an army of ants, you can smell the new growth and feel the world busy as it emerges from its winter's rest.

Waneeda holds out a hand to catch some blossoms. "It's almost like the planet's getting all dressed up for Earth Day, isn't it?"

Not that long ago, Clemens's response to that question would have been that every day is Earth Day, but now what he says is, "I guess that I have to admit I was wrong." Not about the destruction of the planet, of course, but about things like the Earth Day celebration. They turn up the school drive. "I wasn't a hundred percent on board with Cody's ideas to start with, but now I'm kind of changing my mind. Maybe they're not as frivolous and shallow as I thought." Given all the enthusiasm and general hullabaloo, it has to be said that Cody's laid-back, just-turn-off-that-light method has more merit than Clemens imagined. "Not all of them, at least." And what, in the end, is wrong with making saving the world seem like fun? "Even all my parents' friends are coming to the fair, and the closest any of them get to anything green is playing golf."

"I guess Joy Marie was right," says Waneeda. "You catch more flies with organic, fair-trade honey than you do without."

"So maybe people really are starting to be aware, which is better than if they weren't." Clemens's smile shrugs. "Well, you know . . . a lot more aware than they were last year."

And last year—long before she freed her hair and exchanged her sweatpants for flowing skirts and started planting potatoes—Waneeda would have said, *Well, that wouldn't be hard.* But now what she says is, "Like me."

"Not like—" Clemens's sentence breaks off like a twig in a heavy wind and he stops short, squinting ahead of him in a who-stuck-the-Statue-of-Liberty-in-the-middle-of-the-track? kind of way. Only it isn't, of course, the Statue of Liberty that he sees.

"What are those men and trucks doing over there?" asks Waneeda. "Are those chain saws? Is that a *crane*?"

"They can't be," says Clemens. "We got a stay of execution. They can't do anything until after the vote, and that's like a month away."

Needless to say, he doesn't go on to say what else the things they see might be if they aren't men, trucks, chain saws, and a crane. Instead, he starts moving again, slowly, as though it's been a few weeks since he used his legs, but now he is walking not toward the school but the huddle of trees near the tennis court.

"We got all those signatures," Clemens mumbles. "We won the appeal. . . ."

It is Waneeda who starts to run.

Chapter Forty-one

Clemens makes a spontaneous decision

The beauty of this day hasn't been lost on Maya or Sicilee, either. Maya has been taking her time this morning, pedaling slowly and enjoying the sunshine and the new-green breeze, and Sicilee has stopped twice—once to pet Bob the Jack Russell and once to watch the ducklings on the pond. It is safe to say that, despite the fact that neither of them has seen any snails this morning or would recognize a lark if it landed on her head, today both Sicilee and Maya are inclined to agree with Robert Browning that all is pretty right with the world.

This is not an opinion they are going to have for long.

They arrive at the entrance to the campus within seconds of each other. Like dogs trained to associate the clinking of a metal bowl with supper, the sight of the school immediately makes both Maya and Sicilee think of Cody Lightfoot. Out of habit rather than hope, Sicilee pauses at the bottom of the drive to smooth out her skirt and check her makeup in the tiny compact she keeps in her pocket. Also out of habit rather than hope, Maya glides to a stop behind her, getting off her bike and smiling to herself as she takes off her helmet and runs her fingers through her hair.

It is as she's about to stride past Sicilee that Maya notices Clemens and Waneeda, walking slowly in the wrong direction. Where are they going? Neither of them is likely to have a game of tennis or a run around the track before the first bell. And then she sees the men and the machines over at the edge of the school grounds.

"Do you see that?" In her surprise at what it is she sees, Maya forgets that she doesn't usually speak to Sicilee unless it's snidely or totally unavoidable. But the sight of the stump grinders, saws, and cranes is as shocking to her as finding a bunch of white men on their land must have been for the Lenni Lenape. "They're going to cut down those trees!"

Sicilee looks over. "But they can't do that. We all signed Clemens's petition. The town's going to have a vote."

Maya tightens her grip on the handlebars. "Then what do you think those chain saws are for?"

"But they can't be going to cut down those trees," Sicilee says again — as if just the repetition will make it true. She is experiencing one of those moments when even though you know what is happening, you don't want it to happen with such an intensity that you refuse to believe that it is. "There must be some other explanation."

"And what's that? They're going to mow the lawn?" In the distance, Waneeda suddenly starts to run. By now, Maya, too, has heard enough of Clemens's arguments for saving the trees to have been persuaded. She rolls her bike forward. "I'm going to see what's going on."

Sicilee snaps her compact shut. "I'm coming with you."

Clemens is talking to the foreman, a large, bored-looking man in a yellow vest and matching hard hat. Waneeda stands beside him, looking like she's about to lose her temper. The other men in the crew, likewise dressed in yellow vests and matching hard hats, lean against their trucks, drinking coffee from paper cups and looking amused.

Clemens's voice, though calm, is strong and clear, as though he is not a skinny boy in baggy corduroys and a faded flannel shirt over one of his homemade T-shirts, but a grown man himself, bursting with righteousness and reason.

"You're not listening to me," Clemens is saying. "These aren't *just* trees. They represent every single thing that we've destroyed on this planet. Every animal, bird, fish, insect, and plant that's vanished from the Earth forever because we thought it was our right to do whatever we wanted with them. Because we wanted to wear their skins to show off our wealth. Because we hunted out of greed, not need. Because we wanted the land where they lived to build something that we'd then rebuild in twenty years."

"Whoa . . . whoa . . ." The foreman holds up his hands, palms out. "I think you're getting a little carried away here, son."

"You're the ones who are getting carried away," says Clemens. "Look at you!" One hand sweeps across the huddle of trucks, equipment, and men. "You look like soldiers. Man used to be in harmony with nature, not at war with it. These trees are a reminder of that. They're a symbol. They're a warning. They—"

"I know, I know." The foreman's sigh is as heavy as the thud of a felled oak. "I heard you the first time. But like I've been trying to tell you, none of that crap cuts any ice with me or my men. We have a job to do."

"But they promised to reconsider," Clemens fairly wails. "We got thousands of signatures. The town council agreed to have another meeting."

"Well, I guess they had their meeting without you," says the foreman. "Because I've got my orders. Those trees are coming down."

"Do you always follow orders?"

Clemens and Waneeda turn around to see Sici-lee, looking like a walking garden in her floral suit and matching shoes, striding toward them. The foreman, of course, has only to raise his eyes over their heads to see the unlikely source of this outburst.

But the next outburst comes from Maya.

"Would you follow orders if you were told to burn down the school?" she says, wheeling the pink-and-blue bike to a stop beside Waneeda.

The men leaning against the trucks snigger softly; the foreman gives another of his dead-tree sighs.

"Look, ladies," he says, "as I've been trying to tell your friends here, I'm not the one you've got the beef with. I don't make the decisions. I just carry them out."

"But you can't cut down these trees." Sicilee doesn't come to a stop but continues walking until (because the shoes decorated in flowers are four-inch platforms) she is staring the foreman right in the eye. "Do you know how *old* these trees are?"

"Five hundred years. At least." The foreman sounds so weary you'd think he'd been alive for those five hundred years himself. "And before you get going, I know all about how if they could talk they'd tell us all about the Indians and the pigeons and what Paul Revere looked like and how we should eat berries and not McDonald's and stuff like that. But they can't talk, honey. No matter what your friend thinks, they're just trees."

"There is no such thing as 'just trees,'" contradicts Sicilee. "Trees store carbon dioxide. Every time you cut one down, you release those emissions into the atmosphere. You—"

"Don't you kids hear right? They're going to plant *more* trees. More trees than we're taking down."

"But these trees are special," snaps Waneeda. "They're living history."

"Not for much longer they aren't," says the foreman.

All the other men laugh in a way that even those who love them most would call unkind.

Although Dr. Firestone may see Clemens as a hot-headed activist, in reality he has always been more of an eco-worrier than an eco-warrior. He watches the documentaries and reads the books and articles; he makes T-shirts and writes letters and instigates petitions. But, except for joining one climate-change march last spring (carrying a sign that said: THERE IS NO PLANET B), that's all he's done. Until now.

"Oh, yeah?" What's the sense of only talking if all your talk is going to get you is lies or laughter? "We'll see about that." And Clemens turns and hurls himself at the nearest tree, wrapping his arms around it as far as they'll go.

The crew erupts in whoops of laughter.

"Whoowhee!" shouts one of the men. "Looks like we got ourselves a real tree hugger here."

"Too bad you can't get your arms around it!" shouts another.

"Ah, geez . . ." The foreman groans. "Don't start with this crap, sonny. We can pick you off that tree like you're no bigger than an ant."

Waneeda takes a step forward. "We know our rights," says Waneeda. "You lay a hand on him and we'll have you for assault."

"Christ . . ." The foreman pushes his hat back on his head and wipes his forehead with his sleeve, as though he already knows just how long and difficult this day is going to be. "Look, we don't want any trouble. Just come away from the trees and go to your classes and we'll forget this ever happened."

"Forget *what* ever happened?" asks Sicilee.

"Nothing's happened — yet," adds Maya.

The foreman pulls his phone from his pocket. "I'm gonna have to call the cops, you know."

"What are they going to charge us with?" asks Clemens. "Trespassing on school property?"

Chapter Forty-two

Dr. Firestone isn't the only one up a tree

It isn't the police who are called first, but Dr. Firestone.

He marches across the campus in his dark gray suit, brightened by a tie that is a tumble of flowers startlingly similar to the pattern on Sicilee Kewe's linen suit. As this is a serious matter, calling for all his years of professional experience, Dr. Firestone isn't smiling, but he looks no more worried than a man whose breakfast has been disturbed by the buzzing of a fly. Dr. Firestone doesn't want to call the police. Police at a high school never make parents or school boards feel good about the school or the way it's being run. And now, of course, is an especially delicate time, with the new budget coming up for a vote. Dr. Firestone, however, is sure that there's no need for law enforcement. It is, after all, only Clemens Reis, born troublemaker, going off the deep end as usual — once more disrupting the smooth running of the machine that is Clifton Springs High School (as well as the machines that have come to bring down the small grove of oaks). Clemens, though a thorn in Dr. Firestone's side, is a thorn he feels he can pull out by himself.

The foreman walks out to meet him, and he and Dr. Firestone stop together some distance from the target of trees, the yellow hard hat leaning toward the principal's graying head as they discuss the situation in low voices.

By now, of course, the situation is a little more complicated than it was originally. Instead of one scraggly boy plastered against the trunk, Clemens has been joined beneath the ancient oak by Waneeda, Sicilee, Maya, and Maya's bicycle. Dr. Firestone had assumed from what he'd been told over the phone that Clemens was by himself. A lone voice crying not in the wilderness but at the tennis courts, easy enough to drown out. Still, although he hasn't looked at them closely, Dr. Firestone can see that the three other figures under the trees are all girls. Girls, in Dr. Firestone's opinion, do not lead rebellions. So no problem there.

Nodding, Dr. Firestone straightens up, pats the foreman's shoulder in a don't-worry-I'll-take-care-of-this way and walks calmly but authoritatively toward the trees and their protectors.

"Well, well, Mr. Reis, fancy seeing you wrapped around a tree." Dr. Firestone is not a man to waste a smile, but the corners of his mouth do twitch. "I was under the impression that your views had matured in the last few months. That you'd learned some moderation. . . ." He shakes his head, as if sad to find that another illusion has been shattered by the hammer of time. "But I see we're back to our old extreme methods."

The corners of Clemens's mouth don't twitch at all. "I'm not being extreme, Dr. Firestone. I'm employing direct action. You know, like the Boston Tea Party? Those guys didn't have any sense of moderation, either."

Dr. Firestone is not about to get into a debate about historic protest movements with Clemens. They could be here all morning. "I hope you're not seriously comparing yourself to our Founding Fathers, Mr. Reis."

"Of course not," says Clemens. "I have no intention of taking up arms."

Dr. Firestone shifts his attention to someone he considers easier to deal with. Maya Baraberra is just the type to think that wrapping herself around a tree is cool, but she is also the type who is more about image than principles. "I must say, Ms. Baraberra, I'm surprised to see you here." The shadow of a smile flickers across Dr. Firestone's face. "It's not like you to break the rules. I'd expect you to be in class by now."

"I would've been in class," says Maya in a way that makes the principal wonder why he's always thought of her as a model student. "Only they decided to chop the trees down today after promising that they wouldn't, so I'm here instead."

Dr. Firestone blinks. "I see. . . ." He shifts his attention once again, still hopeful that he'll find someone who isn't determined to give him a hard time. Waneeda has always been so much a part of the background in school life that he has no idea who she is, which makes her at least a possibility. "Well, well," he says, his eyes on her. "I've never known *you* to cause any trouble before."

"We're not causing trouble." Waneeda's expression is the facial equivalent to digging your heels in the ground. "It's the tree crew that's causing the trouble."

Dr. Firestone isn't listening. His gaze falls on the last protester with a jolt of surprise. "Ms. Kewe!" Finding Sicilee among the troublemakers, looking like she's just stepped out of the pages of *Teen Vogue,* is no less astonishing than finding the First Lady knocking down pins at Clifton Springs Lanes would be. And she looks happy to see him! "What in heaven's name are you doing here?"

"I'm saving the planet, of course." Sicilee's hair swings over her shoulder like a beam of sunshine. "That's why we're all here."

"Is it?" Lulled into a false sense of security because he isn't aware that Sicilee smiles the way others breathe, Dr. Firestone rocks back and forth very gently. "Well, I'm sure that's very commendable . . . very commendable, indeed. You know that I like to encourage our students to participate in the larger world. But I'm afraid that at the moment you're not actually saving the planet, Ms. Kewe.

What you're doing, I'm afraid, is causing a nuisance and an obstruction."

"You have no right to cut down these trees," says Clemens.

"But we aren't just cutting them down, son." Dr. Firestone shakes his head at such a foolish misconception. "You may not be aware, but the council has promised to plant three trees elsewhere in town for every one tree that's removed here."

"Five-hundred-year-old trees?" asks Waneeda.

Dr. Firestone chuckles as if he's delighted to find that she has a sense of humor.

"But we presented a petition," argues Clemens. "We've lodged an official appeal. We're supposed to be waiting for the meeting in May to have a second vote."

"Oh, I see. . . ." Dr. Firestone's smile relaxes a little. All is clear. He understands. "I'm afraid there's been a terrible oversight. I don't know how it could have happened. You should have been informed that the appeal was rejected after all. The decision to go ahead was made in a special session of the town council."

A connection exists between Clemens, Waneeda, Maya, and Sicilee, due to the fact that they all belong to the same club. But up until this moment it has been a superficial connection at best—no more significant, really, than the connection between a random group of people, all of whom like root beer or peanut-butter-and-banana sandwiches. Now, however, thanks to the hypocrisy and deceit of the town council, the school board, and the administration, their connection takes on a new depth. Clemens, Waneeda, Sicilee, and Maya all exchange the same look. *Who the hell does he think he's kidding?* Such is the power of flagrant injustice to forge bonds.

"But that wasn't the deal," says Maya.

"Oh, but I think that if you look back at the records, you'll find that it was." It is one of Dr. Firestone's natural gifts that he always sounds reasonable and right—even when he is actually being neither. "Everything was agreed months ago. Long before your little petition."

"No, that's not true," says Waneeda. "The deal was that there was going to be public consultation and debate."

Dr. Firestone shrugs helplessly. *Don't blame me,* his expression seems to be saying. "Well, I'm afraid that the opportunity was there, but no one availed themselves of it. And now it's too late. The council's decided to go ahead with the sports complex. As planned and previously agreed."

Even Sicilee is looking serious by now. "And?"

"And I would like you all to get out of the way and let these men do their job." Dr. Firestone bestows on them one of his PTA smiles. P-r-i-n-c-i-*p-a-l,* as he likes to say. The principal is your pal.

"What if we won't?" asks Waneeda.

As if by some unspoken agreement the girls all move closer to one another.

"Yeah," chorus Maya and Sicilee. "What if we won't?"

"Ladies . . ." purrs Dr. Firestone. "I'm sure that you don't want any trouble at this juncture in your high-school careers."

"But what if *I* do?"

The principal frowns at the three girls in front of him. And then he looks up. He hadn't noticed Clemens scrambling into the tree.

Chapter Forty-three

Last man standing

After Dr. Firestone (muttering threats and promising to make Clemens regret his rash behavior) storms off to confer with the foreman again, Clemens climbs a little higher, demonstrating a physical agility of which only Mrs. Huddleston, who has seen him scamper over her back fence on more than one occasion recently, was aware. He'll never get back down without help or breaking a leg, of course, but that's a small price to pay for the annoyance he's causing. Serves them all right for being so untrustworthy. From his perch, Clemens can see Dr. Firestone and the foreman, standing side by side, both holding their cell phones as if they're grenades. Dr. Firestone has been on and off his phone any number of times since he took up his position next to the foreman. Who did he call? The police? The National Guard? Mr. and Mrs. Reis? *Come and get your son out of this tree or the only college he'll get into will be in Peru?*

It isn't long before a crowd starts to gather. People walking past stop to see what's going on. Neighbors, noticing the groups of onlookers, come out to see what they're looking at. Passing cars slow down and then pull over. Within mere minutes, the number of people with dogs, toddlers, their bedroom slippers still on, or leaning against vehicles on Greaves Road, could be in the *Guinness World Records*. Clemens looks down through the lacework of leaves on the growing throng and smiles. An audience is what he needs. Publicity. Witnesses. Complications. It's too bad he didn't think of this before.

Clemens leans against the trunk, more being held than holding on, enjoying the feeling of being in the sky—wondering who else has sat up here to think or dream and what they saw. Not someone arriving with a tray of coffees in paper cups and a box of doughnuts for the men determined to destroy this tree, that's for sure.

Clemens sighs. It really is too bad that he didn't think of it before. There are a lot of good things about spontaneity, but now he realizes that there are a few drawbacks he didn't think about in the heat of the moment. There have been tree sit-ins that have lasted more than a year, but those demonstrations were planned in advance, based on strategy, not impulse. Clemens, of course, acted on the spur of the moment. He's made no preparations. He has no plan. How long does he really think his demonstration can last? It could get a little lonely, sitting in

319

a tree—no matter what its age or how many its memories—not to mention uncomfortable. He has no food or water, no bathroom, nowhere to sleep. What happens if it rains? What if, in this age of climatic uncertainty, the temperature suddenly drops or a freak tornado hits Clifton Springs? The girls have positioned themselves close to the base of the tree as guards, but Clemens knows that if he leaves the tree even for a few minutes, when he returns, Waneeda, Sicilee, and Maya will have been taken away, and there'll be no getting back up. Making his great act of rebellion no more than an empty gesture.

And then he sees a tall, lean figure, coatless and bagless, nonchalantly strolling across the school grounds.

Clemens leans down through the leaves. "Here comes Cody!" he hisses. Clemens is so used to being a minority of one that it didn't even occur to him that as soon as Cody heard about what was happening he'd walk out of the building and join him. Thank God. And Cody always has some scheme or angle. He always has a plan. "Here comes Cody!" The cavalry is on its way.

The girls have been standing close together, tense and angry and uncertain, not knowing what to expect and not knowing what to do should anyone try to move them away. But at the sight of Cody they immediately relax. Like Clemens, they think that Cody is here to help.

Sicilee claps her hands. "I knew he'd show up. He'll make them understand."

"Dr. Firestone listens to him," says Maya.

"Dr. Firestone *likes* Cody," says Waneeda.

Cody gives them one of his loose, hey-man waves as he ambles across the lawn, and they all wave back. But he doesn't so much as glance toward the trucks, where the principal and the foreman are smiling slightly over their coffees.

"Doesn't he have to talk to them to make them understand?" Waneeda asks as Cody fails to make the crucial change of direction. "How come he's coming over here?"

"Maybe he wants to talk to Clemens and us first," suggests Maya. "You know, so he knows where we're coming from."

Waneeda frowns. "Shouldn't he know that already?"

Which is, of course, a good point.

The reason Cody doesn't go directly to Dr. Firestone to dazzle him with his logic and persuasive eloquence is because he and the principal have already spoken, in some detail and at some length. After Clemens took to the tree and the girls gathered at the base, Dr. Firestone had Cody pulled from his homeroom to speak to him on the phone. "Clemens is your friend," said Dr. Firestone. "See if you can't talk some sense into him. The last thing I want to do is have to bring the police into this. Tell him that. Make him understand that I'm thinking only of him. This kind of thing isn't going to look good on his record, you know." Dr. Firestone would hate to see Clemens's future ruined over something as childish as climbing a tree. Cody Lightfoot is not someone whose view of the world is ever obscured by anyone else. His interest in the Environmental Club has always been as much about what it could do for him as what he could do for it. And so, as he approaches the huddle by the tree, what he's thinking about is the other thing Dr. Firestone would hate to see happen besides the destruction of Clemens Reis's future. "You've put so much time and effort into the Earth Day preparations, Cody," added the principal. "It'd be a real shame if that was jeopardized because of a stunt like this."

As he nears them, Sicilee, Waneeda, and Maya surge forward to meet him, all talking at once.

Can you believe that they're doing this? They lied through their teeth. . . . They're, like, totally going back on their word. . . . Thank God you're here. . . . You have to help Clemens. . . . You have to make Firestone listen to reason. . . .

"Whoa, whoa, whoa." Cody laughs, good-humored and affable even in a crisis. "I know all about it."

"Who told you?" asks Waneeda. "Has the rest of the club heard, too?"

Although two questions have been asked, Cody answers neither. "You know what they say," says Cody. "Good news travels fast, but bad news travels faster."

"People are always sitting in trees in California, right?" asks Maya. "What do we do next?"

"I think you should talk to Firestone," says Sicilee. "See if you can't get him to call a truce."

Cody shakes his head. "The man I want a word with is our brother in the tree."

"But Sicilee's right," protests Maya. "If you talk to Dr. Firestone first—"

"We're counting on you to make him change his mind," interrupts Waneeda. "He listens to you."

Cody raises his hands like a speaker trying to still the applause. "What we all have to do here is be reasonable and calm." He lowers his voice and winks in such a way that each of them thinks he's winking at her. "We wouldn't want Clem to fall out of that tree." And then he pushes through them until he is standing directly under the branch where Clemens sits like a very large squirrel. "Hey, my man!" Cody gazes up. "What're you doing up there?"

Clemens stops smiling. "What do you think I'm doing?"

"You're missing first period—that's what you're doing." Cody laughs so Clemens will know that he's joking. "And you're annoying the hell out of Dr. Firestone and those dudes with the trucks."

"Good." Clemens doesn't join in the laughter. "Because they're absolutely annoying the hell out of me."

Cody nods, but it is not, of course, a gesture of agreement. "Thing is, bro," he says slowly, almost drawling,

"I think you kind of have to look at it from their point of view, you know? The reality is that they're not against *you*, dude. They're just doing what they do."

Clemens's eyes narrow. "Which means?"

"Which means they're not persecuting you or your trees. They're just doing their jobs."

"They're just doing their jobs?" repeats Clemens. Now he does laugh. "So I take it you didn't come out here to join me, is that right?"

"No can do." Cody makes a helpless gesture, not a million miles away from the one made by Dr. Firestone not so very long ago. "I'm not saying that I think you're wrong or anything, Clem. You're right in the footsteps of a noble tradition. Civil disobedience is part of our history, right? It's one of the things that's made us a symbol of hope for the downtrodden and the oppressed. That whole no-taxation-without-representation scene . . . the suffragists . . . Martin Luther King. . . . But it's not always the coolest thing to do. And I think this is one of those times when you have to go with the flow, not swim against the current."

Although Cody isn't looking at them, Waneeda, Maya, and Sicilee are all looking at him. Sicilee and Maya, who have hoisted Cody on a pedestal of dreams, are clearly shocked to watch him not simply fall off, but jump. Even Waneeda, whose feelings for Clemens have made her critical of Cody, looks surprised and somewhat shocked.

"Excuse me." Waneeda taps him on the shoulder. "Are you saying that you think we should just give up? After all the work Clemens put into this?"

Cody doesn't turn around. "Don't think of it as giving up," he says to Clemens. "Think of it as recognizing that this is one of those times that you just can't win."

"Wait a minute." Maya moves closer. "What happened to protecting the Earth being the most important thing anyone can do? What happened to that?"

Cody still doesn't turn around. "You can always fight another day," he shouts up through the leaves. "But you've got to pick battles you know you can win."

"Excuse me," says Sicilee. "Maybe I misunderstood you, but I could swear I heard you say that principles are more important than opinions."

Even the fact that Sicilee is standing on his foot doesn't make Cody glance over at her. "I mean, let's be practical here, Clem," he goes on. "You have no food, no water, no shelter, no bathroom. So you have to come down from there eventually. Probably sooner rather than later. And then it's going to be boom, boom, chop, chop—*adiós*, ancient vegetation."

Maya grabs him by the arm. "But that's no reason for us just to give up right away," she insists. "The least we can do is put up a fight."

Cody finally looks over at her. "I like your spirit," he says, sounding remarkably like an adult telling a child that he really likes the necklace they've made out of pasta tubes colored with poster paints. "I really do. Just like I admire Clemens's spirit. But you're missing the dock here and going straight into the marsh."

Only yesterday Maya would have said that Cody Lightfoot could never irk or annoy her. She would have been wrong, of course.

"Why can't you just speak English?" she snaps. "What's 'going straight into the marsh' supposed to mean?"

"It means that you're not looking at the bigger picture." Cody himself is looking at Clemens again. "There's more at stake here than a couple of trees."

"Fifteen," says Sicilee. Fifteen trees that were old when her great-great-grandfather, just a child, was getting on the ship to America.

"Fifteen trees that can never be replaced," adds Waneeda.

"What bigger picture?" says Clemens. Cody's face gazes up at him like a reflection in a pool, but it isn't the reflection of anyone Clemens recognizes. It's certainly not a reflection of himself. "These trees are symbolic of the thousands of trees being cut down every day all over the world. How much bigger can the picture get?"

"Think of the club, man," Cody urges. "Think of Earth Day. All the work we've done . . . all the goodwill and support we've built up . . . all the publicity. Everybody loves us."

Some people are starting to love him a little less.

"*Loves us?*" sneers Maya. "What happened to loving the planet? When did we ditch that?"

"Earth Day?" repeats Sicilee. "The bigger picture is *Earth Day?* I thought the bigger picture was the Earth."

Waneeda doesn't tap Cody's shoulder this time. She thumps it. "What are you talking about, all the work *we've* done? You haven't done any work. All you ever do is talk. Just like you're talking now."

It's as if Waneeda has knocked down the first domino in the wall that made Cody seem perfect.

"Goodwill? Support?" Sicilee's laugh is stretched and high. "It's me and Maya and the others who've gotten all the support. All the goodwill. I didn't see you trudging all over town getting donations."

"And I got just as much publicity as you," says Maya. "I'm the one who had her picture on the front page of the *Clifton Springs Observer.* 'Supporters Rally Around Plastic Girl.' I'm the one who was ridiculed and almost arrested."

But it's as if all their words are no more than the rustle of leaves.

"Can't you see that it's going to mess up everything if you don't get down from there?" Cody pleads. "You're making us all look like a bunch of lunatic Earth Libbers, Clem. You're making us look bad."

Clemens gives a strangled laugh. "No, *you're* making *us* look bad."

Cody ignores him. "We're going to lose everything here." He has never sounded so passionate nor so sincere. "Dr. Firestone'll shut us down faster than you can say *ecological disaster*. Don't you care about the club?"

"Don't you?" asks Maya. "OK, maybe you don't want to get up there with Clemens, but you could at least give him some moral support."

"Like what?" Cody's laid-back charm has started to fray. "Hold hands around the tree with you guys, singing 'We Shall Overcome'?"

"Don't worry—you won't be holding hands with me." Although Waneeda has been described as a large and lumpen girl whose movements bring to mind the bear more than the chimpanzee, she suddenly grabs the lowest branch and swings herself into the tree.

"Or me!" Maya scrambles after her.

"You guys aren't leaving me down here." Sicilee, the girl guaranteed to be voted most sophisticated of her graduating class, hauls herself up after the others in her one-hundred-percent-organic linen designer suit. Her floral platform shoes fall to the ground, narrowly missing the head of Cody Lightfoot, the only one left standing under the tree.

"That's it!" Dr. Firestone comes running toward them, waving his cell phone. "Now you've really gone too far. I'm calling the police."

"That's fine by me," says Sicilee.

"Me too," says Maya.

Each of them already holds her own phone in her hand.

"For God's sake," groans Clemens, "can't you two go a few minutes without calling someone? What are you going to say? That you're in a tree?"

Sicilee ignores him. "I'm calling my mother." Her voice is loud and clear, and her smile is lodged on Dr. Firestone like a laser beam. "She knows a lot of people in the media."

"And who are *you* calling?" Dr. Firestone demands of Maya. "Don't tell me that your mother knows a lot of people in the media, too."

"No, not one," says Maya. "But her brother's a lawyer."

Chapter Forty-four

The spell's been broken

It is a bright and unseasonably hot afternoon. The sun shines down from a cloudless sky, making the noisy crowds below seem to shimmer. The blue and green balloons and flags that decorate Clifton Springs High School on this special day sway in a well-mannered breeze, and the sounds of people celebrating the existence of their planet fill the air.

Sicilee, Kristin, Loretta, and Ash sit together at one of the tables set up in the courtyard, talking and laughing excitedly—and often at the same time. In honor of the occasion, each of them is wearing one of Clemens's handmade T-shirts, and they all look as if they're enjoying themselves. They are best friends again.

Cody Lightfoot was wrong. His prediction that the tree protest would destroy the Environmental Club, cause Earth Day to be canceled, and heap ridicule, embarrassment, and derision on Clemens and anyone foolish enough to join him turned out to be so far from the truth it was in another country. Ms. Kimodo, on the other hand, was right. Ms. Kimodo, also summoned by the principal, arrived only minutes after Sicilee, Maya, and Waneeda joined Clemens in the tree. Ms. Kimodo, unlike Cody, immediately gave the tree-sitters her support. "I'm sorry, Dr. Firestone," said Ms. Kimodo, "but not only do I feel that these students have both legal and moral right on their side, I think you'll find that the community as a whole will stand behind them, too. I know I certainly do." Which is what happened. Thanks, in large part, to Mrs. Kewe's many friends in the media and Maya's Uncle Fabio, the protest forced the tree cutting to be abandoned and made celebrities of Maya, Clemens, Sicilee, and Waneeda.

The press arrived before the police — setting up their cameras and recorders, pulling out notebooks, sticking microphones in the faces of anyone who didn't move out of the way. Dr. Firestone, as unprepared for them as he would have been for the ghost army of Genghis Khan, was surprised to find himself cast as the villain. He was no longer, apparently, anyone's pal. He was a man who broke promises. A man who tried to have students who had Law and Right on their side arrested. A man who showed no respect for either history or the environment. "An Unlikely Group of Eco-Warriors Puts Principles Ahead of the Principal" read one headline. "Brought Together by Love not Dogma" read another. Clemens, Waneeda, Sicilee, and Maya were treated as heroes—photographed, interviewed, and even singled out for special praise by the governor of the state for their courage and character. Sicilee herself was featured on the six o'clock news, leaning comfortably against an ancient trunk and looking (as the reporter pointed out) not like a fanatical environmentalist but a model on a magazine shoot. "Is this the face of anarchy?" asked the anchor as he introduced the story. "Or is this the face of the next generation, demanding its right to a future?" All of which has made Sicilee even more popular than she was before. Celebrities are forgiven a lot.

At the moment, Sicilee is sipping an organic tea, Kristin is finishing her veggie burger, Loretta is rearranging her environmentally friendly purchases, and Ash is nibbling a vegan cookie that, against all predictions, doesn't taste like sand.

Earlier, they watched the day's first screening of a documentary on climate change, presented by Clemens (who everyone agreed was a lot nicer and far less creepy than they'd thought).

"That movie really makes you think, doesn't it?" says Ash. "I never knew all that stuff about the glaciers and the polar bears and everything."

Sicilee makes a face over her cup, though there is nothing wrong with her tea. "At least the polar bears weren't hanging by one foot from a meat hook being clubbed."

Sicilee was on the committee that chose the films to be shown today and sat with her eyes closed or filled with tears through the one on meat production.

"Stop!" orders Kristin. "I don't want to hear any more about that. It's really gross."

Finished with her cookie and her movie review, Ash sniffs at the plant she bought her mother for her birthday. "It reminds me of something." She frowns, wrinkling her nose. A balloon that looks like the Earth seen from space waves above her head. "But I can't think what."

Kristin, too, is looking thoughtful. "You know, this burger isn't so bad." She sounds surprised. "I know it's supposed to be really good because no animals were tortured and it saved the planet a ton of water and cow farts and everything, but it actually tastes OK. I mean, with the mayo and ketchup and pickles and everything, you wouldn't really know it wasn't real if no one told you."

"Oh, um, duh . . ." Sicilee rolls her eyes, but she is laughing. "Sweet Mary, what have I been trying to tell you guys?"

"OK, OK." Loretta, too, is laughing. "I'm not going to, like, start eating tofu, but some of this Green stuff's not so bad. It's not all bean sprouts and Jesus sandals." She pats the shopping bag (hemp, not plastic) on her lap. "I got some pretty awesome things today. That velvet top with the crushed flowers? It's, like, perfect for Rupert's party next week."

"Merciful Mother!" shrieks Sicilee. "I haven't even started thinking about what I'm wearing to that!"

"Well, you'd better." Kristin smirks. "You want to look nice for Abe, don't you?"

"Oh, please. It's not a big deal," says Sicilee, but she raises her cup to her mouth and swings her hair so the others can't see the expression on her face. "It's just a friendly date."

Abe called her the night after the sit-in. Apparently watching her being led away by the police had made him see her differently. He said she was a lot feistier than he'd given her credit for and asked her out.

"Oh, my, my . . ." mutters Loretta. "What's that old saying? Two's company and twenty's a crowd?"

Cody Lightfoot and a small herd of smiling girls from the year below are ambling across the courtyard together.

Sicilee watches them pass like someone watching a movie she's seen before but doesn't really remember. To think she tried so hard to impress Cody Lightfoot! She must've been out of her mind. It's as if she'd been under some kind of spell.

"Hey, you know what this smells like?" Ash's nose is still in the plant. "It smells like that plug-in air freshener my mom uses." She gives another happy sniff. "I think she's really going to like this."

Chapter Forty-five

Waneeda can't remember that she ever had the teeniest crush on Cody Lightfoot

Waneeda and Joy Marie sit together in the shade of the T-shirt stall, which they are running while Clemens oversees the showing of environmental documentaries in the auditorium.

Waneeda makes a drainlike sound as she sucks up the last of her iced tea through the straw. "Look at him, grinning and shaking hands," says Waneeda. "You'd think this whole thing was his idea, the way he's strutting around."

The "him" Waneeda's referring to is none other than Dr. Firestone, and it is fair to say that, as he moves through the crowd in his summer suit and an eye-catching tie that features a picture of a gnarled oak very like the trees he was so eager to chop down, Dr. Firestone is definitely enjoying the success of the day.

"At least he didn't make us cancel the fair," says Joy Marie.

Joy Marie is being far too generous. Dr. Firestone had no choice but to let the Earth Day celebrations go on as planned. He'd already been presented in the press as less than honest, out-of-touch, and unreasonable. After all the publicity and the governor muscling in, canceling the fair would have added "vindictive" to the list of his faults.

"And now there's no way he can shut us down. Especially not after today." Joy Marie leans forward on her elbows. "I mean, can you believe how many people have shown up? I figured that all our parents would come and people like that, but it looks like most of the town's here."

"That's thanks to Clemens, too," says Waneeda. If Clemens hadn't climbed into that tree—and if he hadn't given such an eloquent interview about trees and their memories to the local paper (reprinted in every major newspaper on the eastern seaboard, including the *New York Times*)—there is little doubt that there would be far fewer people at the Earth Day celebration and that most of them would be relatives of club members, friends of relatives of club members, and Mr. Huddlesfield's bowling team.

"I think that's a little unfair." Joy Marie gives her a sideways glance. "Cody had something to do with it, too, Waneeda. He was the one who got it all started, you know."

Waneeda harrumphs. "You mean that he got everybody else to get it started."

"I think he did a little more than that," argues Joy

Marie. "He won over Dr. Firestone . . . and he got the electric company to sponsor Earth Day and—"

"Anything Cody did, he did because it made him look good," cuts in Waneeda. "Cody Lightfoot's like fireworks. All show and no substance."

Joy Marie doesn't quite manage to stifle a spasm of laughter.

Waneeda glares. "What's so funny?"

"You are. You used to be a member of the Cody Lightfoot fan club. Remember?"

"No," says Waneeda. "No, I don't. I remember saying that I thought he was attractive, but you'd have to be blind and in Toledo not to notice that."

"Really?" Joy Marie sips at her own iced tea. "I could've sworn you joined the club because of Cody."

"I joined because you were pressuring me. That's why I joined." Waneeda straightens the stack of T-shirts in front of her. "And anyway, as soon as I got to know Clemens . . ." She shrugs. "Well, you know . . ."

"Well, you'll be happy to hear that Cody's not shedding any tears because you've found somebody else," says Joy Marie.

Waneeda turns in the direction Joy Marie is looking. Cody Lightfoot is standing at the solar-heating stall, surrounded by a gaggle of girls.

For the life of her, Waneeda can't remember what she ever saw in him.

Chapter Forty-six

All systems normal

Maya's friends—all of whom have been having a great time at the Earth Day celebration—have stopped by to see her. With Alice's help, Maya's been running the children's workshop. Making art out of junk. To inspire them, she set up a stall with the whirligigs and mobiles she made out of things she rescued from the recycling center. The result is a cross between an invention by the cartoonist Rube Goldberg, who specialized in drawing complicated machines to perform simple tasks, and Aladdin's cave.

"Man, this is so cool." Brion whistles. "You're selling these things, right? My dad would love one for the backyard."

"I always knew you were talented, Maya," says Mallory, "but I never knew you were *this* talented."

Maya smiles shyly. "It's more inspiration than talent. Once I started, I just couldn't seem to stop."

"But when did you make all this stuff?" asks Shayla. "It must have taken hours and hours."

Maya doesn't say that she made it in those dark days after her Be Kind to Our Planet Night, when she kept pretty much to herself for a while. Maya, like Sicilee, is happy to have her friends back. Especially since it was they who came to her and not the other way around. A certain way of dressing might make you cool. A certain kind of music might make you cool. Reading certain books might make you cool as well. But nothing does the job as well as having a photo of you being led away by a policeman published in the daily paper with the headline, "Clifton Springs Students Climb Up for the First Amendment." There's no making fun of her now. Celebrity is, indeed, forgiven a lot.

"Well, you know . . ." Maya shrugs. "I kind of stopped watching so much TV, so I did this instead." She gives them all a big smile. "You know what they say: use less . . . reuse . . . recycle."

"Maybe we should all give up TV." Finn laughs. "These are totally amazing."

"Man, this rules so bad." Jason's eyes move back and forth as though he's committing the pieces to memory. "Has Zin seen it? He's got to give you an A for this."

Maya looks at her watch. "He's supposed to be here at three to judge the Junk Art competition."

"Well, that's not long." Jason leans over her shoulder,

also looking at her watch. "Why don't I hang out with you? Give you a hand here?" There are a few small children still glueing bits and pieces on painted boxes and tying plastic bottles together with colored string. "I want to see his face."

"That's OK. I'm here," says Alice.

"Don't you want to look around?" asks Jason. "You've been stuck here all day."

Alice blinks. It's never before occurred to her to think of Jason as being especially thoughtful. "Well, I . . ." She glances at Maya. Maya has an oh-my-gosh expression on her face. "Yeah," says Alice quickly. "That's cool. I'll see you guys later."

After the others leave, Jason says, "I guess that wasn't very subtle, was it?"

"What?" Maya starts walking through the junior artists, picking up discarded containers and scraps and putting them back in the bins. "Practically telling Alice to go away?"

Jason grimaces. "I wanted to get you alone. You know, so I could apologize for the way I've been acting."

Maya retrieves a handful of old CDs from the grass. "You mean being rude and obnoxious and torturing me? You want to apologize for that?"

"Yeah." He kicks a cork toward her foot. "You know, because . . . I know it's going to sound crazy, but I think I was jealous."

"*You* were jealous? What of? Me eating lentils? Or me riding my bike to school?"

"Lightfoot." Jason is scouring the grass for more corks, and he is mumbling. "I thought, you know . . . I thought you had the hots for him."

"Me?" It is a testament to how much things can change in a short period of time that Maya isn't acting at all. "You thought *I* liked Cody?"

"Yeah, well, you know. . . . He is pretty good-looking."

"Do you think so?" asks Maya.

It is another testament to how much things can change in a short period of time that although, at this very moment, Cody Lightfoot is walking past them, smiling that smile that not so long ago would have turned her toenails to glue, Maya doesn't even see him.

Acknowledgments

As the characters in my novel discover, it is sometimes easy to feel very alone when you decide to "go Green." You look around and everybody's eating hamburgers and filling their plastic shopping bags with things that aren't very friendly to the environment. They may love their dogs and cats — give them names and personalities and dress them up for major holidays — but they don't spend much time worrying about the life of your average battery chicken. They may accept the fact of climate change, but they don't think a lot about trying to at least slow it down.

When I did the research for this novel, however, I realized that there are a lot of concerned and aware people and groups, eager to share information with the world — and even more eager to try to save it. And I'd like to take this opportunity to thank them for being out there. Thank you.

In addition, I thought I'd like to mention some of the many books, films, and websites I found that helped me the most.

Books: *The Last Green Book on Earth?* by Judy Allen, illustrated by Martin Brown (Red Fox, 1994); *What's in This Stuff?: The Essential Guide to What's Really in the Products You Buy in the Supermarket* by Pat Thomas (Rodale, 2006); *Endgame, vol. 1: The Problem of Civilization* and *Endgame, vol. 2: Resistance* by Derrick Jensen (Seven Stories Press, 2006); *How It All Vegan: Irresistible Recipes for an Animal-Free Diet* by Tanya Barnard and Sarah Kramer (Arsenal Pulp Press, 2002); *Not on the Label: What Really Goes into the Food on Your Plate* by Felicity Lawrence (Penguin Books Ltd., 2004); and *Fast Food Nation: The Dark Side of the All-American Meal* by Eric Schlosser (Harper Perennial, 2005).

Websites: www.vegansociety.com; www.vegsoc.org; www.peta.org; www.revbilly.com (web home of the dynamic—and very funny—Reverend Billy and the Church of Life After Shopping); and www.seashepherd .org (official site for the dedicated Captain Paul Watson and crews of the Sea Shepherd Conservation Society).

Documentaries: *Food, Inc.* (directed by Robert Kenner, 2008); *An Inconvenient Truth* (directed by Davis Guggenheim, 2006); *What a Way to Go: Life at the End of Empire* (directed by Timothy S. Bennett, 2007); *The Age of Stupid* (directed by Franny Armstrong, 2009); *Whale Wars* (from the *Animal Planet* series, 2008); and *The Witness* (directed by Jenny Stein about the Brooklyn animal-rights champion, Eddie Lama, 2000). *The Witness,* though thought-provoking and very moving, was probably the most entertaining. Some of the documentaries I watched, I have to honestly say, were pretty distressing. One of the best, *Earthlings* (directed by Shaun Monson, 2005), is the film Clemens shows that turns Ms. Kimodo into a vegetarian in my novel. I closed my eyes a lot when I watched it.

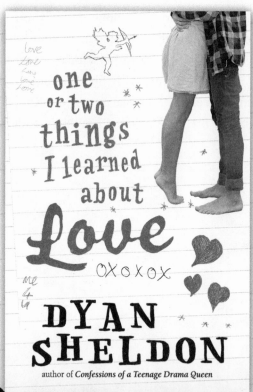